P9-BYY-884

THE STRIVER

A Selection of Recent Titles by Stephen Solomita

DAMAGED GOODS
A GOOD DAY TO DIE
NO CONTROL
A PIECE OF THE ACTION
THE POSTER BOY
TRICK ME TWICE
MONKEY IN THE MIDDLE *
CRACKER BLING *
MERCY KILLING *
ANGEL FACE *
DANCER IN THE FLAMES *
THE STRIVER *

* *available from Severn House*

THE STRIVER

Stephen Solomita

This first world edition published 2014
in Great Britain and 2015 in the USA by
SEVERN HOUSE PUBLISHERS LTD of
19 Cedar Road, Sutton, Surrey, England, SM2 5DA.
Trade paperback edition first published
in Great Britain and the USA 2015 by
SEVERN HOUSE PUBLISHERS LTD.

Copyright © 2014 by Stephen Solomita

All rights reserved.
The moral right of the author has been asserted.

Solomita, Stephen author.
  The striver.
  1. Gangsters–New York (State)–New York–Fiction.
  2. Drug traffic–Fiction. 3. Usury–Fiction. 4. Noir
  fiction.
  I. Title
  813.5'4-dc23

ISBN-13: 978-0-7278-8462-6 (cased)
ISBN-13: 978-1-84751-554-4 (trade paper)
ISBN-13: 978-1-78010-601-4 (e-book)

Except where actual historical events and characters are being
described for the storyline of this novel, all situations in this
publication are fictitious and any resemblance to living persons
is purely coincidental.

All Severn House titles are printed on acid-free paper.

Severn House Publishers support The Forest Stewardship Council™ [FSC™],
the leading international forest certification organisation. All our titles that
are printed on FSC certified paper carry the FSC logo.

Typeset by Palimpsest Book Production Ltd.,
Falkirk, Stirlingshire, Scotland.
Printed and bound in Great Britain by
TJ International, Padstow, Cornwall.

ONE

Teddy Winuk came out of the bathroom to find Sanda Dragomir sprinkling breadcrumbs on the window sill. Despite a cool breeze that rippled through the pink curtains to either side, she wore a silk T-shirt that barely covered her ass. Her perfectly round, perfectly smooth ass. Her magnificent, for-profit-only ass.

As though reading his mind, Sanda bent slightly at the waist and the purple T-shirt lifted far enough to confirm what he already knew. She wore nothing beneath. Teddy bit at his lower lip. She's a whore, he told himself, a worker, an earner, a small piece of the puzzle I've been assembling for as long as I can remember.

Sadly, as Winuk admitted, most of the puzzle pieces were still in a jumbled heap off to one side. But this section was definitely complete. Talk about a time-consuming, low-return activity. Whores were more trouble than they were worth. Besides which, now that he was moving up, he wanted to shed the pimp label. Teddy's peers consigned pimps to a category in the criminal hierarchy only a bit above child molesters. This was a fair assessment, in his opinion, given the casual brutality demonstrated by most pimps, though not in his particular case. Teddy managed four high-end escorts, the deal between them a matter of mutual consent. He'd made that clear from the outset.

'You can walk away anytime you want. No hard feelings.'

Teddy started across the room, but stopped himself after a couple of steps. He'd never felt a moment's desire for the other three girls, yet he could barely keep his hands off Sanda, even now.

'I got some bad news for you, Sanda. Or maybe good news, depending. I'm gonna cut you loose.'

Sanda turned to stare into his eyes, her own laughing blue eyes for once serious. She brought a hand to her face as though brushing away a slap, then dropped it to her side. Teddy found the pose theatrical, which was only to be expected, theatre being the most important part of any sexual transaction more elevated than a quick blow job underneath the Williamsburg Bridge.

'For what do you punish me?'

Rather than answer, Teddy spun around and headed for the closet by the door. He slid his navy pea jacket off a hanger and put it on.

'Where am I to go, Teddy?'

Teddy responded with a shrug, then took an H&K 9mm from the jacket's outer pocket and stuffed it inside his belt. He had other problems to deal with, pressing problems of the most urgent kind, life and death problems.

'Do whatever you'd do if I turned up dead last night.' Squeezed between high cheekbones and a prominent forehead, Teddy's green eyes were small and pinpoint sharp, especially when he allowed them to harden, as he did now. 'Tell the other girls to never mention my name again. You, too, Sanda. If I hear you're talkin' up my business, I'll make you wish you never left Romania.'

Message delivered, Teddy headed for the street, taking the single flight of stairs two at a time, graceful as a gymnast despite his bulk. He crossed the apartment building's lobby, pushed the door open and stepped onto the sidewalks of Greenpoint, Brooklyn. As the November air washed over his face, he breathed a sigh of relief. An Arctic front had swept down out of Canada to bathe New York in the first cold air of the season. The temperature, this early in the morning, was just above freezing.

Teddy pulled a black watch cap over his head, but didn't button his coat. On the whole, he preferred cold weather because it was a lot easier to conceal a gun beneath a coat or a jacket. Which is not to say that Teddy packed heat as a matter of habit. The penalty for a concealed gun in New York, three years in a state prison, was too harsh for that. But right now, while Johnny Piano and his boys were looking to beat him to a pulp, the rewards more than balanced the risks. Johnny Pianetta ran one of the last all-Italian crews in the city. In fact, Johnny Piano owned a house in the Northside, a small Italian enclave just a mile away. And it was Johnny who'd given him that nickname, Teddy Winks, which he hated.

At seven in the morning, Teddy had time to kill, a common occurrence for a man who never slept more than five hours a night. Five hours was enough, though, enough to refresh him. Teddy had the energy of three men and no talent for leisure – two of his biggest advantages, at least in his opinion.

He liked being outside, no matter the weather, constantly on the move when he didn't have an appointment. Now he ambled down Ash Street, past the Brooklyn Ice Cream Factory toward the Pulaski Bridge connecting the counties of Brooklyn and Queens. For the most part, Greenpoint was a mixed neighborhood of apartment buildings, three-family homes, factories and low-rise warehouses. But just here, only a few blocks from Newtown Creek, the irretrievably polluted body of water that separated the counties, industry predominated. Not behemoths – there were no auto plants or steel mills in Greenpoint. The businesses here, like Hong's Seafood Company and Sightline Fabrications, focused on small-scale services, with long hours of hard work the common thread binding them.

Having grown up in Greenpoint, Teddy found the odd mix familiar. It seemed that no matter where you lived, you couldn't avoid the noise of the workaday world, forklifts lugging goods to and from eighteen wheelers, a cement mixer turning in a construction yard, the eerie whoop of a diesel engine starting up, the sharp hiss of released air brakes. All of this as basic to him as trimmed green lawns to suburbanites, a class he generally despised.

The nights, when the businesses closed down, were different. Nights and weekend mornings at seven o'clock. Now steel shutters covered every window and door, while the sidewalks and streets were empty, the frigid air absolutely still. Otherwise, Teddy would never have heard the faint sobs. But he did hear them, coming from behind one of the Pulaski Bridge's concrete footings.

Hyper-alert by nature, Teddy made the first jump instantly: not a threat, not to him.

And therefore not his business, right? He started to move on, but found the sobs unnerving. They sounded like his sister's the first time their stepfather went into her room.

'Shut the fuck up.'

Followed by the thud of a descending fist. Followed by the requested silence.

Teddy had killed three men in his life. Tadeuz Gorowski, his stepfather, was the first. Now he took a step toward the concrete pillar, then another and another. He had no idea what he'd do, but he was anxious to find out. He was curious.

The answer wasn't long in coming and once again Teddy evaluated the situation in an instant. The woman was on her back, lying on the bare pavement. Her eyes were swollen shut and blood dripped from a wound to her scalp. The man knelt between her legs, thrusting into her. His hands gripped her ankles. Drops of sweat flew from his soaked hair.

Play the white knight? Or mind your own business? The dilemma was rendered meaningless by the rapist being Carlo Pianetta, Johnny Piano's son.

'Hey, Carlo,' Teddy said.

Though initially startled to find himself looking at a man condemned to a severe beat-down, Carlo immediately reverted to the hard-ass he imagined himself to be.

'This ain't your business.' When his threatening tone produced no detectable result, he quickly added, 'Forget about her. She's a whore.'

The conflict between Teddy and Johnny Piano was simple. For the past two years, while he built his business, Teddy had been paying tribute. But not anymore. Fuck the guineas. They'd never thrown him any work, never offered him a piece of their action. Meanwhile, he was expected to fork over a piece of his own action every week. And to kiss their asses, too.

Carlo returned to his frantic thrusting. The woman now lay unmoving. Teddy couldn't see past her swollen lids, but he was pretty sure her eyes were unfocused. If she was aware at all, she was merely enduring.

'I'll be through in a few minutes,' Carlo said. 'In case you wanna take a turn.'

Teddy didn't react on instinct. He made a decision – reasoned, in his view – before he drew the semi-automatic from beneath his belt and fired a hollow-point round into Carlo Pianetta's skull. The bullet clipped off the top of Carlo's left ear as it plowed through bone, then brain, then bone again. It exited behind his right ear, drawing the expected plume of human tissue in its wake.

Carlo remained upright for a moment, as though considering the implications. Then he crumpled, every muscle limp, his body little more than an empty sack of bones.

'I'll tell your daddy to say hello,' Teddy muttered, 'when he meets you in hell.'

That was enough. Gunshots attracted attention, even in industrial neighborhoods like this one. Teddy grabbed the spent cartridge, then double-timed the single block to Newtown Creek and tossed the 9mm forty feet out. His eyes searched the sidewalks and alleyways as he went. His ears listened for the wail of sirens, but the streets remained empty, the cold air quiet. Gradually, he settled down, so that by the time he reached his destination twenty minutes later, his thoughts had turned to the ramifications. Johnny Piano couldn't ignore the murder of his son without looking weak. Someone had to pay. But that person didn't have to be Teddy Winuk. No, no, not at all. That person might even be one of Teddy's competitors, a case of the enemy of my enemy being, if not exactly my friend, at least an unwitting ally.

TWO

Andy Littlewood strolled into his son's kitchen two days later at eight o'clock in the morning. He muttered a greeting, poured himself a cup of coffee and sat down at a small wooden table. The table was painted a particularly repulsive greenish-gray, as were the four chairs surrounding it. Boots, of course, would never consider changing the color, or covering the table's cigarette-scarred surface with a tablecloth. Yet the room was neat, the floor swept, the stovetop clean, the ancient sink, its porcelain worn micron thin, freshly scrubbed. Andy Littlewood was as close to Boots as a father can get to a son, but he didn't pretend to understand his only child's many contradictions.

'I have to eat fast,' Boots said. 'Lieutenant Sorrowful called about a body underneath the Pulaski Bridge which I need to attend forthwith.' He opened the oven door, removed a cookie sheet bearing a pair of nicely toasted onion bagels and laid the sheet on a burner. Then he dropped four well-stirred eggs into a cast-iron skillet. Boots wore his gray suit pants, a matching vest and a light-blue shirt. A red tie hung loosely beneath his collar.

'I should already be gone, as a matter of fact.'

Boots cut the eggs in half with the edge of a spatula and flipped the halves. Only a few seconds later, since both men liked their eggs a bit loose, he shoveled each of the halves onto the bottom of a sliced bagel, replaced the tops and threw the sandwiches onto plates. He carried the plates to the table and dropped into a chair. 'The bagels have been sittin' around since Saturday. It was this morning or never.'

'You always did have a way of makin' your old dad feel special.'

Andy lived above his son in a two-family home on Newell Street in Greenpoint, a home Andy owned. He'd only come downstairs to discuss Boots's role in his wedding. Andy's marriage to Libby Greenspan would be celebrated in two months and Boots had volunteered to walk Libby down the aisle.

Boots merely grunted before biting off a chunk of his sandwich. He was in a testy mood and he'd remain that way until Thanksgiving if the past was any indicator. For reasons Andy was never able to comprehend, Boots's relationship with the New York Yankees went beyond fanaticism. For Boots, winter began with the final out of the final game and lasted until opening day in April. The Yankee's season having concluded on an especially dismal note only two weeks before, Boots was as edgy as a heroin addict in the early stages of withdrawal.

'That's the curse of livin' where you work,' Boots observed. 'If it's Monday morning and there's nobody around, you're definitely gettin' the first call.'

'Tell you what, Irwin.' Andy was the only person on the planet allowed to use Boots's given name. 'Why don't you wrap up the sandwich and leave the dishes to me?'

'That'd be a good idea if I hadn't already finished it.' Boots shoved the last bite into his mouth and rose from his chair. 'Here's one thing I never figured out,' he said. 'A crime in progress, a robbery, a burglary? I can understand the rush. But dead bodies don't move. You can take your time and they'll still be layin' there when you arrive. They're patient that way.'

Boots slipped on his shoulder harness, eased his Glock into the holster, then shrugged into his suit jacket and pulled up his tie. 'I had a partner once, talked about the dead cryin' out for revenge. But me, I don't think murdered people sit on clouds waitin' for their killers to be punished. I think they know that dead is forever and it's time to move on.'

'So you're sayin' that justice is for the living?'

But the door was already closing and Boots on his way, taking his foul mood with him.

THREE

Boots was right. The body lay where it had fallen, its temporary resting place altered only by ribbons of yellow tape that ran from the bridge footings to a chain-link fence enclosing a small yard. All of the space beneath the city's many bridges belonged to the city, of course, but much of it was leased to private businesses. This particular slice was currently being rented by Amoroso Construction. Amoroso used the yard to park its smaller vehicles. Boots noted three pickup trucks, several sedans, a mud-spattered Payloader, two yellow backhoes and a grader. Each bore the Amoroso emblem: a stylized letter A, shiny gold, on a blood-red background.

Thoroughly familiar with the logo, Boots knew the scene would have to be carefully preserved. There could be no mistakes here. Amoroso Construction belonged to Johnny Pianetta, a self-styled Mafia Don with a hand in every criminal pursuit this side of international arms trafficking. The NYPD's Organized Crime Control Bureau would definitely come calling, and sooner rather than later.

'Yo, Boots, have a doughnut.'

The offer came from Sergeant Craig O'Malley who worked

alongside Boots in the Sixty-Fourth Precinct, universally called the Six-Four. O'Malley stood next to his cruiser. He was a large man, but his driver, Boris Velikov, towered above him. The Bulgarian was stuffing a powdered doughnut into his mouth. Though he couldn't speak, he waved a hand the size of a baseball mitt in greeting.

'Where's the body?' Boots asked.

'Behind that pillar.'

'How about the car over there? You check it out yet?'

O'Malley didn't ask what car Boots referred to. The 2013 Lexus GS was the only car parked on the block.

'Never gave it a moment's thought, Boots. Maybe that's why you're a detective and I'm still workin' patrol. But I'll get to it in a minute.'

'Let Boris handle it, if he can stop eating. I want you to take me to the body.'

'What's the hurry? Carlo Pianetta's not goin' anywhere. Have some coffee.'

Although he'd made the same argument to his father, Boots said, 'Call me untrusting, but I wanna see for myself.'

O'Malley tracked the line he'd taken when he first inspected the crime scene, leaving Boots to follow in his footsteps.

'The paramedics responded, but I held them off,' he explained. 'Carlo was as dead as dead gets and I didn't want them contaminating the scene. Boots, I knew this was gonna be trouble from the beginning. Amoroso? Johnny Piano's outfit? Bad news, Boots, and when I laid eyes on the body . . .'

O'Malley didn't bother to complete the sentence. They'd rounded the pillar and Boots could see for himself. Boots had known Carlo Pianetta from birth. Both he and the Pianetta family attended the same church, a blasphemy that Boots was forced to endure. Boots had been hearing Mass at Our Lady of Mt. Carmel all his life.

'We need backup,' Boots said, 'before Amoroso's workers arrive. And let's rope off the block all the way to the water. Nobody in or out.'

Boots wouldn't lead the investigation, of this much he was certain. And more than likely, no higher authority would seek his insights. Nevertheless, he examined the scene carefully.

Dispatched by a single shot to the head, Carlo lay on his right side, his body limp now that he'd come through rigor mortis. That meant he'd been dead for at least thirty-six hours and probably more. Although the cause of death screamed mob execution, Carlo's pants and boxer shorts were bunched around his ankles, an inconsistency that demanded its own attention.

There being no good reason for an immediate answer to the obvious question, like what exactly Carlo was doing when he bought the farm, Boots knelt to examine the entrance wound and the surrounding tissue. The hole left by the bullet was round and neat, with none of the tissue damage associated with a contact or near-contact wound. On the other hand, the left side of Carlo's neck and face was speckled with gunpowder residue, little black dots that looked like warts, which meant the shooter had been somewhere between three and six feet away.

Boots rose, then took a deep breath as he shifted his attention. He was standing within a yard of where the shooter had fired the single round that took Carlo's life, if not on the exact spot. He swept the dark asphalt with his eyes, looking for shoe impressions, but the surface was too smooth. If any faint impressions existed, the Crime Scene Unit would have to find them.

About to back off, Boots took one more look, a habit he'd cultivated many years before. The effort rarely produced any good result, but this time his diligence paid off when he found an irregular stain just a bit darker than the asphalt, maybe four inches long and two inches across, a bloodstain. The stain was only a few feet away from Carlo's body, but it wasn't his blood. Carlo's blood, along with bits of bone, brain, hair and skin, extended for a good eight feet from the side of his head. No bit of it reached within two yards of the smaller stain.

On impulse, Boots again dropped to one knee, this time to examine Carlo's hands. He found dried blood on the man's knuckles and fingers. Par for the course. Carlo's reputation for brutality extended back to his childhood when he terrorized his schoolmates on the playground. In that way, at least, he differed from his old man. John Pianetta embraced the use of violence to solve problems, but there was no indication that he enjoyed the pain he caused. A means to an end, that's all violence was for him, his victims' humanity irrelevant, if not entirely unsuspected.

*   *   *

Satisfied, Boots retreated to O'Malley's cruiser in time to snatch the last doughnut. Two more cruisers had arrived, and six cops now stood before the chain-link fence enclosing the yard. Boots carried the doughnut and a paper cup of overly sweetened coffee to where O'Malley stood.

'So?' O'Malley asked. 'Whatta ya think?'

'Three questions.'

'Shoot.'

'Who reported the body?'

'An anonymous tip called to the Six-Four.'

Called in, Boots noted, not to 911, but to the Sixty-Fourth Precinct. 'Man or woman?'

'Man.'

Two items caught Boots's attention. First, the body couldn't be seen from outside the fence. Second, the phone numbers of local precincts weren't publicized. Unless the caller was a cop, he'd have to look the number up. So, why not call 911? More than likely because incoming calls to 911 were not only recorded, the caller's number was captured as well.

'What about the car?' Boots asked Velikov. 'You run the plates?'

'Yeah, it's registered to the scumbag in question.'

'Carlo Pianetta?'

'The one and only.'

Boots wolfed down the last of the doughnut, then called Detective Lieutenant Carl Levine, his commanding officer at the Six-Four. Levine's nickname was Lieutenant Sorrowful, in part because his droopy face resembled that of a bloodhound with a toothache.

'The vic,' Boots explained, after briefly describing the scene. 'He's Carlo Pianetta.'

'Johnny Piano's kid?'

Boots shuddered. He hated the nicknames these jerks gave themselves. 'Yeah,' he said, 'that's him.'

'Shit,' Levine said.

'My sentiments exactly. And the worst part is that Borough Command will definitely take the job away from us. It'll go to Homicide or OCCB.'

Boots had no desire to be a hero. His concern had always been with the overall security of the small neighborhood where he worked and lived. But this particular murder wasn't about to vanish. Johnny Pianetta lived only a mile away. And like Boots, he made his home territory his place of business.

'Johnny,' Boots continued, 'he's gonna tear up the neighborhood lookin' for whoever hit Carlo.'

'Unless he knows right away,' Levine pointed out. 'It could be that Carlo had a beef with someone and his old man's aware of it.'

Boots took a moment to consider the oddities: Carlo's pants around his ankles, the small bloodstain, the blood on Carlo's hands. Best guess, Carlo had been surprised in the act of . . . of sex, at least. But why behind a pillar in the shadows beneath the Pulaski Bridge? Unless Carlo was doing something he needed to hide.

'I'll pass the info up the chain,' Levine said. 'Meanwhile, I don't have to tell you to fill in every blank.'

'You don't actually, but you always do.'

Boots attempted to fill in one of those blanks when he examined Carlo's Lexus. He found the front doors open and conducted a quick search, including the glove compartment, under and behind the seats, then finally the trunk. He found nothing out of order, noting only that the keys were in the ignition. Whatever Carlo was doing under the bridge, he hadn't expected to spend a lot of time doing it.

As he closed the trunk, Boots's cell phone rang. Lieutenant Sorrowful with the anticipated bad news.

'OCCB is on the way,' he announced. 'They're expecting to find the crime scene undisturbed.'

FOUR

As Boots settled down to wait – most likely until he was summarily dismissed – he found himself wanting a cigarette. The craving rushed over him, as cravings had been rushing over him since he quit more than a year before. Cops spend a lot of time waiting and Boots had always filled that time with a smoke, sometimes two or three. Now . . .

Boots took out his cell phone, checked the little green battery to make sure he'd remembered to charge it, and called in to the Six-Four. He greeted the sergeant who answered the phone, then asked for a patrol lieutenant named Nouza Mahoud. A second-generation Egyptian, Mahoud was resolutely gung-ho on America. He told you how much he loved his country somewhere in the course of every conversation, as if his loyalty was perpetually in question.

'Hey, Lou,' Boots said, 'you got a minute?'

'Sure, what's up?'

'I need to know if someone reported a gunshot near the Pulaski Bridge on Saturday night or Sunday morning. You mind checkin' the log?' Boots hesitated, then decided to sweeten the pot by offering a little piece of gossip. The job ran on gossip. 'We got a stiff here. It's Carlo Pianetta.'

'Whoa.'

'Exactly. Which is why I need to move before the bosses arrive.'

'In that case, you came to the right man. I was on duty Sunday morning, maybe at seven thirty, when the job was dispatched to . . . to Six-Four Boy. Yeah, that's it. That would be Lily Bremer and Louie Fallanga. They were patrolling Boy sector that morning.'

'Who called it in?'

'Gimme a second.'

The second turned into several minutes and Boots found himself growing impatient. The Crime Scene Unit had arrived and white-suited cops were busy scouring the yard, hoping, maybe, that the perp dropped his wallet. Several Amoroso workers had also come by to retrieve the company's vehicles. They now stood in a knot on the far side of the street, eight of them dressed in canvas pants and heavy boots, smoking the cigarettes Boots craved. Six months ago, he'd have found an excuse to stand in their midst, to put his nose within a few feet of a little second-hand smoke. Now he felt only a moment of regret. The decision to quit was a concession to oncoming middle age, but succeeding hadn't made him any younger.

A black Chevy Caprice pulled up just as Lieutenant Mahoud came back on the line. The uniformed officer who exited the back seat wore the polished bars of a captain.

'You there, Boots?'

'Here and ready, Lou.'

'The report of a single shot fired was logged in at 7:42 on Sunday morning by a 911 operator. According to the operator, a citizen named Hal McDermott heard a shot and ran to his window. He didn't see anything, but he called 911 anyway. Six-Four Boy responded and called in a 10-90, unfounded, at 8:24.'

'Where does McDermott live?'

'Box Street. That'd be about a block from the Pulaski Bridge.'

Boots caught a little break here. Lily Bremer was currently at the scene. In Boots's view, only a small number of cops had a serious interest in the art of policing. For the rest, it was cover your ass and cash your check. It was hunker down until the magic pension kicked in, along with the lifetime medical benefits.

Lily Bremer's flag had been planted in the aggressive-policing camp for almost two decades. Tall and bony, her skin was the color of warm caramel, a sharp contrast with her bright green eyes. Boots associated Lily's accusing gaze with that of Sister Mary Dennis, the nun who'd caught him stealing a candy bar in the school cafeteria. Back when he was eleven years old.

'Hey, Lily . . .'

'You don't have to tell me, Boots. We messed up.'

'You can't win 'em all.'

Lily Bremer didn't have to be asked for an accounting. The 911 call established the time of death in the homicide of a mob figure. Everything she and her partner had done and seen on Sunday morning would become part of the case file. Criticism might easily follow, but if she was ever to find a sympathetic ear, she was talking into it right now.

'We interviewed the citizen – Hal McDermott – first thing. McDermott told us that he heard what he took to be a gunshot and went immediately to his window. He looked up and down Box Street, but didn't see anything, not even a passing car. Most citizens would've let it go right there, but he called 911 and we got the job, me and Fallanga.'

They were interrupted by a tractor-trailer, a tanker, gearing
down as it approached the haphazardly parked cruisers. The rig's
engine roared each time the driver changed gears, throwing up
twin plumes of black smoke through the exhaust pipes behind
the cab.

The truck was headed for an oil storage depot on the far side
of the bridge, a partnership between Exxon and the Kuwaiti
government called Alltel Enterprises. Alltel didn't do business
on Sunday, but there must have been a security guard somewhere,
and security cameras, too. Oil storage depots with their enormous
tanks were prime targets for a terrorist attack. Blow one of those
tanks and the fire would burn for a week.

Boots glanced to his right. The still unidentified captain was
coming straight toward him. A pair of detectives dutifully trailed
behind.

'We crisscrossed the surrounding blocks for a few minutes,
but . . .' Lily shrugged. 'No bodies, not even a pedestrian we
could ask about the shot, so we called it in as unfounded.'

'Detective Littlewood?'

Boots turned to his right and raised a hand while Lily made
herself scarce. 'That would be me.'

'Captain Karkanian, OCCB. You want to bring me up to date?'
Karkanian was three inches taller and several years younger than
Boots, with a full head of coarse black hair and a unibrow so
thick Boots half expected it to wriggle.

Boots tried not to resent the man's presence, or his failure to
introduce his detectives. But the best he could do was conceal
that resentment as he delivered a precise report, beginning with
the gunshot called in by Clark McDermott, concluding with the
arrival of the Crime Scene Unit.

'Sergeant O'Malley, his driver and myself were the only
personnel past that gate before CSU showed up.'

'Good work, Detective. We'll take it from here.'

A black Cadillac Escalade tore onto the block just as Boots
reached his own car, a battered 2002 Ford Taurus. The Escalade
stopped in the middle of the street and five men, including Johnny
Pianetta, exited. As they double-timed in the direction of the
crime scene, Boots slid into the little Ford. He'd been expecting

Johnny Piano to show up. In fact, he'd been keenly anticipating an opportunity to confront the man. Boots hated gangsters in general and Johnny in particular, this despite a relative tolerance for the common criminals he ordinarily pursued.

Johnny Pianetta relentlessly cultivated a bogus persona. He gave generously to the church, sponsored a Little League team and belonged to a dozen organizations, at all times proclaiming himself a defender of the neighborhood, civic virtue personified. Forget about a loansharking operation that collected debts by any means necessary. Forget about peddling dope, coke and speed to street dealers who sprayed bullets into crowded playgrounds. Forget about extracting tribute from a host of equally violent street criminals.

When a fire consumed the sanctuary at St Stanislaus, John Pianetta was among the first to contribute to its rebuilding. His picture had appeared in the *Daily News*: Local Philanthropist Saves Polish Church.

Boots kept his own count, attributing six hits over the last few years to Johnny's loansharking operation and three additional murders to a heist that went wrong. That was in addition to the dozens of men who'd turned up in emergency rooms with broken bones, and the dozens more who'd overdosed on Johnny Piano's drugs.

Most neighborhoods in New York, as they came into being, had reserved some core of upscale housing for the neighborhood's lawyers, accountants and doctors. Not Greenpoint. One and all, its kids were the offspring of working-class parents only a paycheck or two from poverty. As teenagers, they walked a narrow line while they considered their adult opportunities. Most survived the endless temptations. They either went on to working-class jobs, or graduated college and promptly moved away. But others gave up early on, drifting into drugs and crime, helped by men like Johnny Piano who made sure narcotics were readily available in every one of the neighborhood's schools.

This was the same John Pianetta who showed up on Sunday at Our Lady of Mt. Carmel in a suit and tie. Who showed up with an uncle, two cousins and two sons, each of whom dreamed only of replacing him somewhere down the line.

Boots reached for the gear shift. He'd been dismissed and he had every reason to leave, to let the inevitable confrontation play out. But it was already too late. His equilibrium had shifted and he couldn't walk away. Boots had a big problem with his temper, a sin he confessed to Father Gubetti every Easter when he took Communion. Usually, he made an effort to control himself, but not this time.

Boots got out of the car and signaled to O'Malley and the Bulgarian. 'Show time, boys,' he said.

FIVE

Johnny Pianetta was screaming in Captain Karkanian's face. And why not? Why not indulge himself, given that his oldest son, his heir apparent, was dead? His people expected him to throw a little tantrum, including the six workers who'd come up to join his regular crew. Meanwhile, the opportunity to embarrass a cop, an officer, didn't come along every day. Johnny didn't know exactly what the bars on Karkanian's uniform represented, but the man's arrogance struck him. The asshole was used to having his orders followed, which was probably why he kept repeating himself.

'I'm sorry for your loss, sir, but you can't enter a crime scene.'

'That's my yard and my son.' Johnny's shout loosed tiny drops of spittle that sprayed the cop's face. The vision so delighted him that he decided to try it again before he shoved the man aside. But then he saw Boots Littlewood, flanked by two cops, one an absolute giant, coming up from his left.

For reasons he'd never bothered to examine, John Pianetta craved respect, from his peers in the crime business and from the community at large. That's why he cultivated his successful businessman image. Forget about Amoroso's paper profits being as phony as a politician on the stump. Forget about the bribes he paid to city project managers. Forget about the bribes he paid to city inspectors. John Pianetta was a pillar of the community, a position the community had chosen to acknowledge.

But not Boots Littlewood.

Pianetta was six years older than Boots and they'd barely known each other as kids. They'd have gone their own way as adults, too, if they didn't attend the same church, John every Sunday and Boots when he wasn't working. Inevitably, their paths crossed from time to time, arriving or leaving. Inevitably, Boots passed by without so much as a glance, his contempt obvious.

Wiseguys like Pianetta had little to fear from precinct detectives. Even if caught in the commission of a crime by some local cop, mobster prosecutions were routinely transferred to the Organized Crime Control Bureau or the FBI. And local cops weren't allowed to investigate the mob, or any of the major gangs, because the NYPD believed street cops to be easily corrupted. And not without reason.

Bottom line, Boots wasn't a threat and he could stuff his tight-ass attitude. The schmuck was just another working-class moron. Most likely, he'd spend his last years nursing a can of warm beer in a Florida trailer park.

Pianetta barely had time to put these ideas together before Boots stepped between the gangster and Captain Karkanian.

'Move the fucking car, John,' he said. 'You're blockin' traffic.'

'That's my kid,' Pianetta said. 'I got a right to see him.'

'Fine, we'll let you identify him in the morgue. And while you're there, you could help with the investigation by givin' us an interview. But you're not goin' a step further this morning. If you don't move the car, I'll have it towed.'

'Goddamn it . . .'

'Stop yourself right there. What you said? It's blasphemy, and I'd appreciate you watchin' your tongue.'

Pianetta stared into the detective's blue eyes for a moment before he realized that Boots was amused. The scumbag was playing John Pianetta, a man who'd put more people in the ground than he could remember, and he was doing it in front of Pianetta's crew and his workers.

What Boots deserved was a serious lesson in manners, a lesson that Pianetta, unfortunately, was not, just now, prepared to administer. Johnny Piano had grown soft over the years, his gut expanding even as his muscle mass shrank and his net worth grew. Indulgence was his middle name, in food and women both.

The net effect hadn't troubled him because he routinely kept at least two layers of insulation between himself and the use of violence. But there were no layers between himself and Boots Littlewood at that moment, only a few inches of air, and they both knew it. As they both knew that Boots was large and fit and not prepared to move. There'd be a brawl if Johnny Pianetta didn't back off, one Boots Littlewood was doing everything in his power to provoke.

From a piece-of-shit precinct cop, this was the ultimate humiliation, especially given the number of witnesses. This was the kind of humiliation you had to do something about. Like your oldest son being murdered.

The driver of an enormous eighteen-wheeler chose that moment to lean on his air horn, scattering a dozen pigeons feeding on doughnut crumbs. Pianetta opened his mouth, but didn't speak. In part because he wasn't prepared to shout. In part because there really wasn't anything to say. The negotiations were over. In fact, they'd never gotten started.

Pianetta jerked his head at a kid named Stefano Boco, Stevie Bold. 'Move the car,' he growled, the words seeming unnecessarily loud when the air horn suddenly cut off. For just a second, he watched Boco hustle away, then turned back to face Boots.

'Now you're makin' sense,' the cop said, his stare no less amused. 'I mean, you want us to get to the bottom of this crime, right? You want to see the perpetrator brought to justice, right?'

But Johnny Piano wasn't playing Detective Littlewood's game. His entire life had been about juice, who had it and who didn't. One animal's predator was another animal's prey, and right now he was the rabbit, Boots the wolf. Or wolves, really. The giant standing to Littlewood's right was holding a nightstick, tapping it against the side of his leg. A vein on the side of his neck pulsed with every beat of his heart and his little black eyes glittered with desire. You'd have to kill him to stop him.

'Yeah, justice, Boots. That's what I want. But I'm not gonna get it from you, am I? Last I heard, you weren't good enough to investigate murders. You do purse snatchings on Bedford Avenue.'

Boots didn't dispute the jibe. The overall point of this exercise was to prevent Johnny from seeing Carlo with his pants around his ankles. No clues for the bad guys. Nevertheless, he got in one final jibe of his own.

'Carlo's Lexus,' he said as John Pianetta turned away, 'it's goin' to the crime lab. You'll get it back when the techs are through with it.'

Pianetta didn't react. 'You men,' he said to his workers as he hauled himself into the back seat of the Escalade. 'Forget the equipment. Get your asses out to the job on Bushwick Avenue. I don't care if you gotta dig out the potholes with your fucking hands. You don't work, you don't get paid.'

SIX

Captain Karkanian was on Boots Littlewood before Johnny Piano's Escalade cleared the block. Boots had inserted himself into the confrontation, pushing Karkanian aside. That was his first mistake. Knowing the gangster personally was his second. Did Pianetta back off because Boots intimidated him? Or because Boots had passed a subtle message about wrong time and wrong place?

Karkanian had taken three civil service exams in order to reach his current rank. If there'd been a fourth, he'd have already passed it. But from here on, promotions were by appointment only. One mistake, say if you let a relationship between a gangster and a street detective go unremarked, and you'd remain a captain until the day you retired.

'Detective, a word.' Karkanian led Boots away from the uniformed cops. 'The rest of you go back to work. Nobody on the scene, nobody on the side streets.'

'So, what's up, boss?'

Karkanian took his time, hoping to intimidate the detective whose name he couldn't remember. No such luck. The Organized Crime Control Bureau and the Detective Bureau operated independently, each controlled by one of the city's eight Chiefs. Technically, Karkanian had no authority to command any detective not directly assigned to Organized Crime, rank be damned.

That the man John Pianetta called Boots understood this was obvious at a glance.

'You want to explain what happened a few minutes ago?'

'Well, basically, I've been lookin' for an opportunity to beat the crap out of John Pianetta for the last ten years.'

'And you thought you'd get it by pushing me out of the way?'

'Actually, Johnny's a realist. I knew he'd back off and I just wanted to make sure he didn't get a look at the crime scene.'

'I see. And you and Pianetta are . . . are what? Cousins?'

'No, it's just that his family and mine attend the same church and we can't help but run into each other.'

'Then maybe it's time you found another church.'

'My family's been going to Our Lady of Mt. Carmel since before I was born. I was baptized at Mt. Carmel. It's where my mother's funeral took place. I have as much right to it as some piece-of-shit gangster.'

Karkanian repressed a smile. Somehow, he'd pushed the right button. The cop was really pissed. 'Tell me your name again.'

'Detective Littlewood. And I'm through answering personal questions. You wanna conduct an interrogation, talk to my lawyer at the DBA. As for John Pianetta, sure I wanted to humiliate him, and it did my soul good, but I was also sending him a message. See, Johnny's gonna look to get revenge. On the right guy if possible, on the wrong guy if necessary. The way he makes a living, he's got no choice. I was tellin' him that if the blood flowed on my turf, I'd take it personally.'

Two vehicles pulled onto the scene, interrupting the conversation. Both were familiar to Boots. The first was a van that bore the seal of the Medical Examiner's Office on the side. The man driving was a death investigator. He'd do exactly what O'Malley, Boots and Captain Karkanian had already done. He'd examine the body and the circumstances under which it was found. Only then would he take the next step, calling in a wagon to transport the body to the morgue where it would receive the mandated autopsy.

The second vehicle was a midnight-green Chrysler 300. The cop driving it, a detective, was named Jill Kelly, called Crazy Jill by her admiring peers. They'd had an affair in the not very distant past, Boots and Jill, a torrid, if inevitably doomed, affair.

Jill Kelly could not be contained, much less possessed, and Boots had known that from the beginning. He might as well try to grab the tail of a comet.

Boots watched Jill pull to the curb, watched the front door open and her legs slide out. Then she was coming toward him, her confident stride as familiar as the auburn hair and the indigo eyes.

'Hey, Boots, the eye, it looks good.'

A year before, Boots had taken a beating that left him with a drooping eyelid. A plastic surgeon had repaired the damage only two months ago. The work had taken all of twenty minutes. The scar on his forehead was another matter. All the cures involved numerous visits with no guaranteed results.

'I should've done it earlier,' Boots said. 'The surgery was a piece of cake.'

Jill nodded before moving on to Captain Karkanian. 'And my condolences, too,' she called over her shoulder.

'Condolences?'

'About the way the Yankees' season ended.'

Boots laughed all the way to Sgt. O'Malley's cruiser where a second box of doughnuts had magically appeared. The Bulgarian hovered over the box, his attitude protective, but he gave ground when Boots arrived.

'I can't believe the asshole punked out,' he said, referring to Johnny Piano. 'Ruined my whole morning.' When Boots didn't reply, he added, 'That boss give you a hard time?'

Boots picked up a doughnut, then put it back. His weight was on the rise, his gut beginning to bulge despite the hundreds of sit-ups he did every week. Jill's comment, followed by that mischievous smile, didn't help either. Riddled with injuries, the Yankees had stumbled through the season, finishing well out of playoff contention. Nor were their prospects for next season in any way encouraging. The Yankee greats, men like Mariano Rivera and Derek Jeter, sure to make the Hall of Fame, were rapidly aging. They wouldn't be any younger by opening day, if they were around at all.

'Boots, you there?'

'What?' Boots glared at the Bulgarian for a moment before he remembered that Boris was six inches taller and fifty pounds heavier, a weightlifter who regularly juiced and was subject to extreme manifestations of 'roid rage.

'If you remember, Boots, I asked if that jerk gave you a hard time.'

'Yeah, but it was my own fault. I would've driven away, only I couldn't resist bustin' Pianetta's chops. That's what luck's about, right? No matter how hard you try to avoid trouble – and you can trust me on this because I've been trying hard from my first day on the job – you can't control luck. If Sorrowful had called my house five minutes earlier, I would've been in the shower and never heard the phone.'

'Damn, but I wanted a piece of that gangster's ass,' the Bulgarian replied. 'I wanted to smash his fucking face.'

SEVEN

Teddy Winuk strode up to the Tuscano Food Market as if he owned it, which, in a way, he did. He found Recep Babacan and Shuresh Banerjee, his main men, waiting for him on the sidewalk. Born in the United States, Recep's parents had immigrated from Turkey in the 1980s. Shurie was brought to the U.S. as an infant from India by his illegal mother. He wasn't eligible for citizenship, but that hadn't stopped him from embracing the American dream. Shurie was all about accumulating money. As soon as possible and by any means necessary.

Shurie needed guidance and control, which Recep cheerfully provided. Never mind Shurie's family being Hindu and Recep's Muslim. This was America, the new America where immigrants came from all over the world, Teddy Winuk being a good example. You got along to get ahead if you had a brain, if you were ambitious, if you wanted your place in the sun. The old-school mobs, especially the Italian mob, were on the way out because they were easy targets. Any time an Italian committed a crime, the whole country just assumed he was mobbed up.

And speaking of guineas, Teddy spotted Ben Loriano through

the window. Ben was standing behind the counter, smiling at a lady buying a handful of tomatoes.

Little Ben also wanted his place in the sun and Tuscano Foods was the path he'd taken. The market specialized in high-end cheese, produce and groceries, much of it imported from Italy. Lots of thirty-dollar bottles of olive oil, fifty-dollar bottles of balsamic vinegar, pecorino-romano cheese at twenty-four dollars a pound.

Ben had located Tuscano on Bell Boulevard in the upscale neighborhood of Bayside. The rent was bearable this far from Manhattan, and while his customers weren't rich by New York standards, they were prosperous enough to indulge a need to be sophisticated, not to mention discriminating.

'We're all on the same page, right?' Teddy asked. 'You don't say a word. You don't raise your hands unless I tell you to. We're just gettin' acquainted.'

Teddy kept his eye on Shurie while he spoke. Shurie tended to become upset when denied the fruit of his ill-gotten gains. No matter how many times it was explained to him, he couldn't grasp the simple notion that excessive violence was an indulgence as likely as not to put him behind bars. Meanwhile, he still lived with this mother.

'I'm good,' Shurie said.

The door opened and Ben's lone customer walked out.

'Time to rock and roll, boys.'

Tuscano had three employees on duty, one busy stocking shelves with groceries, the other two pulling boxes of strawberries from a crate. Teddy ignored them, walking directly up to an unsuspecting Ben Loriano.

'I've got good news and bad news,' he said.

'What?' Ben Loriano's thick eyebrows curled into little umbrellas that echoed the layers of deep wrinkles on his forehead. 'What?' he repeated.

'The good news is that you don't owe Rafi Lieberman a single penny. The bad news is that you owe me instead. Forty thousand dollars.'

Ben Loriano began to sweat, then and there, as if the drops were only waiting for a chance to make their escape. His brown eyes kept shifting to Recep, whose expression was now as empty as a drawn window shade. By contrast, Shurie bounced on the balls of his feet as he tried to contain himself. To Teddy Winuk, he looked more insane than threatening. But insane was good, too.

'I want my money,' Teddy said.

Loriano's mouth finally tightened as he folded his arms across his chest. A show of defiance was called for, but when he spoke, he couldn't manage to bypass the constriction in his throat. 'I haven't heard nothin' from Rafi,' he finally said, his voice a near whisper.

'Rafi's in Sloane-Kettering. He's got third-stage bowel cancer. What the docs figure, between the surgery, the radiation and the chemo, he might last another two years. That's why he decided to liquidate his assets and retire.'

Every word true. Luck had reared its head again, real bad luck in Rafi's case. The way Teddy figured, there's a bullet in the air and you're walking toward it. How close? How soon? Rafi was forty-nine years old when he got his diagnosis. That said, one man's trouble can be another man's opportunity. Winuk had acquired the Loriano debt for the bargain basement price of fifty cents on a dollar. Now all he had to do was collect.

'I need to check this out,' Ben said. 'With Lieberman.'

'I understand, Ben. My name's Ted, by the way. Now, what I'm gonna do is come back one day next week and you're gonna have forty cases of Frantoia Olive Oil – just like those bottles on your shelf, the ones that sell for thirty-five bucks – stacked up and waitin' for me. That'll cover the vig for the past month and give you plenty of time to check with Rafi.'

'It's too much,' Ben said. 'I'll go out of business.'

'Well, you can always pay the vig with cash. Let's see, ten percent interest times the four weeks you're overdue . . . equals sixteen large. You have it?'

Loriano turned his head down as he tried to absorb the extent of his troubles. Winuk didn't press the man. A month had passed since his last payment and Ben hadn't gotten so much as a phone call. If he'd come to believe that he was off the hook? Well, you couldn't blame him.

'I ain't got it,' Ben admitted. 'I mean the cash.'

'No big deal. I got a wholesaler in Staten Island ready to take the oil.'

'I can't get the oil, either. I got no credit.'

'Ben, I wanna be clear about this. You don't wanna bullshit me when I'm tryin' to be nice. Look around.'

Teddy let his gaze drift across the shop, which, to his untrained eye, reeked of prosperity. The freshly painted walls above the shelves were decorated with dancing vegetables, eggplants and tomatoes with legs. The new faux-marble floor didn't have a single scratch or a scuff mark. High-end produce topped every table and display. The chrome and the glass on the cheese counter gleamed. Plus, Rafi had examined Tuscano's books prior to issuing the loan, the one that allowed Ben Loriano to satisfy a pair of especially aggressive bookmakers. Tuscano Foods had produced a substantial profit in each of the past five years, despite the recession.

'Another thing, Ben. No more gambling until you pay off the debt. I can't have you riskin' my money. I hear you're gambling, I'm gonna take it hard. I'm gonna take it as you spittin' right in my face.'

The confrontation finally caught the attention of Ben's employees. They'd paused in their work and were muttering to themselves, unsure of what, if anything, to do.

'Look,' Ben said, 'I don't have the cash. I need some time.'

Teddy picked up a Cadbury bar, casually peeled off the wrapper and took a bite. 'Tell me something. Did Rafi Lieberman force the money on you when you originally contracted this debt? Did he shove forty grand into your pocket? Or did he not even know who the fuck you were until you went up to him said, "Please, Mr Lieberman, I'm in bad trouble. Could you loan me some money?"'

Teddy held up his hand. 'Don't say anything. I seen assholes like you a thousand times. You think life's a free fucking ticket. You think the bill's never gonna come due, that you'll just stumble through your dumbass life without having to pay. Shit, you probably even think you shouldn't have to pay at all, that you're somehow being cheated by a big, bad loan shark. You think you're a fuckin victim when you knew the deal going down. I got no respect for that.'

Teddy stepped behind the counter and walked straight up to the much smaller Loriano. 'You wanna call yourself a victim, that's fine, as long as you accept two things. First, the bill *has* come due. Second, you're *gonna* pay it. You don't, I'll hurt you until there's nothing left to hurt.'

One of Loriano's employees finally made a move. He started across the store, a good citizen riding to the rescue.

'Recep,' Teddy said.

A wrecking ball with arms and legs, Recep Babacan stood five-ten and weighed 230 pounds. He ducked under the oncoming employee's clumsy roundhouse right and drove a well-practiced left hook to the man's ribs. Ted watched the jerk drop to the floor, writhing like a snake in a pan of hot oil. The other two employees also watched, open-mouthed and wide-eyed. Lesson received, they didn't move.

'Next week, Ben. I'm gonna show up at a time of my own choosing and there better be thirty cases of olive oil in your storeroom. And you should consider yourself lucky. I could force you to sell the store and pay off the whole debt at once.' Teddy laid a hand on Ben's shoulder, the gesture meant to calm the man. 'Now, when you're alone and thinkin' over what happened here, try tellin' yourself this. If I'm a good boy, I'll come through fine. That guy named Ted? He's a businessman. Bankruptin' my little shop is not in his interests. Besides, I know I have to pay my debts. It's only fair.'

Teddy, Recep and Shurie piled into Teddy's 2009 Chevy Impala, Teddy in the back with Recep driving and Shurie riding shotgun. There was nothing special about the black sedan, no mag wheels, no pinstripes, not even a spoiler on the trunk. Under the hood, it was a different story. Teddy had acquired the car at an auction of police vehicles, then had a Hungarian mechanic put it in perfect working order, going so far as to replace the seats and the dash, and have the supercharged V8 engine completely rebuilt.

Teddy was determined not to make himself an obvious target. Beamers or Benzes were out, as were giant SUVs, gold chains, hip-hop gear and tattooed teardrops. On the other hand, concealed strength, like all that concealed horsepower ready to go at a moment's notice? Cards, in Teddy Winuk's opinion, were meant to be played close to the vest.

As they approached the Long Island Expressway, Teddy gave Shurie his marching orders for the day. They had sixteen commercial refrigerators sitting in a warehouse, the proceeds from a hijacking. Those units needed to be sold before the cops traced them.

'You told me they'd be easy to off, Shurie,' Winuk said. 'You told me you had connections with half the Indian restaurants in New York and we'd be rid of them in a week. Meanwhile, it's been two weeks and they're still sittin' there.'

'I know what I said, Teddy. I just need to meet up with this one guy.'

'And?'

'Three days. I promise.'

'Good, because I don't wanna have to do this myself. I don't have the time and I'm sick of the fucking excuses. Get it done.'

Teddy watched Shurie squirm. Though he'd been known to challenge men twice his size, Shurie, for some mysterious reason, was afraid of his boss. Or maybe he submitted simply because he was grateful. Barely out of his teens and headed for prison, with deportation certain to follow, Shurie had been running wild when he met Teddy Winuk. Now he clung to Teddy like a suckerfish to the belly of a shark.

'Recep, you do collections. Take Pablo with you. I'm gonna look in on a friend of mine, see if he's in need.'

Teddy had money out in Brooklyn and Queens, most of it loaned to small businesses, little grocery stores and jewelry shops. These were true mom and pop operations and the loans were fairly small. Teddy Winuk had no desire to overburden his debtors. If you lent out more than a man could pay, you'd never see your money again. On the other hand, if the debt was too great to be repaid quickly, but not altogether crushing, you could make a decent living off the interest. Still, collecting was a pain in the ass, lots of stops, lots of excuses, lots of threats, lots of tantrums. Not to mention the occasional beat-down when a lesson had to be taught. One thing about Teddy Winuk, if he couldn't get his money out of your wallet, he'd take it out of your ass. Soft was not an option for loan sharks.

Recep slid a CD into the car's sound system as he eased the Impala onto the Expressway. Hassan al Asmar, an Egyptian pop singer. If Recep and Shurie were together again tomorrow, fair being fair, Shurie would throw on some bollyrock, maybe Kolkata.

Teddy spent half his time maintaining the peace, but the potential gains were spectacular, at least in his estimation. Recep and Shurie and Mutava and Pablo, his four main men, hailed from different communities with different customs. That made for competition. But they could also reach into their neighborhoods to tap the vices that made criminals like Teddy succeed. New York was the most cosmopolitan city on the planet, home to immigrants from every part of the world, immigrants and their children. Like the native born, a certain percentage wanted to gamble and whore and use drugs and borrow money.

Teddy had earned an Associate's Degree in business at Manhattan Community College. That didn't make him Mitt Romney, but he'd internalized the part about supply and demand. Of course, there were hurdles related to language and custom, hurdles he fully intended to surmount by appealing, not to the immigrants themselves, but to their Americanized children. And he'd be the first of his kind to do so, the early bird in search of the worm.

Recep put the Chevy into the middle lane and kept it there. Slow and steady, Recep had jumped on Teddy's bandwagon because he lacked the brains, not to mention the ambition, to move up on his own.

'The Armenian, Asep Marjanian,' Recep said. 'He's been short two weeks in a row. If he's short again . . .'

'Does he wear a watch, a wedding ring?'

'Yeah.'

'Take 'em. And tell the prick, next time you'll take his car.'

Teddy settled against the back seat while Hassan al Asmar warbled away, some kind of sour, stringed instrument echoing his warbles in the background. Teddy didn't understand a word and he turned his thoughts to John Pianetta. Having personally tipped the cops, Teddy was certain that Pianetta knew about his kid's fate. All well and good, but now there had to be a next step, something a lot better than waiting for the shit to come down. Teddy's main goal was to stay ahead of the game. To act, not react.

The Impala bounced through a series of small potholes and

Recep eased off the gas. 'What I think I'll do about Marjanian,' he declared. 'I think I'll make him beg.'

And there it was. Teddy rolled down the window and let the cold breeze wash over his face. One thing about the guineas, they loved humility. For them, it was as much about kissing the ring, everyone knowing his place, as it was about the money. Not that the money didn't count. No, the money definitely counted, but the bended knee didn't hurt, either.

EIGHT

After leaving the crime scene beneath the Pulaski Bridge, Boots Littlewood checked in at the Six-Four, where he received word that a burglary suspect he'd been looking for, a kid named Alviro Chacon, had been arrested by a pair of uniformed patrolmen. Chacon now awaited Boots's attention in one of the squad's interrogation rooms.

Boots was eager to confront Alviro, but understood that time was on his side. Better to let the kid stew. Inside the squad room, he went directly to his desk and began to prepare a DD5 report describing his activities, from receiving Lieutenant Sorrowful's call to Karkanian's dismissal. As usual when he wrote up his reports, the computer slowed the process. It was so easy to add or delete that he found himself changing his words almost before he finished typing them out. That wasn't true when he used a manual typewriter. The typewriter forced him to organize his thoughts, knowing that whatever he put down would be handed over to the defense. Knowing that he might someday have a criminal defense lawyer ask, 'And would you tell us, Detective, what lies beneath that whiteout?'

Finished, Boots strolled over to Lieutenant Sorrowful's office.

'The good news,' he told Levine, 'is that we're off the hook. OCCB's gonna handle the investigation.'

'And the bad news?'

'Lily Bremer and Lou Fallanga. They took a shots-fired complaint on Sunday morning, spoke to the guy who made the original call, drove around for a few minutes, then called the report unfounded. Knowing Lily, they made an honest effort – the body was behind a bridge footing and couldn't be seen from the street – but the bosses might have other ideas.'

'That's a problem for patrol, not us.' Levine swiveled in his chair and arched his back, a bulging disc being one of his many physical complaints. He glanced at the photos on his desk, photos of his two children, a girl and a boy. The little girl wore a sparkling gold pinafore over black tights. The little boy wore a soccer uniform. He held a ball in his hands and his wide grin revealed a pair of missing teeth on the right side of his mouth.

Boots looked down. Something about the way Levine kept returning to the photos left him embarrassed for the man. Like he'd just revealed a secret that Boots would rather not know. Lieutenant Sorrowful's kids were in their thirties and lived far away. He barely knew his grandchildren.

'So, that's it?' Levine asked.

'I should only wish. You remember I told you about my being acquainted with the Pianetta family.'

That caught Levine's attention. 'Keep going, Boots. And don't leave anything out.'

'But you do remember, right? I told you that the Pianetta and Littlewood families attend the same church?' Boots spread his hands, inviting a response, which eventually came in the form of a grudging nod. 'Well, John Pianetta showed up at the scene. Demanding to see the body.'

'Don't tell me you braced him?'

'Yeah, I did. So now there's a captain at OCCB who also knows me and Johnny attend the same church. His name's Karkanian.'

'Did he confront you?'

'Briefly.' Boots took out a little packet of Tic Tacs and shook a few into his hand. 'I told him exactly what I told you.'

'That you go to church together?'

'There's no together to it, boss. In fact, if lowly precinct detectives were allowed to investigate wiseguys, I'd have already found an excuse to take the scumbag off the street.'

Levine was prepared to let the matter drop. The incompetency of the bosses down at the Puzzle Palace was taken for granted in the precincts, a self-evident truth beyond dispute. Boots on the other hand, had more to say.

'They like gettin' their pictures in the paper. I'm talkin' about the deputy chiefs at OCCB. All they care about is headline arrests, fifty suspects rounded up in five cities, the bosses, the under-bosses, a whole crime family in custody. This is not something you can do in a hurry and their investigations take years. Meanwhile, the mutts stay on the street, committing one crime after another.'

Both men were aware of a distinct possibility here. Cops and criminals did not associate with one another, the only exception being cops working undercover. Of course, if Boots was telling the truth, if he and Johnny Piano only ran into each other at church . . . well, you can't choose your neighbors. But Karkanian had nothing beyond the detective's word for his relationship with Pianetta. Plus, Karkanian lived in the ultimate cover-your-ass world. It would come as no surprise if he decided to report the 'relationship' to Internal Affairs, let the headhunters worry about it.

Boots and Levine were right, on one level. Captain Viktor Karkanian didn't know Detective Boots Littlewood. But the reverse also held true. Boots didn't know Karkanian, either. That point was driven home when a knock on the door to Levine's office was followed by Jill Kelly's appearance.

'Hi,' she said. 'Hope I was expected.'

The phone on Levine's desk gave off a series of bird-like cheeps, the last one echoing faintly in the small office. He looked at the phone for just a moment, then snatched it up. The conversation that followed was as one-sided as it was quick.

Jill kept her eyes on Boots throughout. He knew what was coming. Was he eager? Reluctant? Or just annoyed?

'That was Inspector McDowd at Borough Command,' Levine announced. 'Boots, you're on temporary assignment to OCCB. That means you don't work for me, so get your ass out of my office while I decide how to distribute your cases to my already overworked detectives.'

Boots led Jill to his desk in the squad room. 'You here to keep an eye on me?'

'Yeah.'

'And you don't care?'

'No.' Jill was ready to let it go at that, but changed her mind when she saw her partner's expression harden. Though she'd never tell him so, not least because they were incredibly incompatible, she'd come close to falling in love with him. Boots had never revealed the slightest desire to control, contain, dominate, subdue or tame her. Nor was he inclined to beg for her attentions. When she stopped calling, he'd drifted back to . . . No, he'd simply resumed the life he'd never strayed from in the first place. He'd remained his own man, before, during and afterward.

'OCCB,' she explained, 'is so far from the streets that it might as well be a corporate sub-department. Did you know that every phone tap has to be actively monitored? You don't start the recorder, then come back later to see what you captured. No, you have to sit there and listen to some mob mama talk about her hairdresser for two hours. You have to listen to wiseguys talk about the price of real estate in Syosset. One night, I spent two hours in a blazing hot attic listening to Joe Duranga and Sal Micchiono compare the virtues of a Lexus to an Audi. In the end, Sal decided to buy a Cadillac. I thought I'd go crazy.'

Boots's laughter rocked the little room. No human being on the planet was less suited to the tedious pace of Organized Crime investigations than Crazy Jill Kelly. No wonder she'd jumped at the chance to work an active investigation. Keeping her superiors apprised of her new partner's corrupt practices was simply the price she'd have to pay. In this case, being as Johnny Piano and Boots had no corrupt relationship to uncover, and she knew it, the price was too small to worry about.

'Yo.' The shout came from inside an interrogation room. 'Like I'm glad you po-pos are havin' a good time, but I been in this fuckin' room for three damn hours and I gotta take a piss. Swear to God, *maricon*, I'm ready to whip it out and let go in the corner.'

Jill glanced at a closed door. 'Who's that?'

'That's someone I gotta take care of before I do anything else. Gimme a minute here.'

The minute turned into ten as Boots led a short, thin boy from an interrogation room to a bathroom down the hall. The boy returned with a package of cheese puffs and a can of orange soda.

'I wasn't gonna run,' the boy said. 'I woulda come back.'

'That's good, Alviro. Because if I had to go out and find you again? Take it to the bank, this particular cop holds grudges.'

Boots set the boy on a chair bolted to the floor, but didn't handcuff him to the chair. He closed the door behind him as he left the tiny room. 'That's the FUCK YOU burglar,' he said. 'He doesn't know it yet, but he's gonna confess.'

'A burglar? Boots, tell me you won't delay investigating the death of a mob figure for a mope who steals television sets?'

Boots sat down behind his desk as Detective Connie Sherman entered the squad room. Sherman hesitated when he saw Jill, then nodded to Boots before crossing to his own desk. A moment later, he was on his computer, typing away.

'Carlo Pianetta's gonna have to wait until I nail this particular burglar. Alviro's creeped twenty apartments. He steals whatever cash and jewelry he can find, along with a TV or a laptop, or sometimes both if the television's not too big. You understand, his victims are all working-class people. They can't replace these losses by snappin' their fingers.' Boots slipped out of his jacket, unbuttoned his shirt and loosened his tie. 'But that's not the worst of it, Jill. Alviro trashes the apartments, slices the cushions on the couch, slices the mattresses, tears up letters and photographs. Then he spray-paints FUCK YOU on the walls so you have to put on ten coats of paint to cover it up.'

A smile tugged at the corner of Jill's mouth. Did Boots Littlewood think removing his jacket transformed him into an average Joe? Between the shoulder rig and the bunched muscle in his shoulders and neck, he looked even bigger without the jacket. Bigger in a menacing way that screamed cop.

'How can you compare property loss to the loss of life?' she asked. 'A few years from now, this jerk's victims will barely remember what happened. But there's no "few years from now" for Carlo Pianetta. He's dead.'

Boots didn't expect cops who worked special squads to understand precinct life. Those units moved all around the city, a few months here, a few months there. They never hung around long enough to meet the citizens they protected and served. The bosses stationed at Borough Command or the Puzzle Palace were even more handicapped. Statistics dominated their working lives, especially the ratio between complaints and arrests. Some hadn't come within spitting distance of the streets for decades.

'Let me explain it like this,' Boots finally said. 'When someone in the family dies, someone else has to go through their belongings. Everything, right? You have to decide what to give away, what to throw out and what to keep. My dad wasn't up to it when mom passed, so the job fell to me. Lemme tell ya, I wasn't in such great shape either – Mom was our rock – but it had to be done. So I went at it one afternoon when my dad was out of the house. I don't know what I thought going in, but what I found were her treasures.'

Boots drummed his fingers on the desk. This was a place he'd never gone, not even with his father. 'I found 'em in a box tucked way back in the closet, a bunch of love letters tied up with a ribbon, some costume jewelry and a few porcelain figurines. The letters were from a boyfriend she had in 1962, before she met my father and they left Ireland. I think Mom was about fifteen at the time. The letters didn't really amount to much. He'd love her forever, she was the love of his life, nothing could tear them apart. The usual adolescent garbage.' Boots finally met Jill's eyes. 'I don't wanna drag this out. The jewelry also wasn't much, or the little figurines either, but when I finally looked around, I realized that everything in the apartment was a treasure to my mother. The furniture, the good silver, the good dishes, the photos in the living room –which she called a sitting room to the end of her days – these were all her treasures, the life she'd built up. Now imagine her comin' home one day to find everything destroyed by some kid with anger management issues. Imagine those letters ripped up and tossed to the floor like so much toilet paper. Imagine the jewelry missing, the figurines smashed. It'd be like takin' her whole life away, my father's, too. It'd be like they got wiped out by a hurricane, only without being eligible for a low-interest loan from the government.'

Jill started to interrupt, but thought better of it. 'Go ahead, Boots.'

'Now this kid's committed a couple of dozen burglaries in which he destroyed his victims' treasures, but I've got exactly one I can hang around his neck. A witness saw him coming out of an apartment building with a TV in his hands, a witness who knows him. You're sayin I should book him and walk away. But if he's only got the single charge, the judge'll set a low bail, or maybe even release him on personal recognizance. Keep in mind, the kid just turned seventeen and most judges don't take burglaries too seriously. On the other hand, if I get a confession, I can charge him with enough counts to make the prosecutor and the judge think twice.'

Slightly out of breath, Boots grabbed a case file and headed into the interrogation room. Jill waited until the door closed behind him, then made her way to a small window. This was a one-way mirror that revealed two small chairs and a table, the only furniture in the room. The chair behind the table was occupied by a teenage boy. He stuck his chin in the air and crossed his legs as Boots took a seat, a show of defiance that didn't fool Jill Kelly, who had a predator's nose for weakness. Alviro's dark eyes were fearful and sad as he watched Boots roll up his sleeves to reveal a pair of obscenely thick forearms. The kid's life, all seventeen years of it, had taken a bad turn somewhere in the past and it was about to get a lot worse. Go, Boots, go.

NINE

Teddy Winuk opened the door to the Poseidon Lounge on North 11th Street and took a tentative step inside. He drew a deep breath as he glanced around, then marched off to a stool in the shadows at the far end of the bar. Teddy wasn't fooling himself. The Poseidon was home turf for the Pianetta crew and the few late-afternoon customers, including Mike Marciano, the Rock, were carefully evaluating his sudden appearance. Marciano was John Pianetta's tax collector. Teddy found his presence at the Poseidon encouraging. Despite the tragedy, Johnny Piano and Company had opened for business.

Al Zeno, the tavern's ancient bartender, put down his racing form and made the long walk from the other end of the bar. He looked exactly like the ex-pug he was, with a flattened nose, thick scars along both brows and hearing aids in his ears. Not the disappearing type. Al's hearing aids were large enough to serve as speakers for a rock band.

'So, whatta ya want?'

'Heineken.'

'Tap?'

'Bottle.'

Teddy forced himself not to look around as Al shuffled off. He'd chosen the role of penitent, not to mention supplicant, and he intended to stay with the script no matter what the provocation. Not that he expected trouble. The expectations were all on the other side. The wops played a simple game: I can disrespect you any time I want, but you can never disrespect me. All Teddy had to do was observe this simple rule and he'd be fine. Or so he hoped.

On reflection, while reviewing his best moves earlier in the day, Teddy had admitted that he, too, played the game. You couldn't allow strivers on the lower rungs of the ladder to disrespect you, ever. But Teddy understood that respect was something you extorted from people who feared you. The guineas believed respect was due them.

Teddy settled down to wait. The Poseidon was lit by track lights that reflected dimly in the walnut paneling, and by the lights behind the bar, a system designed to keep the booths along the wall in deep shadow, as the cork floor and acoustical drop ceiling were designed to muffle sound. At the other end of the bar, a small television was running a close-captioned account of yesterday's races at Aqueduct.

The wait turned out to be short. Within a few minutes, the Rock sidled up to him. Marciano didn't sit. He stood behind and just off Teddy's right shoulder.

'You got a lotta nerve comin' here. You got balls of steel, which I might just decide to remove with a fuckin' blowtorch.'

Teddy looked down at the bar. He kept his shoulders slumped and his voice low. 'I heard what happened on the news,' he said. 'I don't wanna add to your troubles.'

'Add to my troubles?'

'Yours and John's. I'm here to pay what I owe ya. I woulda paid sooner, but I came up short last month on my collections.'

The excuse was bullshit and both men knew it. Teddy was making a simple offer. If the Rock pretended that Teddy hadn't defied him and his boss, Teddy would hand him an envelope with five thousand dollars inside. With the promise of more envelopes to come. That would take the heat off while he planned his next move.

Mobsters being as greedy as private equity capitalists, the Rock didn't ponder the offer. He confined his skepticism to a single hard look, then said, 'In my office.'

Teddy rose and followed Marciano across the bar and down a narrow hallway to a small office that reeked of stale tobacco. The room's two windows were sealed with brick, the better to foil OCCB and FBI listening devices.

Marciano dropped his bulk into a leather chair on the far side of a massive wooden desk. 'Take a seat.'

Teddy laid the envelope on the desk. 'I did a couple of deals last week. If things work out, and I have no reason to think they won't, I'll do better next month.'

'That's good to hear.' The Rock put on his reading glasses, then made a little production out of opening the envelope. He hefted it, sliced the top with a small pocket knife, separated the edges and peeked inside. Finally, he slid the envelope into the center drawer on his desk. He didn't actually count the money, the assumption being that Teddy wouldn't have the balls to shortchange Mike Marciano.

'So, whatta ya doin'?' Marciano said. 'How come you been avoidin' me?'

The Rock's short face was all jowls and furrows. When he raised his brow, as he did then, his skin settled into a series of parentheses on either side of his face. He'd been fearsome once, a thick-chested bull of a man. Not anymore. Like his boss, the Rock had softened, though not, of course, in his own estimation.

Teddy dropped his eyes. 'Ya know . . . I mean, I didn't have the money and I didn't know how you'd . . . how you'd react.'

'C'mon, Teddy, don't bullshit a bullshitter. We're in this thing together. That's the whole point. You come to me, say you can't pay the tax, I'm gonna arrange for a loan.'

A loan at ten percent interest per week.

'Next time,' Teddy said. 'I'll remember.'

'Are you tellin' me there's gonna be a *next* time?'

'No, no. We're doin' good now. There won't be any more problems, I promise. Like I said, you got troubles of your own. I don't want you to worry about me.'

'Worried? Do I look like I'm worried?' When Teddy failed to respond, the Rock transitioned to a lecture he routinely delivered to his hard-pressed debtors. 'You gotta pay your taxes, just like you would if you were a square john and worked for a paycheck. In return, you get connected to us and nobody fucks with us. If somebody tries to muscle in, we take care of the problem. In other words, with us watchin' your back, you could operate freely. You don't have to be lookin' over your shoulder every minute, wonderin' who's comin' up behind ya.'

Having heard this lecture before, Teddy let his mind drift. Not that he disputed the facts. Order was good. Turf battles were bad. Besides, Teddy himself was busy establishing the same order in a Queens neighborhood dominated by Indian immigrants and their children. Shurie, acting as their point man on his home turf, had approached the neighborhood's small and mid-level dealers. He'd keep them supplied with whatever they sold, from weed to OxyContin, at competitive prices. Even better, he'd front the drugs for a short time. In return, he wanted only one thing. He wanted to become their exclusive supplier.

Did they sense the trap? Probably not, any more than a bug on a leaf senses the oncoming tongue of a hungry frog. Then again, Shurie's pitch wasn't exactly an offer. The neighborhood was being organized, to everyone's benefit. Go along or stop dealing. Never mind that in the long run you'd become an employee. Never mind that if you ran up a little debt, the Teddy Winuk crew would own your sorry ass. Just go along.

'So, like I'm sayin',' the Rock continued, 'everybody pays it up, including me. If there's someone at the top, somebody who only collects, I ain't met him and I don't expect to. Me, I pay my taxes and I'm glad for the opportunity.'

When Teddy finally looked up, he had to stifle a laugh. The Rock had put on his sincere face, mouth and jaw firm, chin dropped. Meanwhile, his dead black eyes might have been carved from obsidian.

'Like I said, Mike, I know you got troubles enough. I don't want to add to your problems.'

'My problems?'

'With Carlo gettin' . . .'

Marciano's expression instantly hardened, a simple trick that Teddy knew well. Still, the dead eyes were a lot more convincing in this context.

'What happened this morning, to Carlo, it didn't have anything to do with you, right?'

'Jesus, Mike, I . . .'

'Forget what I said, kid.' Marciano leaned back in his chair and spread his hands. 'You're not stupid enough to hit a made man like Carlo. But there's a favor you could do for us. To, like, ease the family's suffering.'

'Name it.'

'If you should hear anything, any loose talk about Carlo? Even if you think it's bullshit, let us know. The family would owe you, Teddy, and the family always pays its debts.'

'Yeah, no problem. I'll keep my ears open.'

'I appreciate that. And I'll see you next week.'

Teddy had the doorknob in his hand when the Rock dropped the hammer. Not real hard, not hard enough to hurt. The envelope, after all, was in the drawer. Just hard enough to remind.

'I heard you bought Rafi Lieberman's accounts. That true?'

'Some of them, but yeah, I cut a deal with Rafi.'

'That's good, Teddy, and I can see that you're goin' places, which I got no objection to. But you shoulda told me up front. You wanna be trusted, you gotta trust. The way it is now, I feel I gotta watch you.'

TEN

'If you're goin' out, I'm gonna go with you,' Tommy Frisk said. 'It ain't safe out there.'

'No need, Tommy,' Corry told her brother. 'I'll be all right.'

'You don't look all right.'

And that was the truth. Corry Frisk had passed a good half-hour in front of the bathroom mirror, about as long as she could bear standing upright. Swollen to mere slits, her eyes and the right side of her face, when she started, were the color of an overripe plum. Maybe even a rotting plum.

This was a deformity that a thick layer of concealer had failed to conceal. Her skin was now a shade of lavender she associated with the handkerchiefs her grandmother carried in a tiny, beaded purse.

What she ought to do, being as she was safe here, was hole up until she halfway healed, then get her sorry ass out of town. Tommy had army buddies down in Florida. Buddies who'd put them up, no questions asked.

That was the sane thing to do, a course of action Corry would definitely take if she lived in a sane world. If she wasn't a heroin junkie, for example. Or if Tommy hadn't been blown up one too many times in Afghanistan.

Five to be exact, and he still had all his limbs, which was unnerving because a whole chunk of his mind had gone to hell and stayed there. By last count, there were eight guns in his one-bedroom apartment, including an M249 machine gun that had to be a major felony waiting to happen.

On one level, Corry was sympathetic. Her own post-traumatic stress disorder was ongoing. She couldn't stop replaying her . . . Corry couldn't find an adequate word for what happened to her. Assaulted? Raped? No way. Not even close.

Corry's brain wouldn't stop rerunning the whole chain of events, from when Carlo Pianetta pulled up on Navy Street to the bullet that blew Carlo's brains all over the asphalt. Sometimes in sequence, sometimes a piece here, a piece there. Especially the moment when she knew, as she knew the sun would rise, that Carlo was going to beat her to death and dump her body in the river. In truth, she'd never been more certain of anything. Never.

What actually happened didn't matter. Every time her brain dragged her back to those minutes before the guy showed up, the certainty returned. She was going to die and there was nothing to be done about it.

It was like they were already closing the lid on her coffin. Rest in peace, whore.

The issue, the big issue, which Corry somehow had to face, was that she'd recognized Sir Galahad. She didn't know his last name, but she'd seen him once or twice at a bar where she hooked before Stat put her on the street. His friends, one of whom was bargaining for her services, had called him Teddy.

Corry had been a fool to get into the car with Carlo. He'd seemed straight enough, but she'd been warned about him, and not once, but twice. So, what could you say? Corry Frisk had fucked up again? Gee whizz. Somebody tweet Beyonce.

It seemed, to Corry, that the stakes just kept getting higher. For the whole of her life, every minute, every second. And now she was playing for the biggest stakes of all. Corry had been watching the news all day, especially the part about Carlo with his pants down. Carlo was a big-time mobster – that's what they were saying – and his even bigger-time father would be after a little payback. Make that a lot of payback.

If John Pianetta put things together, he'd look to Corry for answers. Hell, he might even blame her. After all, if she wasn't out there being raped and beaten half to death, Carlo would still be alive.

Big stakes, all right. A blunder here would be the last one she'd ever make. As if she wasn't in enough pain.

One step at a time, Corry told herself, first things first. She watched her brother jam a pistol behind the waistband of his jeans. Tommy was a handsome boy, his face bright and youthful, even after four deployments. But he was also a walking time bomb and ordinary people shied away from him. The long hair didn't help, or the stringy beard, or the camo gear . . .

Corry doubled over as a spasm tore at her gut. Even beyond the pain, she was sick and getting sicker and the only fix was a fix. The *only* fix.

'You wanna protect me, little brother?' she asked, knowing very well that what Tommy really wanted was a mission.

'Whatta ya think, Corry? You're my sister and somebody kicked your ass and you won't tell me who . . .'

Corry waved him off. 'All right, all right, I hear ya. And I could use the protection, which I admit. But you're gonna have to lose the hair, lose the beard and dress like a civilian. The kinda war we're in, you don't wear a uniform.'

It was threatening rain when sister and brother stepped out of a thirty-unit apartment house on 90th Street in Jackson Heights. Corry wore one of Tommy's ponchos, in basic camo, of course. The hood practically covered her face, especially if she kept her head down, which she would do anyway.

Corry's face throbbed with every step, but she never paused. The rhythm of her legs remained constant, if a bit ragged, as she covered the few blocks to the elevated subway stop at the junction of Elmhurst and Roosevelt Avenues. Tommy walked on the far side of the street, no doubt mentally rehearsing his quick-draw technique.

Corry was on the way to meet a working girl named Shoona. If Shoona was true to her word, she'd be carrying twenty bags of heroin for which Corry would pay double the going price on the street. Corry didn't begrudge Shoona the profit. But if Corry Frisk could add two and two, so could Shoona. Maybe she wasn't bringing Corry's medicine. Maybe she was bringing John Pianetta.

If so, Corry intended to go down fighting. For once in her miserable fucking life.

Shoona was seated alone at a table, munching on a slice, when Corry stepped inside Solliano Sicilian, a pizza shop on Elmhurst Avenue only feet from the subway stop.

'Girl,' she said, 'what happened to you?' When Corry didn't reply, she added, 'Like that, huh? Well, I expect you're in a hurry, so let's move on.'

Shoona carried the remains of her slice into an intermittent drizzle. She hesitated, then raised a butterfly-festooned umbrella big enough to shield a minivan. Drawing Corry into the umbrella's shadow, she passed over a Ziploc bag containing twenty glassine envelopes.

'You been to a doctor?' she asked.

'Fuck the doctor,' Corry said. 'I got my medicine right here.'

ELEVEN

By the time Boots and Jill finally headed out, at four o'clock, the skies above were rapidly darkening and it had begun to drizzle. It would rain hard that night, a cold, November rain certain to leave the city's many homeless residents scurrying for cover. Doorways, awnings, subway cars, anything but a shelter system that ran by a simple rule long associated with prison life. The strong collect, the weak pay.

In no hurry, Boots drove his ancient Taurus along North 12th Street, the ball fields of McCarren Park to his right, a series of construction sites to his left. The Northside was changing fast. The three-story homes that once dominated had been torn down, replaced within months by sleek apartment buildings with floor-to-ceiling windows. The developers were already selling condos at prices no one he knew could afford.

For the most part, Boots avoided the pity parties his neighbors regularly attended. Williamsburg and Greenpoint had undergone many changes over the years, one group muscling in, another moving out. Poles, Jews, Irish, Italians, Puerto Ricans and Dominicans had fought too many turf battles to count. But if the actors had come and gone, the two neighborhoods had remained working class throughout. No longer. Hundreds of people had been displaced and dozens of businesses uprooted to provide housing for young professionals who'd never work in the small factories and warehouses that provided the natives with a paycheck. But they just might buy up those factories in order to build even more unaffordable housing.

There was nothing to be done about the situation, of this Boots was certain. Here, too, the strong and powerful devoured the weak and helpless. Boots could only hope that his street wouldn't be included in the next wave of development. In any event, with Jill Kelly sitting beside him, Boots was content. The smoke curling up from a cigarette didn't hurt. Nor did that amused look only a step from sultry.

'Did you have it all planned, Boots?' Jill asked, her tone playful.

'All what?'

'You urged the prosecutor to fight for a high bail after you told Alviro he could rely on you to do exactly the opposite.'

'I only said that to get his confession.' Boots was prepared to drop the matter, what with Alviro being in his personal rear-view mirror, but finally relented as he eased the Ford around a truck delivering sheetrock to a construction site. 'Remember I told you that Alviro cut up the cushions and mattresses in the apartments he trashed?'

'Sure.'

'Well he did the cutting with his own knife, one of those combat knives where you can flick out the blade with your thumb. It was found in his pocket when he was picked up. Bad news if someone had come home unexpectedly, which is why I want him off the street for as long as possible. Most burglars don't carry weapons.'

Jill tossed her cigarette out the window. 'Bottom line, never trust a cop?'

'Bottom line, don't destroy other people's homes and not expect to pay a high price when you're finally apprehended. I've been after this kid for a long time. The way you saw him this afternoon? Scared out of his little mind? Trust me, the Alviro who spray-painted those walls bears no resemblance to the terrified Alviro trapped in the box. They might as well be unacquainted.'

Boots turned east on Kent Avenue and followed it to Franklyn Street. Behind him, newly erected apartment buildings along the waterfront stretched back to the Williamsburg Bridge. Ahead, squat, flat-roofed cubes built a hundred years ago lined both sides of the road. These buildings, from the grimy brick to the artless graffiti, had yesterday written all over them.

'You wouldn't want to tell me where we're going?' Jill asked.

Boots answered her question with one of his own. 'Explain it to me again. What's your assignment?'

'I've been sent to keep an eye on you while OCCB investigates Carlo's murder.'

'Well, you're doin' a fine job.' Boots turned his head to look at her, a smile playing at the corners of his mouth. 'But if OCCB's handling the investigation, where we're goin' doesn't really matter. Hell, we could go to the movies and nobody would give a damn. Or even notice.'

Jill stared out through the windshield. Having decided to cover his ass, Karkanian had dispatched Jill to spy on Boots. Or maybe his aim was to rid himself of Jill Kelly, a general pain in the ass and a poor detective to boot. Either way, at no time had Captain Karkanian expressed a desire to have Jill and Boots investigate the murder of Carlo Pianetta.

'Where's your sense of adventure?' Jill asked.

'I locked it in a safe the last time someone took a shot at me. If my memory serves, you were there at the time.'

'C'mon, Boots, admit it, we had a lot of fun.' Jill laid her hand on her new partner's shoulder. 'Do you remember the time I pretended to be a hooker and you picked me up on the street? Do you remember telling me to get in the backseat? Do you remember . . . Why Boots, your face is getting all red. Your neck, too. If I didn't know better, what with the round head and the buzz cut, I'd think I was looking at a giant erection.'

Boots sighed. 'We're heading for the crime scene,' he admitted. 'I want you to see something before the rain washes it away.'

The sun was all but down by the time Boots pulled to a stop behind a Sixty-Fourth Precinct RMP. Two cops, Louis Fallanga and Lily Bremer sat inside, their mission to protect the scene in case the Crime Scene Unit wanted another shot.

Boots took a flashlight from the trunk of his Taurus, then approached the two cops. 'You on punishment detail?' he asked.

'I'm on overtime and I have a kid who needs braces,' Lily said. She jerked her chin at Jill, who stood by Boots's Taurus. 'That who I think it is?'

'That's Jill Kelly.'

'Crazy Jill. If I remember right, last time the two of you worked together, you nearly got killed.'

'So did she.'

Boots led Jill into the deep shadows beneath the bridge, past a footing, to where Carlo Pianetta had breathed his last. He played the flashlight's beam over the trail of blood and tissue that extended outward from where Carlo's skull, or what was left of it, had once rested.

'What'd you see this morning?' he asked.

'The victim took one to the head.'

'That's it?'

'I spoke to the ME's investigator. There was just the one wound.'

'The Death Investigator? You didn't examine the body yourself?'

'I took a look, Boots, and like I said, there was just the one visible wound.'

Boots sighed. Jill had never pretended to be a great, or even a competent, detective. Truth be told, she wasn't cut out to be a cop, and probably wouldn't have considered the job if she wasn't descended from a cop family that had deep roots in the NYPD. Or if her father hadn't been a hero detective who'd given his life for the job.

'So, what do you think happened to Carlo?'

Jill shook her head. 'I don't think I want to play professor-student today, but what with a single shot to the back of the head, it looked like a professional hit.'

'Except . . .?'

'Except that Carlo's pants and underpants were around his ankles.'

Boots slid the flashlight beam to the left of where Carlo had fallen. It took him several minutes to find what remained of the blood spot he'd discovered earlier. Someone from the Crime Scene Unit had collected most of the blood, but the outline of the stain was still visible.

'That's what's left of a bloodstain that couldn't have come from Carlo. Like you said, one shot to the back of the skull and the spatter all went in the same direction. When I noticed it, the odd bloodstain, my first thought was that it was deposited by the shooter. But that still wouldn't explain the pants around the ankles. Plus, the shot was fired from behind Carlo, not from where I found the bloodstain. What I finally did, knowing Carlo Pianetta to be a particularly vicious criminal, was check his hands. The knuckles on both his hands were stained with blood, but they weren't cut.'

Boots turned away from the crime scene and began to walk back to his car. Jill put the pieces together as she followed. The puzzle wasn't all that complex anyway. The pants and underwear around the ankles indicated a sexual encounter. The bloodstain and the blood on Carlo's hands indicated the use of force. But why hadn't Boots simply said the word rape? Was he being considerate? Early in her teens, Jill had witnessed her father's murder, then been raped by his killers. Maybe Boots thought she was still fragile, that hearing the word might trigger some kind of PTSD-like response. That was so far from the truth that Jill almost laughed aloud. She'd tracked down the men who killed her father, had enacted the ultimate revenge, understanding all the while that what she wanted most – to alter the past, to bring her father back – could never happen.

'You're thinking Carlo was in the act of raping someone?'

'Someone he'd beaten severely.'

'And then what? She had a gun, or got hold of his gun?'

'Carlo wasn't killed by his victim. The shooter stood behind him and off to one side.'

'A partner?'

'Some kind of gang rape? That's possible, but very unlikely. Given the blood, we have to assume the attack had been going on for some time. If the partner intended to kill Carlo all along, there was no reason to wait. And there's something else. We can be sure Carlo's victim wasn't killed because there's only the small bloodstain.'

Boots and Jill slid into the Taurus as the first drops of rain began to fall. Within a few seconds, the patter on the roof above their heads grew steady. Jill waited for Boots to start the car, then turn on the lights and the wipers. She watched the wipers trace a greasy trail across the windshield before she spoke.

'You think she was taken away?'

'Why? Why not kill her, too? Look, I could be completely wrong, but you have to start somewhere and I'm starting with the most likely explanation. Somebody happened along and caught Pianetta in the act. Though he took the opportunity to make the world a better place by sending Carlo's soul to hell, he had enough humanity to spare Carlo's victim, who then left the scene.'

Jill poked Boots in the ribs. She laughed as Boots flinched. The man was still ticklish. 'I thought cops didn't believe in coincidence.'

'Jill, if coincidences didn't happen, there wouldn't be a word for them.'

Boots put the Ford in gear and pulled away from the curb. 'This case,' he said, 'we don't have a realistic chance of closing it. First thing, in a normal homicide investigation, you interview family and friends. Did the victim have any enemies? How'd he get along with the missus? Was he feuding with the wrong neighbor? But that approach is out because Carlo's whole life revolved around the Pianetta crew, none of whom will give us the time of day.'

'We could look for the woman. If she was badly beaten, she must have sought treatment.'

'That's exactly what I intend to do.'

TWELVE

'I'm surprised you haven't popped the big question,' Boots said as he turned onto McGuinness Boulevard.

'You talking marriage, Boots?'

'I'm asking why, if we're right about what Carlo was doing just before he met the end he so richly deserved, the victim didn't report the assault. I'm asking why, since her attacker was dead, she didn't call for an ambulance.'

Boots reached under the seat and withdrew a bottle of Windex. He rolled down the window, stuck his arm out and sprayed Windex across the windshield.

'Better,' he said. 'Now I can see where we're going.'

'Which is where?'

'Woodhull Memorial Hospital, also known as Hell On Earth. I'm hoping Carlo's vic went to their emergency room.'

Jill stared out through the clean windshield at a young couple huddled under a massive umbrella. In no hurry, they ambled along, arms around each other's waists. The girl had a cell phone in her free hand and she held up its glowing screen so her companion could have a look.

'I don't know if you heard, but there are new medical privacy rules in place. You'll need a warrant to look at medical records and you won't get one. Not for a fishing expedition.'

'Sometimes it's not a matter of askin' the right question. Sometimes you have to ask the right person. Woodhull is where cops interview victims, and where prisoners are taken if they're too crazy to be handled in the house.' Boots paused for a moment, then said, 'I have a lot of friends at Woodhull.'

Ten minutes later, as they got out of the car, Boots and Jill clipped their badges to the lapels of their coats lest they be mistaken for patients. Or victims.

Woodhull Hospital's emergency room easily matched Boots's description. Cacophony first, crying children, scolding mothers, howling crack addicts handcuffed to gurneys. A man standing near the door was giving a passionate address to an audience visible only to himself. A sobbing woman spread her hands before her, a supplicating gesture ignored by the nurses and aides who whizzed past. Several men wandered through the room, jostling other patients, their expressions clearly belligerent.

Underfunded, like every city hospital, Woodhull was located on Broadway, the borderline between Williamsburg and the nearly all-black neighborhood of Bedford-Stuyvesant. Williamsburg's yuppies avoided Woodhull, as they avoided small, dark bars with Spanish names. Except in dire emergencies, they took their private health insurance to Manhattan's private hospitals. Woodhull was reserved for Medicaid patients. It was also, by far, the hospital closest to the Pulaski Bridge.

'This place is crazy,' Jill observed.

'You should see it on Saturday night,' Boots said.

A uniformed hospital cop, a woman, interrupted Jill's reply. 'Hey, Boots, you got a minute?' She kept her eyes on Jill as Boots approached. 'You don't mind, I need to speak to you confidentially.'

Boots shook his head. 'You can speak in front of my partner, Consuela. But first, I have something I want to ask you. Were you on duty Sunday morning?'

'Yeah, I worked a double on Sunday.' Consuela's round face opened into a broad smile. 'I'm payin' tuition fees for three kids in Catholic School. Truth be told, with the hours I gotta work, they spend more time with the nuns than with their mother.'

'I danced that dance with my own kid,' Boots said. 'All the way into college. He bought into a business a year ago and now he's finally livin' on his own dime. In fact, the little prick makes more than I do.'

Though Consuela laughed, her eyes never stopped moving across the emergency room. This was her realm, this lunacy, and from her point of view, peace reigned in the land.

'OK, tell me what you want, Boots.'

'I want to find out if a woman with facial injuries was treated here on Sunday morning sometime after eight o'clock. I'm talkin' about a serious beating, an *obvious* beating.'

'Any race, any age? Gee, Boots, why don't you make it hard for me?'

'Sorry, Consuela, that's the best I can do. So, what was it you wanted to ask me?'

The emergency room door blew open to admit two cops, Sgt. Craig O'Malley and Boris Velikov. They pushed a limping, hand-cuffed prisoner ahead of them. Boots waved, but didn't turn away from Consuela.

'So?'

'It's about my sister's boy, Julio Vargas. The asshole got himself arrested three days ago for stealin' a car. It's killin' his mother. He's fifteen.' Consuela stopped abruptly and drew a deep breath. 'I'm his godmother,' she explained. 'It's killin' me, too.'

Boots nodded. He'd worried about Joaquin making a stupid mistake, one that would follow him for the rest of his life, throughout the boy's high-school years. 'Where'd this happen, Consuela?'

'He and his buddy snatched the car on Jewel Street. They didn't make it to McGuinness Boulevard before they crashed into a stop sign.'

'Was Julio driving?'

'No. But the boy who was really driving, a hoodlum named Rafael Quintera, says he was.'

'So it's one boy's word against the other?' Boots waited

for a nod. 'You wouldn't know the names of the arresting officers?'

'Sorry.'

'Well, I can ask around, but I wouldn't expect much more than a heads up. It'd be different if Julio hadn't already been charged. Now it's mostly up to the prosecutors. And by the way, Consuela, if I hear the kid's a knucklehead, I won't lift a finger to help him out.'

Consuela stared into Boots's eyes for a moment, then turned away. 'I don't remember a battered woman comin' through on Sunday morning, but let me check with the coordinator.'

Left to themselves, Boots and Jill created a small island of calm in the misery around them, a bit of dry land on a flood plain. This was a case of practice makes perfect. Given the amount of time cops spent in emergency rooms during their years on patrol, they either erected floodgates or drowned in the suffering. Just ahead of them, a woman cradled a feverish toddler, his face flushed, his hair soaked with sweat. The bawling child would not be consoled.

The woman called to a passing nurse. '*Mira, mira.*' She didn't protest when she was ignored, but only settled in her seat and patted the child on the back. 'Ai, *niño*. Hush, hush.'

Jill took Boots's elbow in her hand. No matter how ugly Woodhull's emergency room, it was far preferable to sitting on a stakeout for eight hours, or analyzing ten hours of recorded conversation, which you were somehow supposed to accomplish on a single, eight-hour shift.

'The question you asked, about why the victim didn't report the assault?'

'Right, what do you make of it?'

'Well, how do we know she was severely injured?'

'That's a different question, but I'll answer it. First point, Carlo is very fit, very strong and ruthless in a fight. Second point, there was blood on Carlo's shirtsleeves as well as on his knuckles, which could only have gotten there if he'd hit his victim multiple times. Now it's possible the victim's dead, that she was taken away, like you suggested, and killed somewhere else. But if she's alive, she's lying up somewhere. We have one advantage, Jill. Pianetta doesn't know any of the details, which is the main reason I was so determined to keep him away from Carlo's body.'

Consuela chose that moment to return, already shaking her head as she approached. 'Sorry, Boots. No such. We had two stabbings and a gunshot wound on Sunday morning. All the victims were men.'

'That's pretty much what I expected. I'll look into that thing with your nephew and get back to you.'

As they walked toward the door leading into the parking lot, Boots and Jill were approached by a morbidly obese patient in a hospital gown that didn't come within a yard of covering his enormous ass.

'Gimme some money,' he said.

'Fuck off,' Jill returned.

'Say what?'

Boots resisted a powerful urge to drive his fist into the man's gut. If he hit this jerk, he'd have to arrest him and that would mean spending hours at the house writing up arrest reports. Boots had better plans for the evening. He laid his fingers on the man's chest and gently pushed him to the side.

'Like the lady said, fuck off.'

'You touchin' me?'

Consuela appeared at Jill's shoulder. 'Amos Sugarman,' she said, 'you don't get your retarded ass back on the gurney, I'm gonna send you up to the rubber room.'

The man dropped his head and muttered something unintelligible before turning to walk away, his giant cheeks alternately rising and falling with each step.

'The thing about Amos,' Consuela observed, 'is that askin' for money is the only trade he knows.'

Inside the Taurus, Jill yanked a cigarette from her pack and lit up. Boots took a deep breath as he turned the key in the ignition, thinking only a few more hours before she filled his bedroom with smoke.

'We need to make one more stop,' he said.

'Sorry, but you're gonna have to make it without me.' Jill tucked her cigarettes into her purse. 'I need to get home. Why don't you drive me back to the house so I can pick up my car?'

Boots struggled to keep the disappointment out of his voice. 'I do something to offend you?'

'No, and if you want, you can stop by later, but I have to go.'

Boots didn't bother to respond. He would definitely stop by later. Of that, he had no doubt. He'd been dating a divorcee named Berta Blugolovic for the past two months, but the relationship was going nowhere. Just as well. Her criticism of his chosen profession, and the hours it imposed, had been unrelenting. Still, Jill's resigned tone wasn't lost on him.

'You have trouble at home?'

'Yeah, with my mother. If you remember, I told you she was a drunk.'

'I remember.'

'Well, her liver gave out and now she's waiting on a transplant, which she's not gonna get because she won't stop drinking. We have a health aide, Simone, but she takes off at nine o'clock.'

Boots tapped the steering wheel as the memories flooded his consciousness, memories he ordinarily kept at a distance. His own mother had died of cancer only a few years before, died slowly and painfully. Now, with Thanksgiving a few weeks away, he vividly recalled Margie Littlewood's final Thanksgiving. That she wouldn't see another had been obvious to all and the effort to maintain holiday cheer had taken a toll. Along with a significant chunk of his heart.

As Boots piloted the car toward Richardson Street, he tried to imagine the situation from Jill's point of view. A Lone Ranger, suck-it-up type, Jill almost surely resented her mother's alcoholism. Boots had been to the house Jill shared with her mother many times without ever laying eyes on the woman. Yet Jill still went home at night to care for her.

'You comin' by later?' Jill asked when Boots pulled to a stop alongside her Chrysler.

'To your house?'

'My house and my bed.'

'Count on it.'

'Good, I've missed you.' Jill stepped into the rain, started to close the door, but then suddenly leaned back inside. 'She's fifty-five years old, Boots. Fifty-five years old and she's killin' herself. I don't get it. Really. I just don't fucking get it.'

THIRTEEN

Silvio Mussa, universally called Silvy Mussa, walked into his last stop, Carney's Pub, at nine o'clock. He had a job to do, a simple task. Collect the tax, then carry it and the rest of his collections to the Poseidon Lounge and the waiting, not to mention greedy, hands of the Rock. A younger, more ambitious man, a man eager to move up, would have completed this assignment before settling down for a few drinks. But Silvy, at age seventy-four, was neither young nor ambitious. Stabbed once and shot twice, with the scars to prove it, he'd survived enough mob wars to earn a few privileges. Johnny Piano's father was still a bachelor when Silvy made his bones.

Carney's Pub was as phony as its owner, Sean Carney, a fourth-generation American who affected a slight brogue. Sean didn't have to fear being caught out. His tavern on Grand Street was designed to attract Williamsburg's young professionals, not native-born Irishmen. No, Sean considered the pub to be Irish-*themed*: leprechauns pushing gold-filled wheelbarrows, giant shamrocks, a decent collection of hand-carved shillelaghs, Kelly-green walls, the Clancy Brothers and the Wolf Tones on a battered jukebox.

All for show.

Well, the show must go on, Silvy mused as he dropped onto a stool at the end of the bar. His show, of course.

'Chivas, neat,' he told the bartender.

The bar was quiet, as usual on a Monday night, with only a few patrons scattered about. The oldest among them by a good forty years, Mussa didn't feel out of place, although his full head of silvery hair stood out like a beacon. No, not even the most obvious truth, that he'd become an errand boy, an aging house servant kept on out of kindness, was enough to knock him off his perch. In his own mind, he'd be Silvy Mussa, mob warrior, until the day he died.

Silvy was halfway through his second Chivas when Sean

Carney sat down next to him. Although the bar did well, especially on weekends, Sean derived most of his considerable income from a bookmaking operation run out of the pub's windowless basement.

'How's the action?' Mussa asked. Not that he really cared. The tax was the tax, through good times and bad.

'I'm takin' a lot of Jets' money. If it keeps on this way, I'll have to lay some of it off.'

'If you don't have a guy, I could recommend someone.'

'No, I got a guy in Boston. I take his Patriots' action, he takes my Jets'.'

'What about the Giants?' Mussa asked. The Giants were New York's second football team.

'Not this year, Silvy. This year the Giants are straight-up losers and the money splits about even, depending on the point spread.'

Sean moved in close to Mussa, putting his back to his patrons as he slid an envelope into Mussa's open briefcase. Silvy nodded approvingly. One thing about Sean, he knew his place. No bullshit, no poor mouthing, no excuses of any kind.

'Good man,' Silvy muttered before returning to his drink.

Mussa busied himself for the next half-hour with a third scotch and the reflections in the mirror over the bar. Behind him, three young girls flirted with a series of men – boys, actually – rejecting all with the sort of caustic remarks that no woman could have gotten away with back in the day. Meanwhile, after a few abortive attempts to make contact, the unattached males in the bar took the hint and busied themselves with a football game running on the flat-screen over the bar.

Have any of these girls ever met a real man, Mussa wondered. A real man like him. Or him when he was young, anyway. These days, when Silvy Mussa needed pussy – which wasn't all that often, truth be told – he bought it. And not girls this young. No, if he hoped to get any further than wistful desire, even with Viagra, he needed a hooker who got by on her technique, not on her looks.

Mussa glanced at his watch. Ten thirty. He slid off the stool, pausing long enough for the crick in his back to release. In theory, he was expected in the Rock's office by ten o'clock.

'Silvy,' Sean Carney said as Mussa passed, 'I'm thinkin' ya
might want me to call a cab.'

'What, you sayin' I can't drive?'

Carney smiled. 'You're wobblin' a bit is the only point I'm
makin' here.'

'Well, fuck you, too.'

'Same old, same old? A couple of drinks and you're disposed
to fight the world?'

'I already fought the world, ya punk. I fought the world and
I won.'

Carney gestured to the door. 'Tell that to the police when they
pull you over. See if they're properly impressed.'

Silvy touched his jacket, right where the bulge of the gun he
once routinely carried should be. Nothing there. His coat over
his arm, he stepped off, shuffling out of the bar and into a relentless downpour he'd somehow entirely forgotten.

'Shit,' he muttered. His car was around the corner and he could
sprint to it faster than he could put on his bulky overcoat. If he
was still able to sprint, that is, or even walk very fast, which he
wasn't, especially after a few drinks. He finally draped the coat
over his head, pulling it tight around his face. Still, rain spattered
against his forehead and ran down into his eyes. He wouldn't
have seen a tank coming down the street, or heard it above the
pounding of the rain. He certainly failed to notice the man who
trailed behind him. Or that the street ahead was deserted. Or that,
on this residential block, there were no security cameras to be
found.

Still pissed, at the rain and at Sean Carney, Silvy Mussa
jammed his hip against the steering wheel as he got in the car.
If the flash of pain that followed was predictable – lately, his
doctors has been hinting at replacement surgery – it was nonetheless searing, and it took Silvy a moment to remember that he
needed to bring his left leg into the car and close the door. His
soaked coat now sat on his head like a saturated sponge.

Befuddled by age and alcohol, Mussa only managed to arrange
the various pieces after a struggle. A waste of time, as it turned
out. As he reached into his pocket for his keys, the window beside
him exploded into a million tiny pieces. He jerked away, a matter
of instinct, raising his hand to cover his face. A few seconds

later, when he dropped his hand, he found himself looking into the barrel of a gun.

'Gimme tha' briefcase, man.'

Silvy stared, not at the man's face, which was covered in any event, but at the rosary draped around the man's neck, a mix of black and gold beads with a small metal skull instead of a crucifix dangling from the bottom.

'Whatta you . . .'

The barrel of the gun inched forward until it rested between his eyes, rendering him effectively mute.

'Last chance, Silvy. You don' gimme the *maricon* briefcase, I'm gonna be killin' your *blanco* ass and takin' it anyway.'

Mussa's head jerked at the sound of his name, but he maintained his cool. The funny thing about getting old was that you only wanted to get older. Fuck the infirmities.

'Awright, take it. But I'm tellin' ya that you're makin' a big mistake. And it ain't me. I'm just an old man. It's Johnny Piano who's gonna run you down.'

Apparently unimpressed, the man took the briefcase with his left hand, then fired three .22 caliber rounds into Mussa's body, the first two into his exposed shoulder and the last into his left thigh. Overwhelmed by the unrelenting downpour, the gunshots barely registered, even in his own ears.

Teddy pulled away from curb, taking his time. Beside him, Pablo Santiago, a second-generation Dominican, stripped off the idiotic rosary and wrapped it around the barrel of the gun before jamming both under the seat. The rosary bore the colors of a tiny Salvadoran street gang centered in Greenpoint's Cooper Park Houses.

'Talk to me,' Teddy said as Pablo wiped his face with a towel.

'Piece of cake, baby.'

'Silvy's still alive?'

'Was when I left, but . . .'

No further explanation was necessary. Bullets did unpredictable things after they entered a human body, even small-caliber bullets. 'Did you check in the briefcase?'

'C'mon, Teddy, the briefcase he gave me was the same briefcase he was carryin' when he left Carney's. Plus, it was pourin'. If I would've opened it, we'd be dryin' the money in an oven.'

'Open it now.'

Pablo did as he was told, though he couldn't suppress a scowl. Teddy had four main men. If he'd been running an Italian mob, he supposed they be called capos, since each ran a crew of his own. He tended to view them as minority shareholders in his personal corporation. Pablo Santiago was by far the most difficult of the four, a man who'd rather eat glass than take orders. On the other hand, he was also a man who could be trusted to put three bullets in the body of a helpless senior citizen. Costs and benefits. Weighing and measuring. There was no such thing as a perfect employee, as his Business 101 instructor, Susan Underwood, had explained at length.

'Here.' Pablo yanked a handful of white envelopes from the bag and held them up. 'Satisfied?'

Teddy checked his mirrors, then pulled to the curb. He slid the gun and the rosary into the bag, then put the bag in the trunk. He did this himself, a small concession to Pablo's injured feelings.

'Looks like you fucked yourself,' he observed as he made a right on Meeker Avenue, merging with the traffic headed for a Brooklyn-Queens Expressway onramp at the foot of the Kosciusko Bridge. 'There's gotta be twenty grand in there.'

The remark produced another sulk. Teddy had originally offered Pablo a third of the take, but Pablo had bargained for a guarantee. He wanted three thousand dollars, succeed or fail. A poor choice, but Pablo had a history of poor choices, one of which had landed him in a medium-security prison for several years.

Twenty minutes later, Teddy dumped the gun and the rosary in an enormous dumpster on a quiet street in College Point. He didn't think they'd be found, but neither item could be traced to him in any event.

Teddy's day had begun at five o'clock in the morning, but there was still work to do. He dropped Pablo in Sunnyside, and headed for a twenty-four-hour coffee shop on Manhattan's Lower East Side. Nose to the grindstone. Shoulder to the wheel. Still, when he discovered two lanes closed for repair on the Williamsburg Bridge and traffic backed up for a mile, he found himself dialing Sanda Dragomir's number on his cell phone. So much for resolutions.

Sanda's husky voice had a way of rumbling up from her chest, creating an odd echo, and Teddy found himself instantly stirred when she answered on the third ring.

'Hello, Teddy.'

'Hey, baby, what are you doing tonight?'

'Waiting for you.'

FOURTEEN

Teddy had a habit of making promises he wasn't immediately prepared to meet. Shurie, for instance, had been telling low-level drug dealers in Jackson Heights that he could supply any quantity of anything they wanted. Now the orders were pouring in and they had to deliver and they didn't have enough product. Robert Lorton, the man he was to meet, worked in a pharmaceutical warehouse in Yonkers that supplied almost the whole of Westchester County. Not the big boys, not CVS or Duane Reade or Walgreens, but the many hundreds of independents.

Lorton's message had reached Teddy through a third party. A small quantity of various narcotics, from OxyContin to Valium to Ritalin, could be skimmed from the company's inventory without attracting the attention of regulators. Lorton had no desire to retail these pills. He wanted a single buyer, one man to handle the entire flow.

Teddy loved the whole scheme. Violence ruled in the drug world, actual violence or the threat of violence. You protected yourself with simple ferocity. Fuck with me and I'll kill you. This deal was entirely different. When he finally showed, fifteen minutes late, Mr Lorton radiated paranoia, a middle-aged man so far out of his comfort zone he might have been standing in a prison yard. Once hooked, he could be held in place by fear alone.

'You see that briefcase under the table?' Teddy asked as Lorton worked on his second beer. By then, Teddy had had been maintaining a reassuring smile for so long that his lips were numb. 'Take a look in the front compartment.'

Closing in on fifty, Lorton was all gut and no ass. The press of his distended belly on the edge of the table when he leaned forward produced a breathless grunt, but his hand didn't come within a foot of the briefcase.

Teddy picked up the briefcase and laid it on the seat beside Lorton. 'Try not to be too obvious,' he said. 'But take a look.'

The envelopes Teddy emptied before entering the restaurant had contained as many five- and ten-dollar bills as they did fifties or hundreds, a deficiency Teddy had overcome by stuffing the bills into the briefcase's smaller front pocket so that they could only be seen from the top.

'If you're the supply, I'm the demand,' Teddy said as Bobby Lorton peered down at this display of wealth. 'Let's drink to a happy marriage.'

Teddy sat at Sanda's little Formica table and watched her prepare a late-night snack. Sanda hadn't protested when he called, hadn't asked for an explanation, or even clarification. Just as well because Teddy didn't have an answer that passed his personal smell test.

Sanda turned to him, a plate of fried cheese perogies topped by a mound of sour cream in her hands. As she leaned down to lay the plate on the table, the edges of her semi-transparent peignoir came apart to reveal her small, round breasts. All very calculated, as Teddy knew, but effective nonetheless.

Teddy cut one of the perogies in half, dipped one of the halves in the sour cream and stuffed it into his mouth. Maybe, he thought, this is what I want. Or maybe it's all I can hope for.

Handsome and very fit, with an easy charm when he chose to be charming, Teddy never had trouble meeting college-educated women who talked about their jobs and their friends and their Twitter followers and their Facebook postings, about where they spent their last vacation, where they hoped to spend their next vacation, the next bonus, the next pay raise, the riches they expected to accumulate through talent, hard work and perseverance.

Somehow, they didn't see themselves as the good worker ants they were. Somehow, they imagined themselves to be savage competitors, when they didn't have an ounce of fight in them. Somehow, in the end, they turned him off.

'You wanna quit?' Teddy asked, the question out before he considered the consequences.

'Quit? What am I to quit?'

'Whoring.'

'To do what, Teddy? Clean floors of rich peoples? I am illegal.'

'I can set you up with a decent apartment, take care of your bills.'

'Then I am not to quit whoring.' Sanda flashed her wistful smile, the one that hinted of secrets Teddy would never know. 'I am to be Teddy Winuk's personal whore.'

'You mean you wouldn't be doing it out of love?'

This time Sanda laughed. 'When I arrive in America, I look in my suitcase, but love wasn't there. Stupid Sanda. I must have forgotten to pack this.'

Teddy was still chuckling when he finished his meal and pushed the plate away. 'What if I gave you a job?'

'Job for committing crimes?' Sanda put a finger to Teddy's lips. 'If I am charged with crime I will be returned to Romania.'

'I didn't say there were no risks. But there are risks to what you're already doing, like the chance that you'll make a date with the wrong guy and get your throat slashed.'

'You are doing this for what reason, Teddy? For love with me?'

'Sanda, baby, I've never been to Romania. Hell, I don't know if I could find it on a map. But I left my love somewhere, too. Maybe on a subway car in the Bronx.'

FIFTEEN

Boots hightailed it through the rain, from his car to Frankie Drago's little porch. He rang the bell as he wiped his forehead with a handkerchief still damp from his foray into Woodhull Medical Center.

The porch light came on and Drago's face appeared in a little window on the door. A second later, the door opened.

'Hey, Boots, come on in. You want a beer?'

Boots and Frankie Drago shared a common history that had culminated with Frankie sentenced to a year and a day in prison for involuntary manslaughter, the victim in this case being his sister, Angie. Released only a month before, Drago was already directing the bookmaking operation he'd turned over to a nephew while he was away. The kid had done a good job, according to his uncle, expanding the operation. As a result, Steve Marrone was now a junior partner.

Prison had been good to Frankie, who'd done his time on an honor unit at the Otisville Correctional Facility. Now forty pounds lighter and toned by long hours in the weight room, he felt as if he'd somehow been returned to his youth. He felt vigorous, powerful, ready to meet any challenge. Except, possibly, Boots Littlewood's sour expression.

Boots followed Frankie into the kitchen. He accepted a beer and sat at the table. Nothing had changed in the months since he'd been here. The tail on the Minnie Mouse clock still twitched back and forth. The plastic tablecloth still depicted the glories of ancient Rome. Pale red curtains still covered the windows. Never mind that Angie Drago had died in this kitchen. Or that she'd been the one to decorate the room.

'So, what's up?' Drago asked.

If Boots was the hard-ass detective who dragged a confession out of Frankie Drago, he was also the detective who guided Frankie through the criminal justice system and showed up at Frankie's parole hearing.

'I've reviewed the case many times and I believe Angela Drago's death to be entirely unintentional,' he'd explained to the Parole Board. 'And I was there when Mr Drago made a full confession. At the time, he was about as remorseful as a man can be.'

Boots had been wearing his usual three-piece suit, the vest a bit snug over his broad chest, his blue tie pulled tight against the collar of his white-on-white shirt. Between the clothes and the buzz cut and the big, square face, he'd been every inch the cop. You listened to him because he brought a cop's cold calculation to his argument.

Here it is. Take it or leave it.

Lucky for Drago, the board had taken it, releasing him on his first try, and now Boots Littlewood held Frankie's marker, which he'd continue to hold into the indefinite future. And Boots wasn't shy about collecting debts. The guy had the instincts of a loan shark.

'You heard what happened,' Boots said. 'With Carlo Pianetta?'

'Yeah, he got caught with his pants down.'

'What?'

'C'mon, Boots, it was all over the news tonight. They found him with his pants down. Me, I'm thinkin' he was a homo. I'm thinkin' he was bending over when he bought the farm.'

Boots closed his eyes for a moment. The whole point of confronting Johnny was to prevent him from learning this particular detail. 'What exactly do you mean when you say "all over the news"?'

'OK, I watched the story on the local news at six o'clock. Channel Four, NBC. They claimed the story was exclusive to them, but so what? Bet your mother on this one, Boots. By eleven o'clock, it'll be on every station. And the front pages of the *News* and the *Post* tomorrow morning.'

Calm down, Boots told himself. It's done, finished, over. Some asshole at OCCB leaked the detail to his favorite reporter. Now you have to live with a new set of facts. A far more complicated set of facts. Like the fact that there's only one innocent in this scenario and that's the woman Carlo assaulted. You've been assuming that she's safe, wherever she's hiding, because Johnny Piano doesn't have enough facts to put the pieces together. Now he does. And Johnny isn't stupid enough to conclude that his son was gay. Carlo was a pussy hound if there ever was one. Sex was his only recreation. His wife knew it. His father knew it. Hell, his kids knew it.

'Anything else?' Boots asked. 'Any other little details heretofore known only to investigators? Were there any pictures, for instance?'

Frankie bridled at his reaction to the cop's narrowed eyes and tightened fists. Boots had a volcanic temper when aroused and Frankie instinctively backed off, his tone somehow apologetic though he'd done nothing more than tell the truth.

'No pictures. And really nothing more than what I already said. I mean the station was playin' up the sex angle, which you gotta figure is natural. Nothin' sells tickets like sex.'

Boots twirled the beer bottle between his palms. He'd have to move faster now, much faster, and that meant a lot of guessing. Educated guessing, but guessing nonetheless.

'What about on the street, Frankie? What are you hearin' on the street?' Boots raised a hand. 'No, scratch that. I want to know if you pay off Johnny Pianetta.'

'What kinda stupid question is that? Yeah, I give Johnny a piece. There's no way I could operate in this end of Brooklyn without payin' the tax.'

'You're right,' Boots admitted. 'I take it back.'

'Look, Boots, there's advantages to payin' off. Like a heads-up when Vice targets the neighborhood. Like nobody messes with me because they know I'm connected. Peace of mind, right? That's what I get for the money.'

Boots's cell phone sounded the opening notes of the tune 'Chances Are', the Johnny Mathis version, his mother's favorite song. Annoyed by the intrusion, he took the phone from his jacket and checked the screen. Lieutenant Sorrowful, another messenger with bad news.

'What's up, boss?'

Boots listened for a moment, then said, 'Will do.' When he turned to Frankie, his smile was so nasty it could only have been inspired by infantile delight.

'You know Silvy Mussa?'

'Sure. He's Johnny Piano's main runner.'

'He's protected, right, by the same people protecting you?'

'Of course.'

'Well, someone forgot to watch his back. Silvy's at Woodhull, recovering from three gunshot wounds.'

Frankie's chest tightened. 'You think he was robbed?'

'I don't know, but I'm going to Woodhull to ask him.' Boots finished his beer and laid the bottle on the table. Trailed by Frankie, he walked to the door and stared through the window at the splatter of raindrops on the pavement. 'See, Frankie, the thing we really want to avoid is a mob war and there's only one way to do it. The police have to take Carlo's killer into custody. Otherwise, it's gonna be family feud time. The killing could go on for years with nobody knowin' who's gonna be the next casualty.'

'Fine, but what's this got to do with me?'

'The hit on Carlo? At first, I thought the shooter was somebody with a personal grudge, Carlo being a scumbag of the first magnitude. But that's yesterday's news, what with the assault on Silvy. There's a crew out there willing to attack the Pianetta family, simple as that.'

'And you think I know who they are?'

'No, I'm thinkin' that you speak to a lot of people in your line or work. I'm thinkin' you're gonna hear rumors. I know you're not a rat, but I want you to pass them on to me. Think of it as self-preservation. I mean, you spend every Wednesday at Silky's Bar collecting and payin' off on the week's bets. Have I got that right?'

Frankie could have pointed out that Boots put down a bet on nearly every game the Yankees played, but he didn't want to get sidetracked. 'Not everyone loses, but, yeah, that's the routine.'

'So, how many people know that, Frankie? How many people know you'll be carryin' a bagful of money on Wednesday night when you finally head home? And who might they have told?' Boots tapped Frankie on the chest. 'Believe me, if the people who killed Carlo and shot Silvy aren't afraid of Johnny, they're not gonna be afraid of Frankie Drago.'

Boots left it at that. He'd planted a seed and that, for the time being, would have to do. Still holding his cell phone in one hand, he hustled through the rain to his car, started the engine and turned the heater's fan to full high. The engine was still warm. Thank the Lord.

Relying on memory, Boots tapped out Jill Kelly's cell number. Jill had asked for an adventure and now she'd get one.

'Hey, Boots,' Jill said, 'I hope you're not canceling out on me? I have enough trouble with my self-esteem.'

In fact, as Boots knew, recklessness, not self-esteem, was Jill Kelly's problem. But he didn't argue the point, launching, instead, into a description of the NBC newscast and the assault on Silvy Mussa.

'Right now, there's a cop standing in front of Mussa's door. Nobody in or out except family, which in Mussa's case means no visitors at all. Silvy's wife has Alzheimer's. She's in a nursing home and their only kid, a daughter, lives in Ann Arbor . . .'

'How do you know this?'

'What could I say? I try to keep up.'

In fact, Boots relied mainly on the three graces: Fianna Walsh, Dorota Nitski and Jenicka Balicki. Well into their seventies, gossip was their lifeblood, the nourishment that kept them going. On warm afternoons, they sat in front of Jenicka's apartment and conferred with every passing neighbor. On Sunday mornings, they worked the crowd at their respective churches. On Wednesdays, bingo night, they plied the gamblers at St Anthony's.

Silvy Mussa's wife, Anka, was the daughter of two Polish immigrants who'd moved into Greenpoint shortly before WWII. She and Jenicka Balicki had begun attending Mass at the Polish church when they were children. They'd continued the practice until Anka, in Jenicka's words, couldn't tell the difference between a confessional and a Porta Potti.

'But this is the thing, Jill. When Johnny hears about the shooting, he's gonna go crazy, what with his son already being portrayed as a homosexual. For sure, he's gonna run over to the hospital. For sure, he's gonna have a bodyguard with him, probably armed. For sure, I could use a little backup.'

'Ahhhh.' Jill's little sigh of appreciation went right to Boots's groin, danger being Jill's foreplay of choice. 'Gimme a second.'

When she came back on, her tone was matter-of-fact. 'It's costin' me, but Simone decided she can stay after all. I'll be at Woodhull in about a half-hour.'

'I'll meet you in the parking lot. That good?'

'Actually, I do have a question.'

'And what's that?'

'Would you be terribly upset if I whistle the theme song to *High Noon* as we come down the hallway?'

SIXTEEN

When Boots and Jill came out of the elevator on Woodhull's pre-surgery unit, the atmosphere precluded any serious drama. John Pianetta, his son, Tony, and a third man stood at the end of the hall, talking quietly. Just past them, a uniformed cop lounged against the wall. He stood up straight when he saw their gold shields, but said nothing.

The three gangsters turned when Boots and Jill emerged, but except for John Pianetta's little scowl, quickly returned to their conversation. They didn't look up when the pair walked past them, not even when Boots fixed them with the hardest cop stare in his cop-stare arsenal. Only Boots recognized Tony Pianetta, yet both dismissed him as no threat. The third man, in his mid-thirties, drew closer attention. His eyes were as blank as they were dark.

As Boots had predicted, Johnny Piano's body was being guarded.

Boots and Jill didn't slow until they approached the uniformed cop. Tall, broad and very young, his nametag read Gilden.

'Littlewood and Kelly,' Boots said by way of introduction. 'Is this Silvy Mussa's room?'

'Yeah, he's in there with his wife.'

Jill grabbed the back of her partner's arm. 'You might wanna slow down here,' she said.

Too late. Boots was already pushing through the door. Ahead of him, a woman leaned over the room's single bed. She was in her forties, at most, way too young for Silvy Mussa. Not that she hadn't made an effort. The bone-white makeup and the tight bun did make her look older, but she'd put on that makeup way too thick and the shoulders of her navy sweater were flecked with powder.

The woman's eyes jumped from Boots to Jill, then to their gold shields, finally to the expression on Boots Littlewood's face. She drew back slightly and looked to the side as she considered her options.

'Who are you?' Boots asked.

'Hey, Boots, take it easy. That's my wife.'

The head of the bed rose a few inches to reveal Silvy Mussa's smiling face. The smile was drug-induced, at least in part. His pupils were mere pinpoints. But there was another element, too, one Boots recognized. More scars, more glory. He'd taken three bullets and lived to tell the tale.

Boots drove his foot into the side of Silvy's bed, the jolt hard enough to excite the pain receptors in the man's brain, despite the narcotics. The bullets fired into Silvy's body had fractured several bones in his shoulder and cracked his left femur. This time, when they spoke out, he listened.

'Jesus . . .'

'Stop right there, Silvy. I don't allow anyone to use the Lord's name in vain. And if you were about to call me Boots again, you need to think twice. That's because you're a piece-of-shit gangster and I'm a New York City police officer. My name, as far as you're concerned, is Detective Littlewood.'

Boots didn't wait for an answer. Nor did he notice the amused smile on his partner's face. He grabbed the collar of the blond woman's coat and yanked her through the door.

'Officer Gilden, I want you to search this woman for a weapon and then take her into custody.'

'What?' The woman's broad mouth turned down at both corners until the ends rested to either side of her narrow chin. 'What for?'

'For interfering in a police investigation. I knew Anka Mussa before she went into a nursing home and you're not her.'

Boots finally turned his attention to John Pianetta and his companions. The bodyguard's blank expression hadn't changed, leaving Boots to wonder if it was the only one he had. Johnny Piano and his son, however, were both smiling. They'd pressed his buttons and there was nothing he could do about it.

Or so they apparently thought.

Jill at his side, Boots approached to within six feet of the body-guard. 'You've got a bulge beneath your coat on your right hip that leads me to believe that you're armed. I want you to turn around, put your hands on the wall and spread your feet. If you don't, I'm authorized to use whatever force necessary to make you comply.'

The bodyguard wore a black, microsuede raincoat. Confused by the unexpected command, his fingers moved toward the opening in the unbuttoned coat. The movement was tiny, almost a tic, but did not go unnoticed. Jill Kelly's weapon leaped into her hand, the draw so fast it seemed like a magician's trick.

'Keep your hands apart or I'll kill you,' she said.

There being nothing in Jill Kelly's voice or expression to belie the threat, all three gangsters froze.

Boots, on the other hand, finally relaxed. He'd gotten his own hand to the butt of his weapon before Jill completed her draw. The last time they'd been in this position, he was still trying to unbutton his coat.

'No more warnings,' he said. 'Turn around and put your hands on the wall.'

His expression still unchanged, the man cautiously complied. He'd been here before and he wasn't about to give the woman an excuse to pull that trigger. He spread his hands and feet without being asked and he didn't resist when Boots plucked a forty-caliber Colt from a holster tucked behind his belt, exactly where Boots said it would be. Only after Boots handcuffed him and he was allowed to stand straight did he speak.

'I want a lawyer,' he said, the words directed as much to his boss as to Boots Littlewood.

Jill lowered her weapon to her side. Boots had promised a little fun and that's exactly what she'd had. Not all that much, because the gangsters hadn't posed a serious threat, but a lot more than she'd been expecting when she got home that evening.

And Boots wasn't through, not even close. He walked to within a yard of John Pianetta and said, 'You next. Put your hands on the wall.'

Credit where credit is due, Jill thought. Tony Pianetta stepped up, prepared to put himself between his father and Boots, a tight squeeze that would certainly trigger the use of force Boots had mentioned earlier. Tony was fifteen years younger than Boots. He was also two inches shorter and fifty pounds lighter. The confrontation would be short-lived unless Tony's father jumped in. If that happened, Jill would pull the little sap from the front pocket of her coat and beat him about the head and shoulders until he ceased and desisted.

Much to her regret, it was not to be. John Pianetta put a hand on his son's chest and shook his head.

'Step back, Tony, learn a lesson.' The gangster's tone was cool and controlled, but his reddened face told another story. 'The cops are the good guys, right?'

Boots stripped away Pianetta's coat and jacket, methodically searching through the outside and inside pockets of both. Then he put his hands on the gangster's shoulders.

'I don't know what it is about people like you,' he said as his hands began to move across Pianetta's body. 'You somehow think you can interfere in a police investigation without suffering any consequences. That's arrogance, Johnny. That's vanity, which is one of the seven deadly sins. And yet there you are, at church every Sunday, offerin' prayers to the Lord.'

Boots ran his fingers up and down Pianetta's left leg, taking his time. But instead of repeating the procedure on the right leg, he wrapped his fingers around the man's family jewels and squeezed just hard enough to reveal how much damage he could do if he decided to make a fist.

'Here's what pisses me off the most. You go to church? OK, that's part of the game. I understand. But when you march up to the altar rail and take the body and blood of the Savior in your hands, when you bring the Host to your mouth, when you swallow it down . . . You got no right, Johnny. You got no right at all. Now you take your kid and get the fuck out of here.'

As they watched the Pianettas step into the elevator, Jill poked Boots in the ribs. 'How come,' she asked, 'you failed to mention that anger is also one of the seven deadly sins?'

To Jill's surprise, Boots took the question seriously, pausing for a moment to organize his thoughts. 'I admit,' he finally said, 'to being a half-assed Catholic. When it comes to religion, I'm pretty much like everyone else. Yeah, I'm tryin', only not too hard. But Johnny Pianetta's a cold-blooded murderer. He's killed in the past, many times, and if I'm not mistaken, he plans to kill in the immediate future. There's no salvation for men like that. If the prick ever had a soul, it died long ago.'

'Now you're talking blasphemy.'

'Which is another failing I don't plan to mention when I write up my Daily Activity Report.'

SEVENTEEN

Boots and Jill spent another forty-five minutes taking a statement from Silvy Mussa. According to Mussa, he'd stopped at the location where the shooting took place to buy a newspaper from a little grocery store. For reasons unknown, a man stepped up to his car, broke the window and fired three shots into his body. This man, who never made a sound, wore a ski mask that covered his face and neck. In fact, as even his hands were covered, Mussa was unable to identify his race. He might have been white or black, a Latino or an Asian. He might have been from Mars.

'Sorry, Detective, but that's the best I can do.'

Boots watched Mussa press the little button that controlled his morphine drip, watched the man's eyes flutter and his breathing slow.

'How about height and weight?' he asked.

'Average. Maybe.'

With Mussa's signature at the bottom of a written statement, Boots herded his two prisoners onto the elevator. He relieved Officer Gilden at the same time, ordering him back to patrol. Johnny Piano would soon be privy to facts unknown to the police. This was certain to happen because Boots intended to release Maria Coloroso once they got to the precinct. The basic charge, interfering with a police investigation, was unsustainable. Filing it would only piss off the prosecutors and his boss, a matter of wasting taxpayer dollars on a personal vendetta.

'You could do me a favor,' Boots told Officer Gilden before dismissing him.

'What's that?'

'You know who John Pianetta is, right?'

'Yeah.'

'Well, what happened between me and Pianetta . . .'

'You want me to keep it to myself?'

'Just the opposite. I want you to spread the story, and ask your brother and sister officers to spread it, too. I want the scumbag's humiliation on the street. I want everyone in Greenpoint to know about it.'

Gilden stared at Boots for a moment, a slow smile gradually lighting his features. 'Consider it done.'

It was nearing two thirty by the time Boots finished the paperwork and dropped off Alberto Buffo (whose expression had yet to change) at the precinct's basement jail. Jill had headed home to relieve her mother's home health aide more than two hours before. Initially disappointed, Boots was now looking forward to his bed. He wouldn't get much sleep under the best of circumstances. Find the victim. That was the name of the game both he and John Pianetta would now play. Could she identify Carlo's killer? To answer that question, she'd have to be found.

Work harder. Work longer. Boots had always subscribed to these maxims, but he wasn't fooling himself. Johnny had resources of his own, along with methods of persuasion unavailable to Boots, and more bodies to do the persuading.

As for Boots, he had Crazy Jill Kelly. Jill was a definite asset, given that Boots had humiliated a man who'd staked his entire reputation on not allowing himself to be disrespected. Violent retaliation could not be taken off the table just because Boots wore a badge.

Boots weighed these factors as he left the Six-Four, as much a home to him as his apartment on Newell Street just a mile away. The rain had finally stopped, replaced by a cold wind out of the northwest. Boots started to button his overcoat, but then hesitated long enough to transfer his weapon from the shoulder rig to his coat pocket. A delay in getting past his coat to his gun had almost cost him his life. Above him, tattered clouds sailed before a waxing moon, now concealing, now revealing, a celestial fan dance. Or so Boots thought as he got into his Nissan and drove along the familiar streets, past McCarren Park, then along Nassau Avenue with shops to either side, the bakeries and the laundromats, the hardware stores and the medical offices, Polski Pyza and Devito's Paints.

There was one thing that Johnny Pianetta didn't know, Boots decided as he slowed for the light at McGuinness Boulevard. If anything happened to Boots, Crazy Jill Kelly would almost certainly kill him. Jill Kelly had killed before, the same Jill Kelly who routinely won inter-department shooting competitions, squaring off against all comers, male or female. She would take the mobster out from a rooftop or a window hundreds of yards away, using a sniper's rifle she kept in a locked gun safe.

Boots found a parking space two blocks past his father's house and hustled back through the cold, turning up his collar against the stiffening wind. He paused to look around before taking out his keys with his left hand, then unlocked the door and walked into the living room where he discovered Joaquin watching television. Boots glanced at his watch. It was nearing three o'clock.

'Can't sleep?'

'A little birdie woke me,' Joaquin muttered, his sullen tone precluding further conversation.

Joaquin's long-time girlfriend, Polly Boll, had thrown him out of their apartment a week before. She did this every few months, a matter, apparently, of marking the seasons. This was the autumn fight. Boots didn't resent Joaquin's unannounced appearances. He enjoyed his son's company for the most part and Joaquin didn't indulge in the blame game. In fact, Joaquin seemed mystified by his relationship woes.

'See you in the morning.'

Boots continued along a narrow corridor to the large bedroom in the back. As he entered the bedroom, he flicked on the light, only then understanding what his son had meant by 'little birdie'.

Jill Kelly's slender form stirred beneath the covers, her legs scissoring as they straightened. Then she sat up, rubbing her eyes, and the covers fell to below her navel. Jill had never been self-conscious about her body and she wasn't now. Her nipples stared out at Boots, seeming to scrutinize him. OK, pal, let's see what you've got.

'I thought you were going home,' Boots said as he bent to slip out of his ankle boots and peel off his socks.

'I was, Boots. I was on my way home when I started thinking.'

'About what?'

'About you and Johnny Pianetta. I mean, you really got into his face, and not just once, but twice. Did you see him in the hospital? He was red as a beet. I thought he was gonna have a stroke.'

Jill paused as Boots slipped out of his trousers and his briefs. Boots wasn't all that demure, either.

'You can trust me on this,' she continued, 'because I've been trapped in OCCB for the past six months. Mobster bosses like Pianetta? They're not big on being humiliated in public. Especially not by some cop they see in church every week. So, the way I figure, Johnny's gotta do something. He can't just let it slide.'

'Does that mean you're here to protect me?'

'Actually, I got to thinking that this could be your last night on Earth and I figured you probably wouldn't want to spend it alone.'

'In that, Jill, you were absolutely right.'

Jill sighed as Boots climbed onto the bed and cupped her breasts in his hands. 'Dead Man Fucking,' she muttered. 'Maybe we could turn it into a musical.'

'Great idea.' Boots slid his hands beneath Jill's thighs and spilled her onto her back. 'You get the first solo.'

EIGHTEEN

Teddy Winuk had one failing he couldn't shake. He was simply unable to handle free time. Leisure didn't work for Teddy. He had no talent for hanging out, for relaxing in the company of friends, for killing time. Not even at five o'clock in the morning. Television didn't interest him, neither the infomercials, nor the early news programs that seemed little more than a succession of weather and traffic reports.

Money interested Teddy Winuk. Money and more money. Nothing grabbed Teddy's attention like the potential for gain, especially now, when his expanding operation required him to reinvest every penny he made.

Teddy had two, medium-range goals: to find a legitimate front and to insulate himself from the Jackson Heights drug scene. Tuscano Foods, he'd come to believe, might do for the first of these goals. Ben Loriano was a deadbeat, a weasel, and sure to come up light. He'd have his excuses prepared and he'd make promises and he wouldn't keep them. Then he'd have more excuses.

This was a set of events familiar to Winuk and his boys. What you did with deadbeats was inflict enough pain to keep them on track for at least a few weeks, all the time knowing that the loan, if unpaid, would go on forever. Well-managed deadbeats were a loan shark's best friend.

Teddy slid beneath the covers and laid the back of his head on the pillow. Next to him, Sanda snored softly. Her scent, of salt and musk and perfume, filled his nostrils. He closed his eyes and let his imagination wander. Teddy's best ideas often came to him in moments of imagining, as if the ideas had been patiently waiting in the wings for their cue.

As if his ideas were veteran actors confronting a nervous playwright: 'Relax, friend, it's gonna be all right.'

Teddy's fantasy begins in a car, a Lincoln with darkened windows. Teddy's riding shotgun next to Recep, who's driving. Behind them, Pablo and Shurie play bookends to a terrified Ben Loriano. Loriano's perched on the little hump in the middle of the seat.

Teddy ignores Loriano's pleas as they glide onto the Grand Central Parkway, headed east toward the far reaches of Long Island. That's because they all amount to the same thing, give me another chance, a song Teddy's heard before. A song, in fact, he's committed to memory.

Little Ben's already had his chances, and many of them. He's had lessons as well, harsh lessons. At one point, after Recep pounded on his kidneys, the grocer had pissed blood for a week. Or so he claimed.

Teddy finally breaks his silence as they cross the Queens-Nassau border, as they leave New York City behind.

'Some people never get the message,' he says. 'Sometimes you have to settle for making a point. But that's OK. Points are good, too.'

More pleas, more sniveling. What about his wife, his two children? What will they do without him? How will they survive? Teddy Winuk doesn't know and doesn't care.

The winter sun's been down for many hours and the darkness outside wraps the Lincoln in a perfect anonymity, each passing vehicle its own world, its own universe. The headlight beams and glowing red taillights, as they sweep across the Lincoln's windows, only serve to underscore their isolation, Teddy's and Ben's.

Miles pass. The traffic, already thin, grows thinner still as they make their way along a series of highways to Ocean Parkway, a dead-flat ribbon of a road connecting the Meadowbrook Parkway to Captree State Park. To their right, the dunes, the beach and the Atlantic Ocean. To their left, a forest of reeds and the great bay separating the narrow island from the mainland. The few summer communities they pass are almost deserted this time of the year. The occasional lit windows seem as far away as the stars in the sky.

'You remember what I told you about gambling?' Teddy says. 'You remember I told you to stop gambling with my money? You remember I told you what would happen if you didn't?'

'Yeah, I—'

'But just last week you laid five grand on Notre Dame with a bookmaker named Sal Zeno. I know this because Sal is a friend of mine. Sal told me you put up the five thousand in advance because he wouldn't give you any more credit. He told me you lost, like you always lose, like you're the biggest fuckin' loser the world's ever seen. You lost the money you needed to pay your debts. I can't have that, Ben. It sets a bad example for the rest of the children.'

The Lincoln glides to a stop in the middle of nowhere. A high dune blocks the beach and the crashing surf on their side of the road. Across the way, slender reeds tipped by silvery tassels rise to more than seven feet, a wall of reeds, impenetrable but for a narrow trail lost in the shadows.

Pablo and Shurie pull Loriano from the car. The little grocer's face is covered with snot and his bladder lets go before he takes his third step.

'Uh, uh, uh . . .'

Teddy draws a .22 caliber semi-automatic pistol from beneath his belt and presses the six-inch barrel into Loriano's back.

'Move it, Ben.'

The grocer's pleas are now so broken by sobs that Teddy can't make out a word. But Loriano hasn't collapsed. He's staggering forward and he keeps on staggering until they reach a small clearing, an island of sand surrounded by swaying reeds. Then, when his legs give out and he drops to his knees, it's like a gift. He's assumed the position without being asked.

Driven by a sudden gust of wind, the reeds clack together, a sound, in Teddy's ears, very much like applause. He cocks the pistol and places it ever so gently against what remains of Ben Loriano's hair.

'I'm not ready,' Ben moans. 'I'm not ready.'

'Nobody's ready, Ben. That's the whole point. To go through your life pretending it's not gonna happen.'

The slap of the hammer against the empty chamber seems, in its own way, louder than the crack of a bullet. Though uninjured, at least physically, Ben falls forward, still blubbering. His body begins to spasm and he grinds his face into the sand.

'Seven hours from now,' Teddy explains, 'you and me are gonna walk into the office of a lawyer I know, another deadbeat, just like you. He will point to a space on a page and you will sign 51% of Tuscano Foods over to me. You will do this in return for the sum of $44,600, which is the amount of money you owe me. If you have a problem with any of that, tell me now so I can kill you without havin' to chase you down again.'

And what's the little grocer gonna say? Yeah, I got a problem?

Loriano stinks up the car on the way back and they have to ride with the windows partially open. Still, Teddy remembers to be reassuring.

'Don't worry, Ben. You're gonna manage the business, just like you've been managing it all along. And I can pretty much guarantee that Tuscano Foods will show a profit, so you'll get a piece of that, too. In fact, I'm already thinkin' big. Ask yourself, what's preventing you from duplicating your success in a second location? What preventing you except capital? Which you never manage to accumulate because you're a degenerate gambler. But

capital is the least of my problems, the absolute least. I got
more capital than I know what to do with.'

This wasn't strictly true, but what the hell. It was his fantasy
and . . . But, no, it wasn't a fantasy, not at all. It was a plan, one
he fully intended to implement.

As he rolled toward Sanda, Teddy gave himself a deadline for
the entire project: six months. 'Hey, baby,' he whispered, 'are
you awake?'

Teddy leaned over the stove. He had two thick pieces of sour-
dough rye bread, hand cut from a loaf that had to weigh five
pounds, toasting in a pan. He'd smear them with the remains of
a salmon salad as soon as they browned.

Fifteen feet away, perched on a stationary bike, Sanda pedaled
away. She wore a black leotard and her dark, sweat-soaked hair
clung to the side of her head. Yet her breathing, when she broke
their silence, was only a bit labored.

'If you are coming back here tonight I must be telling customers
to cancel. If you are coming back.'

Teddy flipped the bread onto his plate with the toasted side
up. He added dollops of salmon salad and smoothed them with
the back of the spoon. Did he really need this obligation, this
commitment? A voice too loud to be ignored yelled right in his
ear: 'Fuck, no!'

Teddy had been responsible for one human being and one
human being only for the whole of his life. He hadn't seen his
sister in years and rarely thought about her. And though he wasn't
absolutely sure, most likely his mother was already in the ground.

In his first year at Manhattan Community College, Teddy had
taken a required course in business history. They were all there,
all the big boys, each lovingly profiled. Astor, McCormick,
Vanderbilt, Carnegie, Gould, Rockefeller, Morgan, Edison, Ford.
Teddy got the point before completing the fourth biography.
Folks who knew Cornelius Vanderbilt, the Commodore, claimed
that he never had a thought in his life that wasn't about profit.
Ditto for the rest of them. They had families, true, but families
weren't a thing you could get out of back then. It was different
now. Teddy could have all the sex he wanted and none of the
responsibility.

'What I told you before,' he said between bites. 'It holds true. I'll set you up with an apartment and pay your expenses. That would make you my mistress, not my whore. And if you want a job, I'll find something.'

'Teddy, I have asked you if you are coming back this night.'

'Yeah,' Teddy finally admitted. 'Yeah, I am.'

NINETEEN

Jill found Boots in the basement lifting weights. Ordinarily, as Jill knew, Boots preferred to work out with other cops at the Six-Four. He liked the atmosphere, the stupid jibes, the stories, even the smell of human sweat which had permeated the very walls of the precinct weight room. The workouts also enabled him to keep in touch with street cops. If there was a bad actor out there, Boots was sure to hear about him, as Boots was sure to make him a special project if the actor was bad enough.

'How long have you been awake?' Jill asked.

'About an hour.'

'And you went to sleep . . .?'

'Around four.'

Jill nodded appreciatively. The weights, for Boots, served the same purpose as the many hours she spent on various gun ranges. Sooner or later, the streets punished weakness. You had to project power at all times. Physical strength did the job for Boots. He was big and strong and had a temper that quickly gave way to fearlessness. You sensed it before he opened his mouth.

'So, any burglars we need to apprehend before we go to work?'

'No, but there's a turnstile jumper I've been after for years.'

Jill laughed. 'Silvy Mussa. You think the shooter meant to kill him?'

'Nope.'

'So, we're looking at a simple robbery that took a bad turn. Maybe Silvy resisted and the thief shot him to make a point?'

'I don't think that, either.' Boots grunted as he drew the weight bar from his waist to beneath his chin, held it for a few seconds, then dropped the bar to his waist. He repeated the sequence four more times before lowering the bar. 'The shots were fired from a twenty-two-caliber handgun at a distance of less than two feet. If Silvy was shot in the arm and leg, he was meant to be shot in the arm and the leg, which in turns means that he was meant to survive. I think Silvy saw something he was supposed to see, something he was supposed to describe to his boss. The rest was smoke and mirrors.'

'But . . .?'

'But the victim won't tell us what that something is, which makes us spectators. All we can do is wait and watch.' Boots grabbed a towel and wiped his face. 'Give me twenty minutes to shower.'

Twenty minutes later, right on time, Boots came out of the bedroom to discover Jill and Joaquin sitting on opposite sides of the kitchen table. Jill had a cup of coffee in one hand and an unlit cigarette in the other.

'Are you staying for breakfast?' Joaquin asked without turning his eyes away from Jill.

Under other circumstances, Boots might have had mercy on his son. He might have reminded himself, for instance, that Joaquin had been sleeping by himself for the past week. But not this time. This time there was real urgency to Boots's personal schedule. That was point number one. Point number two was the cigarette Jill held in her hand. Boots wanted to make sure they were in the car when she lit up.

'Sorry, we gotta move.' Boots took his coat out of the closet and checked to make sure the gun was still in its pocket. He was hoping to get into the coat before Jill noticed that the holster hanging by his left arm was empty. No such luck.

'Aren't you forgetting something?' Jill asked.

Boots stole a glance at Joaquin as he tapped his pocket. The glance was a message to Jill, but Joaquin had always been quick to spot a tell.

'Is that a gun in your pocket?' he asked. 'Or are you just happy to see Jill again?'

'I trained him to respect his elders,' Boots said to Jill. 'But as you can see, it didn't take.'

'Cut the crap, Boots. Last time you carried a gun in your pocket, your father had to go into hiding.'

'Not this time.'

That part was true. The Italian mob didn't kill innocent family members. Nor, Boots admitted to himself, did the Italian mob ordinarily target cops. But the memories were too much, the memories that jumped into his consciousness just before sleep, the van drawing closer and closer, the shotgun in the window, chunks of mortar and brick dropping onto his head and shoulders. There was no forgetting, not for him. The barrel of that shotgun, that hollow tube, had seemed infinitely dark, a black hole from which there was no escape. And there was another factor at play, one Boots had only begun to acknowledge. Maybe Crazy Jill's insanity was contagious. Maybe she'd infected a dumb flatfoot named Boots Littlewood. For sure, some part of him wanted to confront Johnny Pianetta, now and in the future. Some part of him wanted to make the gangster a special project, consequences be damned. Some part of him knew he'd been wanting this for many years.

TWENTY

B oots drew a deep breath as he started the Nissan. His nicotine cravings had retreated, inch by inch, over the past months. Now they were back, descending on him with the speed and the force of a trapdoor spider on an unsuspecting lizard. Yo, dinner.

'Off to work,' he said as he drew a sharp breath. 'Another day, another dollar.'

Jill stared out the window while Boots, for unexplained reasons, made his way to the Pulaski Bridge, then pulled to the curb. To their left, a single strand of canary-yellow tape fluttered in a breeze much too cold for early November. At the back of the yard, a man in greasy coveralls fitted a socket to one of the nuts on the left front tire of an Amoroso pickup truck. A pair of workmen in jeans and heavy boots stood to either side of him, shoulders hunched, hands in their pockets.

'Carlo was committing a violent rape when he was killed,' Jill said. 'I know that for a fact because I called a friend of mine at the morgue while you were in the shower. They did the autopsy last night. First, the blood on Carlo's hands was Type A and Carlo's blood is Type O. Second, the pathologist who performed the autopsy found vaginal fluids on his penis. They'll test the DNA and the alleged fluids, just not right away.'

'We need to find the victim now,' Boots said after a moment, a point he'd already made. 'And just for the record, I don't believe the shooter would have left her alive if he thought she could identify him. She was probably unconscious by the time he arrived.'

'So, why is she a priority?'

'She's a priority because I know what Johnny will do if he gets his hands on her. That's the difference between normal human beings and men like Pianetta. Most people would consider what she's already been through, about Carlo beating her until his hands were covered with blood. Most people would go out of their way to ease her suffering. Not Johnny. Johnny will hurt her until he's sure she can't help him find his son's murderer. Then he'll kill her and leave her body where it'll be found. All part of the lesson, the one about messing with the Pianetta family.'

Jill didn't question her partner's priorities. Protecting the victim had to come first. But the part about the woman not being able to identify her rescuer struck Jill as coming from the male blind spot. Women commonly retreated from their bodies in the course of a rape, aware and not aware. They played dead in the hope of staying alive, knowing, instinctively, that rapists like Carlo Pianetta were fueled by resistance. Resistance got them hot. Resistance and the pleasure of quelling that resistance.

'The real issue,' Jill said, 'is what happened next, after Carlo was dead. Did the shooter aid the victim? Did he take her away? Drive her somewhere? Leave her to fend for herself? What?'

Boots put the Nissan in gear. 'You want an educated guess, based on a series of educated guesses, any of which has a forty percent probability of being utter bullshit? And which, by the way, we have to accept because we don't have time to run down multiple scenarios?'

'I've been waiting all morning. In fact, your educated guess is the only wish you didn't fulfill last night.'

'Then there's no point to stopping off at my place for lunch.'

'Actually, I've got to be home by three. That was the deal I made with Simone, the aide that let me spend the night with you. It's some kind of parent-teacher day at her daughter's school and she needs to be there by four.'

Boots turned left, drove alongside the bridge for a single block, then down a narrow alley to the edge of Newtown Creek. He stopped the car with the bridge to his left, the expanse of the Alltel Petroleum Depot to his right. Straight ahead, a long oil slick, stirred by the bobbing waters, flashed a brilliant iridescence.

'More guesses,' Boots said. 'I'm saying the shooter was on foot, not driving. I'm also saying that he had a big problem after he shot Carlo.'

'The gun?'

'Yeah, the gun. The neighborhood's a hundred percent industrial next to the bridge. There's not an apartment building within two blocks and it's as quiet as a graveyard on Saturday mornings. Still, he couldn't be sure the shot wasn't reported, which, in fact, it was.'

Boots gestured to the tanks in the depot on their right. The largest of the white cylinders rose a good fifty feet in the air. 'That's Alltel, a joint venture between Exxon and the Kuwaiti sheiks. There has to be half a million gallons of home heating oil, diesel fuel and gasoline stored in those tanks. And there has to be a security detail to make sure nobody steals it.'

Out on the water, a loaded barge, its red decks almost at the waterline, slid beneath the bridge. Boots remained silent as the barge passed them by, its destination one of the many tank farms located along the creek.

'All right, so the shooter couldn't be certain that the shot wasn't overheard and reported,' he finally said. 'He had to take off and he had to get rid of that gun. As it turned out, the police response was slow. The two cops who caught the job interviewed the old guy who reported the shot before they searched for the shooter. But if they'd searched for the shooter right away, if they'd come upon a man walking alone in an industrial neighborhood on a Sunday morning, they would definitely have searched him.'

Jill didn't have to be convinced. 'Why not leave the gun at the scene?' she asked. 'Because it could be somehow traced to him?'

Boots turned the heater down. 'The why doesn't matter. The shooter didn't drop it at the scene, but he knew he had to be rid of it. The first part is certain, the second is a guess. Maybe he kept the weapon because he liked it. Or maybe he decided that he'd shoot it out if he was confronted. But I don't think so. I think he tossed the gun into the water, figuring it was gone forever. And I also think we'll recover the weapon if you convince your boss to authorize an underwater search.'

Jill grinned. Newtown Creek was one of the most polluted bodies of water on the east coast. The SCUBA team would be overjoyed at the news. 'Sorry, partner, but the bosses won't authorize a row boat and a grappling hook on the basis of a guess, educated or not.'

'True enough, Jill, but we can verify this particular guess. Lucky for us.' He pointed to the chain-link fence surrounding the Alltel property, and to the security cameras that topped the fence. 'It's a new world,' Boots said as he backed the car into a U-turn. 'Instant replay for cops.'

TWENTY-ONE

'Don't forget to smile,' Boots said as they approached a guard shack alongside the main gate. 'If security decides not to cooperate, we'll have to get a subpoena for the tapes. That'll take most of the day.'

Alltel functioned strictly as a storage depot. The company owned no vehicles, and thus assumed no liability for its products as they made their flammable way along city streets and highways. On this busy morning, the eight fill stations were all in use.

'How may I help you?' The security guard in the booth was young, polite and firm. His nametag read Zeman. He watched Boots and Jill flash their shields and nodded to himself. 'You look like a cop,' he said to Boots.

Apparently, the same could not be said of Detective Kelly. The look Zeman conferred on her was clearly appreciative. This Boots expected. But Jill's return smile came out of nowhere, a thousand-watt special he was certain she'd never bestowed on Boots Littlewood.

'We need a few minutes with the head of security,' she said.

'That would be Al Hanford. I'll call him.'

Zeman picked up a clipboard as a full tanker pulled up to the gate, made a series of notations and waved the truck through.

'Any chance,' Jill said, 'that you were out here on Saturday morning around seven thirty?'

'No chance whatsoever. The yard is closed on weekends and we don't man the booth. We do have somebody in the office, but when he's not sleeping, he sits in a chair watching the monitors. The security cameras do all the work.'

Altell's offices, including the security unit, were contained in a one-story building made of gray concrete blocks. A pair of corrugated wooden panels flanked the main entrance, the only decorative touch on the entire structure. From the back, where Boots and Jill approached a man standing beside a small door, the building might have been a meat locker.

Boots wasn't surprised. An Exxon-Kuwaiti joint venture sounded impressive, but industrial life in Greenpoint had always been about function. About getting the most out of every buck.

'Detective Littlewood,' Boots said, flashing his ID and his shield. 'This is Detective Kelly.'

'Al Hanford.'

Hanford wore a suit, a cheap suit to be sure, an off-the-rack suit, but he was still out of uniform. He was about fifty, heavily built, with a square, flat face and a two-inch buzz cut that somehow managed to emphasize the fact that he'd kept his hair. He shook hands with both detectives, then announced, 'I was on the job. Twenty-two glorious years in the South Bronx. So, what can I do for you?'

'You heard about the shooting on Sunday morning?' Jill asked.

'Yeah, under the bridge. Some gangster.'

'We think the shooter came your way,' Jill said. 'We're thinking he threw the gun into the Creek somewhere between seven forty-two and maybe eight fifteen AM.'

'You want to review our data? That about it?'

'There's no *about* to it. We're tryin' to make the jump from a theory to a fact. We really need to see the footage and we don't have time for a subpoena.'

'Forget subpoena. As long as you're not asking to copy the data, Alltel doesn't give a damn.' He waved Boots and Jill into the building. 'The company's not worried about theft anymore. The pumps are computerized, so you could only pull off a heist from the inside. The main fear is terrorism. The cameras give us visual access to every corner of the depot, even the loading dock on Newtown Creek. You'd need forty guys on foot to cover what two men cover in a roomful of monitors.'

'What about on Sunday mornings?'

'We only use one man when the depot's closed. Not my choice because I think quiet weekend mornings are prime time for terrorists, but I don't write the budget.'

He led Boots and Jill into his office. The space was just big enough to hold a desk and four metal office chairs with padded seats. Several black cables ran from a desktop computer to six monitors lined up on a shelf. No filing cabinets here. The Alltel depot, including the security cameras, ran by computer.

Hanford waved his guests to a chair, took his own chair and tapped the keyboard in front of his computer. After less than a minute, he turned to Boots and said, 'You remember the old days? A hundred video tapes locked in a cabinet somewhere? It took forever to find the tape you were looking for and even longer to fast forward to the time you wanted to look at. Well, check this out.'

Boots watched Hanford raise a dramatic finger almost to his nose before dropping it on the Enter key. Four monitors lit up, the day and date time-stamped into the lower right-hand corners of each image: 07:42, Saturday, November 4. The views were from the four cameras spaced about a hundred feet apart along the fence, from the corner of Paidge Avenue to Newtown Creek.

The images on the screens were definitely sharper than most of the video tapes Boots had reviewed over the years. Still, nobody would confuse the system with IMAX. The washed-out colors left the scene a series of blotchy pastels. Worse yet, the cameras were angled toward the fence line. That left the middle of the street fuzzy and the far side of street, overshadowed by the bridge, in near darkness. Nevertheless, all three – Hanford, Boots and Jill – saw the figure moving through that darkness, a shadow within a shadow, the moment it came into view at 07:49.

Jill drew a deep breath and her pulse quickened, a reaction she was quick to note. Competition shooting demanded that you slow your pulse, that you fire between heartbeats. Here, she indulged herself, as would a hunter at the first glimpse of her prey, as would a rattlesnake detecting a few stray molecules on the tip of its tongue. Not here, not yet, but definitely out there.

The figure moved from left to right, from monitor to monitor, in that stop motion common to surveillance videos, always at the far side of the street, never more than a shadow. Male, though, for sure, and walking fast, a man with a specific destination in mind. He disappeared at the end, into an uncovered space beside the creek, but then reappeared a moment later, retracing his steps. Still at that fast walk, he crossed Paidge Avenue before turning left, toward the front of the Alltel depot.

'He knows,' Jill said while Hanford accessed data from the six cameras on Paidge Avenue.

'Knows what?' Hanford asked.

'Knows about the cameras, and how to avoid them. Anybody wanna bet that he stays in the shadows on the far side of Paidge Avenue? That we never get a look at his face?'

Nobody covered the bet, which the next few minutes proved she would have won. The two buildings on the far side of Paidge Avenue were both for lease. Unoccupied, there was nothing to steal, and no security cameras. They were fenced, but with corrugated iron that rose above the man's head, leaving his body, once again, in shadow.

At Jill's insistence, Hanford ran the tapes for both sides of the complex several more times, though all knew the videos were worthless as a means of identification. Boots watched the process, vaguely amused. The slow pace of most investigations irritated Jill, as did the many rules and regulations, but she was fully involved now.

'I feel like I have a fix on him,' Jill said.

They were standing in the cold on Paidge Avenue just outside the fence line, Jill and Boots. Jill wanted two things. A cigarette, first. There was no smoking anywhere in the Alltel complex, for obvious reasons. She also wanted to call her boss, Captain Viktor Karkanian, with the news. The shooter could now be placed along the shore of Newtown Creek at seven forty-eight, six minutes after the gunshot was reported.

'A fix?' Boots said. 'How so?'

'The way he moved. He's young, for sure, and strong. Graceful, too. What my old gym teacher called physically gifted. He's also arrogant, and smart enough to spot the security cameras and avoid them. I think, when I finally come across this guy, my radar's gonna start beeping.'

Jill punched Karkanian's number into her cell phone and brought the phone to her ear. 'We think we know what he did with the gun,' she told him a moment later.

An explanation followed, which Boots tuned out. He'd made a lucky guess, but of what significance had yet to be determined. Meanwhile, there was more pressing work to do.

'The search area would be relatively small,' Jill said, now into her pitch. 'How far can a man throw a gun? Fifty feet? I mean, it's not like something people practice.'

Jill stopped for a moment to listen, then said, 'Right, got it,' before hanging up. 'Bad news, Boots. Karkanian wants to see the tapes. We're supposed to wait for him.'

'Not me.'

'And what do I tell the Captain when he arrives an hour from now?'

'Tell him you gave me permission to go.' Boots stared at Jill for a moment, then said, 'You think finding the gun is important, which it is, only not in the short term. In the short term, we want to find Carlo's victim. From that point of view, the surveillance video establishes three vital facts. The shooter was alone, on foot and didn't aid the woman we're looking for.'

'That doesn't tell us where she went.'

'No, it doesn't, but here's a more basic question. Where did Carlo find a victim on a Saturday morning at seven o'clock?' Boots stepped a little closer when Jill lit a cigarette. 'Greenpoint and Williamsburg have become magnets for young people over the past fifteen years. Lots of hipsters, lots of yuppies, lots of unattached women who work hard during the week and party even harder on the weekends. So it's possible that Carlo spotted some girl returning from a night on the town, maybe even a bit inebriated, and forced her into a car.'

'OK, but why didn't she report the attack?'

'Well, that's the question. These women I'm describing, they're daughters of the middle class. When someone does you injury, you don't pick up a weapon and seek revenge. You go to the cops for justice and protection. Meanwhile, we haven't heard a peep.'

Jill walked off a few steps, head turned down, deep in thought. 'She didn't seek medical help at the nearest hospital, either. She went to ground.'

'Which makes her what?'

'A prostitute?'

Boots nodded. 'On Kent Avenue, where all those new condos went up? That used to be a major stroll, especially at night when the factories shut down. I mean for decades, Jill. The yuppies drove the whores off Kent Avenue, but you can still find working girls by the Navy Yard.'

'This is sounding more and more like another educated guess.'

'Wait, it gets worse. I'm thinking the victim went into hiding because she knew Carlo, knew who he was, knew who his father still is. Where do you turn when your attacker is a merciless killer from a family of merciless killers? And here's another question. Where do you go on a Sunday morning when your face is covered with blood? The G train on Manhattan Avenue? The B1 bus on McGuinness Boulevard? I could check with the MTA, talk to the trainmen and bus drivers on duty around eight o'clock. I will, too, if my hunch doesn't work out.'

Jill smiled, even as she shook her head. 'How do you know she didn't call someone to pick her up?'

'I don't, Jill. But I'm not going to start with a hopeless scenario. That's because I'm basically an optimist. Plus, I need to do something to justify my paycheck.'

'God, but you're a smug son of a bitch. You remind me of myself.' She gave Boots a quick peck on the chin, about as high as she could reach. 'Now, tell me about the hunch.'

'There's a shelter for battered women about three-quarters of a mile from here. Open Circle. They do outreach to prostitutes. I know this because I had a major run-in with them two years ago. They'd given refuge to a fugitive, a woman who emptied a Glock into her pimp's skull. Tell you the truth, I was sympathetic. If it was up to me, I would've handed the shooter a medal and sent her off to rehab. But I had to take her out of there and Lila Payton, who runs the place, wanted to force me to get a search warrant. I told her I'd arrest her for harboring a fugitive, but she wasn't impressed. No, she promised to have the media and a thousand protesters on the scene if I made the attempt.'

When Boots stopped abruptly, a half-smile pulling at the corners of his mouth, Jill poked him. 'So, what happened?'

'The fugitive's name was Marina Torres and her sheet went back nine years to her first adult arrest at age eighteen. Talk about misery. Marina's whole life was a misery. But she knew the ropes and what I did was shout over Lila Payton's shoulder.'

'What did you say?'

'I said, "You're not helping yourself, Marina. So stop being an asshole and get out here. You know how this story ends. You've been walking down this road your whole life. And if Ms Payton really wants to help you, she'll find you a decent lawyer instead of pissing off the criminal justice system."'

'Did she come out?'

'Two minutes later.'

Jill ground her cigarette into the sidewalk. 'I'll bet the woman . . . What's her name again?'

'Lila Payton.'

'I'll bet Lila Payton was really pissed.'

'Jill, she was so hot I thought her hair would catch fire.'

TWENTY-TWO

B oots pulled to the curb in front of a check-cashing store on the corner of McGuinness Boulevard and India Avenue. Open Circle was just a block away, in a three-story home on India Street near Manhattan Avenue. Boots wasn't anxious to confront Lila Payton with only a hunch to back his play. Carlo's victim might have gone anyplace without her condition being reported. New Yorkers tended to ignore the bizarre. A battered and bleeding woman on the G train? If she asks for help, fine. If she doesn't, also fine. Privacy first.

Like any of the numerous check-cashing stores in New York, Casablanca Financial Services always had cash on hand. Criminals knew this, of course, but the company had never been ripped off. Inside Casablanca, the staff worked behind a thick wall of bulletproof acrylic and the proprietor, Walid Tufiq, carried a large-caliber handgun on his hip. The many surveillance cameras provided a third layer of protection, cameras in the front, in the back, on both sides and on the roof.

Walid Tufiq was a third-generation American, his Christian grandparents having immigrated to the United States from Morocco shortly after World War II. Like Boots, Tufiq loved the New York Yankees. Like Boots, he bet almost every game. Like Boots, he commonly watched the games at a sports bar named Silky's.

'Hey, Boots,' Walid called out when Boots made his appearance. 'What's up?'

Tufiq's words were muffled by the acrylic wall and Boots put a finger to his ear. Rather than shout, Walid motioned Boots to a door at the end of a row of teller windows. The shopkeeper waited until Boots reached the door, then buzzed him through.

As the two men shook hands, Tufiq said, 'Too bad, too bad.'

Boots nodded, but had nothing to say in return. Walid was referring to the Yankees' season. The thing, in his opinion, spoke for itself.

'I need a favor,' Boots said.

Walid's eyes narrowed. He was a noticeably thin man, with a receding chin and a mousy expression that belied the very large and powerful .357 revolver strapped to his hip.

'Name it.'

'I need to review the video from your security cameras, the one on McGuinness Boulevard and the one on the India Street side. That would be for this past Sunday, from seven forty-two until . . . until maybe nine o'clock.'

'Does this involve the store?'

'Not in any way. It's would be a pure favor, and I'd definitely owe you one.'

'OK, no problem.'

Tufiq's office was larger and better furnished than Al Hanson's at Alltel. Bunched photos of the man's extended family nearly covered the wall behind his desk and his monitors rested on a maple cabinet, not an unvarnished shelf. A white vase on the window sill held a single red rose.

'For my wife,' Tufiq said when Boots's eye fell on the rose. 'To always remember the vows I took.'

Boots tried to imagine having that kind of a relationship with Jill Kelly. It would be like running a marathon over a bed of quicksand.

Walid Tufiq wasn't as fast on the computer as Al Hanson, but he eventually produced the same result. This time the sidewalk and cameras were both in the shade, the resulting image a definite upgrade relative to the footage at Alltel. The time frame, on the other hand, had expanded significantly. How long would it take Carlo's victim to walk the seven blocks to India Street? Better yet, when did she begin walking?

Boots settled down to watch a whole lot of nothing. The stores on McGuinness Boulevard were closed, the sidewalks empty. A few cars and trucks whizzed by, and once a bus. Boots eagerly scanned the windows of the bus, a waste of time. The angled sunlight was focused on the glass, producing a flare that hid the interior.

Walid maintained a respectful silence initially, content to stare at the two monitors. But after thirty minutes, he finally spoke out. 'What do you think, Boots? About where the Yankees are going? A bunch of old, half-crippled men.'

'What I think is that George Steinbrenner's kids aren't as smart as their old man. Steinbrenner built the team by spending money. Understand? He spent money to make money. Back in the 70s and 80s, when the team sucked, they were lucky to draw twenty-five thousand fans. As winners, they filled the stadium every night. They drew three and a half million . . .'

Boots ground to an abrupt halt as a figure on the sidewalk drew closer. He raised a hand to shush Walid, then realized that the figure was a man pushing a shopping cart loaded with his possessions.

'Shit,' he muttered.

'So, what do we do, give up? Do we go back to being second rate?'

'Probably.' Boots smiled, remembering his son, Joaquin. 'I think there's a law that requires kids to believe they know more than their parents. Steinbrenner spent like a drunken sailor. Now he's dead and his kids are in charge. So what do we get? An austerity budget.'

On that gloomy note, Boots settled down, his attention returning to the task at hand. The minutes ticked by slowly, despite the time lapse video that reduced two seconds to one. By eight forty-five, Tufiq had had enough. He excused himself and left the office. Boots's eyes never strayed from the monitors.

The proliferation of surveillance cameras had changed policing forever. Most crimes are committed by offenders working close to home, a fact long ago established by criminologists. If you found a single decent image, and it didn't have to be perfect, you could show it around the neighborhood with the reasonable hope that a tip would follow. But that was only part of the good news. There was also the pleasure of displaying a photo to a suspect and saying, 'Are you gonna tell me that's not you?'

Nine o'clock passed, then nine fifteen. A little voice in Boots's mind began to insist that his quest was hopeless. Softly at first, than louder until, at exactly nine thirty, a figure came into view, a woman, and the little voice was drowned out by a much bigger voice that screamed, 'Yesssssssssss'

Boots's eyes drew the woman forward, step by step, until he could see the blood on her face and the bloodstains on the shoulders and breast of her white coat. The left side of her face was severely swollen, the eye nearly shut, and she listed to one side as she staggered forward, a small, light-skinned woman who might have been Latino. He watched her turn the corner onto India Street, watched her make her slow, steady way toward Manhattan Avenue until she passed out of the camera's field of view.

Five minutes later, armed with a printed photo of the woman, Boots shook hands with Walid, again assuring him that the favor would be repaid should he ever be in need of a favor. Boots's

earnest expression, as he renewed his promise, belied a rising
exhilaration. He was on a roll, two for two, and he found himself
wishing the Yankees were still playing so he could bet the games.
The way he felt now, he couldn't lose.

TWENTY-THREE

S mall trees lined both side of India Street. Planted only a
few years earlier as part of the mayor's Greening the
Cityscape initiative, their branches hung low enough to
obscure the small apartment houses on either side of the road.
Boots knew that Open Circle was on the south side of the street,
but he couldn't see the front door until he was almost on top of
it. Thus, the ongoing situation took him completely by surprise.

Lila Payton stood before the open door. A uniformed security
guard – a necessity in a shelter that included abused women
fleeing violent husbands and lovers – stood behind her. Together,
they faced a man in a black coat.

Even in profile, Boots recognized the man. The hawk nose, a
sharp triangle with a pronounced hook at the end, was a dead
giveaway. Boots was looking at Stefano Ungaro, also known as
Stevie Eagle. In his early forties, Ungaro had been a member of
Pianetta's crew for twenty years, his main function to enforce
the rules.

Maybe Boots would have been able to contain his temper if
he'd had a bit more time to adjust. He'd vowed to do exactly
that more times than he cared to count. The way it was, however,
his resolution vanished the minute he laid eyes on Steve Ungaro.
A hot flush, fierce as sunburn, rose to cover his face and neck
as he pulled to the curb before a fire hydrant twenty feet beyond
Open Circle, as he switched off the ignition, shoved the keys in
his pocket and got out of the car. The gun in his coat went back
into the holster dangling beneath his left arm. The coat, itself,
followed by his suit jacket, went into the Nissan's trunk. Then
he clipped his gold shield to the strap on his shoulder rig, just
so there'd be no misunderstanding.

Boots closed the ground between himself and Ungaro at a fast walk. Lila Payton may have seen him coming. Boots couldn't tell because Ungaro was leaning toward the woman, his face so close to hers that he appeared to be breathing into her mouth. But the security guard saw him clearly enough, saw his gun and his badge. She took a step back and raised her hands, gestures that didn't escape Stevie Eagle, though he misinterpreted their implications.

Ungaro turned to the security guard and said, 'What, you got something to say here?'

A second later, Boots fist crashed into his right ear. The punch was thrown with every ounce of strength in the cop's 220-pound body, a leaping hook that reflected all his years in basement weight rooms.

Ungaro screamed in pain as the shockwave impacted his eardrum. Then he fell, his balance gone, landing on the side of his face. Boots knelt down and yanked the mobster's coat over his shoulders, pinning his arms. This was a wasted effort because the gangster was too dizzy to resist when Boots searched him. Boots was hoping that Ungaro had repeated Al Buffo's mistake. No such luck. The man was unarmed.

Boots finally rose to his feet and faced Lila Payton. 'You don't need to see this,' he said. 'Go inside.'

Formerly a starting forward on NYU's basketball team, Lila Payton was as tall as Boots. She now looked him directly in the eye and brought her hands to her hips. Payton had been dealing with angry men ever since she graduated from college. She didn't allow herself to be bullied and she wasn't intimidated by the cop's violent attack. Payton only complied because she knew Boots was right. What happened next was between Boots and the asshole who'd ruined her morning.

When Payton stepped back and closed the door, Boots snapped a vicious kick to Ungaro's face. He wanted to mark the man, internal injuries being too subtle for gangsters like Johnny Piano.

Ungaro spit blood as he rolled away. 'I'll kill you for this,' he said.

Boots responded by driving his foot into Ungaro's unprotected back, a stunning blow to the kidney that produced a scream.

'Say it again, mutt. Tell me that you're gonna kill me.'

'Fuck you.'

Boots stomped on the back of Ungaro's thigh, then cupped his hand to his ear. This time, except for a heartfelt moan, Ungaro kept his mouth shut.

'I don't know if you heard about this,' Boots said, 'but me and your boss had a conversation over at Woodhull. Did you hear about it?'

Rather than answer, Ungaro tried to get up. Boots let him rise to one knee then snapped out a jab that caught the gangster on the back of the neck. Not the best punch Boots had ever thrown, but hard enough to send the man to the sidewalk.

'I asked you a question. I asked you if you heard about me and Johnny at Woodhull.'

'Yeah, I heard he had some trouble.' Ungaro rolled onto his back, revealing a bloody mouth.

'Did you hear that I told him, in the plainest language, to stay the fuck away from my investigation?'

'No.' Ungaro raised a hand to ward off a blow that never came. 'I mean I didn't know that part, what you actually said to each other.'

'Well, ya know what I think? I think Johnny heard me loud and clear, which is why he sent you instead of comin' himself. But you take him this message. No, forget that. You *are* the message, Stevie. Just go home.'

Easier said than done. Ungaro's inner ear had been thrown into chaos and his stomped-on leg didn't want to support his weight. Boots had to help the man to his feet and then to his car, a late-model Audi that Boots would never be able to afford.

'Drive carefully,' he said.

His hand on his weapon, Boots watched Ungaro settle behind the wheel. Boots hadn't searched the car and his life these days wasn't about taking chances. Only when the Audi turned left onto Manhattan Avenue and vanished did he knock on Open Circle's front door.

The door opened immediately to reveal Lila Payton. The security guard was seated behind her, Payton apparently having decided that Boots was no threat. Boots was tempted to push his way inside and have a look around. He couldn't really fault do-gooders because most of the time they did good. But he couldn't bear the self-righteous attitude, either, the one that seemed to come with the territory.

'In a way,' he said, 'I'm glad that asshole showed up at your door.'

'And why is that?'

'Because now I don't have to convince you. That man? His name is Stefano Ungaro. He works for a gangster named John Pianetta whose son was murdered two days ago. Pianetta's lookin' for a witness to that crime. If he finds her, he's gonna hurt her. It's as simple as that.'

Payton's expression didn't so much as flicker. 'What's that got to do with Open Circle?'

'That's a long story which I'll cut short.' Boots's hand was already in motion when he realized that he'd put the witness's photo in his jacket pocket and his jacket was in the trunk of his car. 'Wait a second. I have something you need to see.'

Boots jogged to the car, retrieved his jacket and jogged back to Lila Payton. His anger had vanished, replaced by a vague sense of guilt about losing his temper again. He felt exhilarated, as well. Life on the edge, as Jill would say.

'OK, no bullshit,' he said. 'John Pianetta? He was guessing about the witness coming here. But not me.' Boots handed the photo to Lila Payton. 'The security cameras at the check-cashing place on McGuinness Boulevard captured her passage at nine thirty on Saturday morning. She came along McGuinness Boulevard from where the murder took place and turned up India Street toward Open Circle. You can see her injuries for yourself. She needed a refuge at that moment, which is exactly what Open Circle is.'

'You know, you're a bully. You were a bully last time I saw you and you're a bully now.'

'Fine, I agree. I'm a bully. I even agree that all cops are bullies. But that doesn't change the simple fact that this woman is in big trouble if Pianetta finds her before I do. Which you already know because you looked into Ungaro's eyes.'

Lila Payton twisted her mouth into what amounted to an amused frown. She'd checked out Detective Littlewood after their first meeting. According to her sources, he had a white knight complex when it came to protecting the neighborhood.

Nevertheless, she didn't have to cooperate. Open Circle's clients depended on the shelter's confidentiality rule precisely because it gave them confidence.

'What do you want?' she asked.

Boots pointed to the photo. 'Her.'

'Why?'

'Because protecting crime victims is what bullies like me do for a living. She doesn't stand a chance on her own, not unless she leaves town, which I don't think she's in any condition to do.'

'Protect? Bullies like you? Tell that to all the murdered women who secured orders of protection and then found themselves unprotected.'

Boots raised a hand before Payton could work up a head of steam. 'Ask yourself this, Ms Payton. Do you really protect the women who come to Open Circle, or is it only a matter of their abusers not being able to find them? Because I'm telling you from the bottom of my heart, you won't be able to keep Pianetta out. He'll burn Open Circle to the ground if he has to.'

'You're asking me for a big favor. You're asking me to trust you.'

'Call it a favor if that's what makes you happy. I'll even go so far as to say it's a favor I'm obliged to return. In fact, if you want, I'll give you the number of my cell phone.'

'I'll take it.' Payton finally smiled, exposing a set of startlingly white teeth. 'But I have to say, I don't think you've cut a very good deal.'

'Why's that.'

'Because the woman you're looking for left here on Sunday morning.'

'What's her name?'

'I only know her first name. It's Corry.'

'Did she say where she was going?'

'To her brother's. But don't get your hopes up. She didn't tell me his name or where he lives.'

'OK, I get the point. But does she use the name Corry when she's on the street?'

Payton laughed. 'I believe you're trying to trick me, Detective.'

'Call me Boots. And the truth is that I give my cell number to just about anybody who asks for it. But you don't have to answer the question because I already know you do outreach to prostitutes. What I don't know is where Corry works.'

'I can only tell you that we first ran into her on Flushing Avenue by the Navy Yard. On cold nights, we sometimes pass out coffee, rolls and advice.' Payton frowned again. 'Sad to say, a lot more of the women take the coffee than the advice.'

Boots was on his phone before he started the Nissan. He'd lost his temper and the consequences, many of which Jill Kelly was far more equipped to handle, had to be faced. But Jill Kelly had problems of her own.

'I'm glad you called,' she told Boots. 'My mom was taken to the hospital and I have to get out of here.'

'You want me to go with you?'

The question caught Jill off-guard. She'd been handling her own problems for many years, neither requesting, nor expecting, support.

'No, Boots,' she said after a brief hesitation. 'You've got enough on your plate. But I'll tell you, I still don't get it. My mom was told that her liver was giving out ten years ago, but she didn't stop drinking, didn't even put on the brakes. It's like slow-motion suicide.'

Boots nodded to himself. Jill Kelly loved life. The thought of deliberately ending it, slow or fast, was utterly repugnant. Which was not to say she was above putting her life at risk.

'I'll stay in touch, Jill. Where'd they bring her?'

'NYU Medical Center in Manhattan. Her doctor's on the staff there. So, how'd you make out?'

'I got a line on our victim. Her name's Corry and she's a prostitute, which is what we figured. I'll start looking for her tonight. What about Karkanian? He show up yet?'

'Yeah, and he's gonna do the underwater search next week.'

'Did he ask about me?'

'Of course, and he wasn't all that pleased to find you gone until I told him about the game you played with Pianetta's testicles. He's not worried about you being corrupt anymore. Now he's thinking you're on a crusade. That worries him even more. In fact, he said, "I don't need any shootouts."'

'And what did you say?'

'I told him shootouts are my specialty, not yours.'

TWENTY-FOUR

With little choice, Boots headed back to the Six-Four after his encounter with Lila Payton. His search for Corry would continue, but not until after working hours when the Navy Yard stroll became active. Meanwhile, he had a debt to pay. Consuela, the security guard at Woodhull Medical, had done him a favor which he was obliged to return. Boots was big on obligation. That's how societies ran, at least in his opinion. You took a favor, you did a favor, everybody made out.

According to Consuela, her nephew, Julio Vargas, had been arrested for stealing a car on November 2nd, four days ago. Boots didn't intend to intervene on Julio's behalf – it was too late for that – only to present Consuela with the facts on the ground.

He began at his computer, entering Julio's name in a search window narrowed to the Sixty-Fourth Precinct. The report came up a few seconds later, leading Boots to nod his head in appreciation. Not all that long ago, he would have spent the better part of an hour hunting for paperwork that may or may not have been properly filed. Or filed at all.

According to Julio's sheet, the arresting officer, a cop named Sylvia Armstrong, had turned the case over to Detective Cletis Small, who happened to be seated at his desk thirty feet away from Boots. Clete was interviewing a kid whose iPhone had been taken by three older kids. One of those older kids had flashed a knife, which made the incident serious enough for the detective's involvement. The Six-Four had a street-gang unit, as required by the bosses, and Cletis was it.

Boots walked over to Clete's desk and raised a finger. 'I need to talk to you about something. I'll be in the weight room.'

Cletis Small was a whippet of man, his body all sinew. Though he pumped iron regularly, he couldn't add weight to his frame.

O'Malley and the Bulgarian, whose massive frames were fueled by steroids, had urged Clete to join the party. A health-conscious Small, who had no desire to see his testicles shrink to the size of lemon pits, had refused.

'That bullshit with Pianetta,' he asked as Boots turned away. 'That true?'

'We had a one-sided conversation,' Boots admitted. 'If that's what you're talkin' about.'

'And you're not worried?'

'No,' Boots said after a moment, 'I'm not.'

True enough, despite the possibility that Johnny Piano might be angry enough to retaliate. For the humiliation, for the arrest of Alberto Buffo, for bloodying Stefano Ungaro. Any of these provocations, all by its lonesome, was enough to invite payback.

Still, he wasn't frightened.

For the next hour, Boots had the weight room to himself. He worked out hard, pushing himself, despite his fatigue. Boots hadn't used the weight room for almost a week and his body was already losing mass. Even ten years ago, his body was quick to restore itself. No more. Now his efforts amounted to little more than a holding action. Nevertheless, the minute he finished with Consuela's business, he was headed home for a nap. It was going to be a long night.

Clete Small was already loosening his tie when he walked into the weight room. A competent detective by anyone's standards, he had a difficult time with cops like Boots Littlewood, who took crime personally. Small never took his job home with him, and never blamed himself for the one that got away. Another day, another dollar, you took the man's money and did the man's job.

Boots continued on, doing shoulder shrugs, while Small changed into a sweat suit and began to stretch out.

'So, what's up?' Small asked.

'You made an arrest four days ago. Two kids for stealing a car which they cracked up on Jewel Street and McGuinness Boulevard.'

'Yeah, I remember. A coupla punks. One of 'em, the kid named Julio, started cryin' when I ran him down. Funny thing, though, he clammed up when I got him into the house. Meanwhile, the other one . . .'

'Rafael Quintera.'

'Yeah, that's him. Rafael was the real deal. Not two minutes after I got him in the box, he was offerin' to rat on his pal. According to him, Julio already had the car when he ran into Rafael at the schoolyard. Rafael didn't know the car was stolen.'

Boots dropped the weight to the floor. He wiped his face with a towel and began to wrap an Ace bandage around his left knee. He'd be doing knee bends next.

'And the cops who made the arrest, they didn't see who was driving?'

'When they happened on the scene, a matter of blind luck, the kids were already runnin'.'

'So, you don't know who was driving, or even if the kids were in the car?'

'We know they were in the car because we found witnesses who saw the crash. But the wits couldn't put either one behind the wheel.'

'So, where's the case now?'

Small fought a sudden resentment. He had no idea what the criminal justice system had in store for Julio and Rafael, hadn't given the matter a second thought since he turned over the paperwork, including Rafael's signed statement, to the DA's office.

'I got no idea.'

Boots, on the other hand, did have an idea. The case, itself, was weak, and if Quintera hadn't ratted on his buddy, they might have both gotten off. The witnesses were unreliable and the cops hadn't seen anything more than two kids running away. As it was, the prosecutors would have to rely on Quintera's testimony. Good news for Rafael, bad news for Julio Vargas.

An hour later, a call to Assistant District Attorney Thelma Blount confirmed his prediction. Quintera had been given limited immunity in return for his testimony. Vargas, in light of his age and his clean record, would be offered probation and several hundred hours of community service. Assuming, of course, that he pleaded guilty and forever stained his record with a felony conviction.

Consuela wasn't happy when Boots called. Her nephew, she insisted, had only committed the crime of being young and naive. Where was the justice? Boots was appropriately sympathetic, but firm.

'If Julio puts the state to the expense of a trial and he's convicted, they're gonna send him away for a couple of years. Fair has nothing to do with it. The plea bargain on the table is the best deal he's gonna get.'

'But it's not right, Boots.'

'Neither is stealing cars.'

TWENTY-FIVE

Boots settled into his nap within seconds of turning out the light in his bedroom. He slept until four o'clock when the repeated sounding of a car horn on Newell Street roused him. He opened his eyes, looked at the clock, muttered 'Shit' and headed for the bathroom. Thirty minutes later, showered, shaved and ready for the street, he walked out of his bedroom to find Joaquin making coffee in the kitchen. Boots initially thought the coffee was meant for him, an act of generosity on Joaquin's part rare enough to merit attention. But then Boots stepped into the living room and saw Father Leonzo Gubetti and his own father seated on the couch.

A parish priest assigned to Mt. Carmel, Leo Gubetti was a Littlewood family friend. He was also Boots's confessor. Ordinarily, Boots would have been glad to see him. Not today.

'So, what's up?' he asked.

Boots expected evasion, but the priest got right to the point. 'This business with John Pianetta. I don't want it brought into the church.'

'Pianetta brings his business into the church every time he hears Mass.' Boots waved off the priest's response. He went back to the kitchen and stayed there until he finished a mug of coffee. Boots didn't intend to disturb his neighbors' peace by challenging Pianetta at Mt. Carmel. God's house was a neutral zone by anyone's definition.

But Father Gubetti didn't know that, not yet, and Boots wasn't above using the priest's uncertainty to needle him.

'I suppose you have a stake in this,' he said to his father as he carried a second cup of coffee into the living room.

'In Mt. Carmel, no. In helping you through your mid-life crisis? Well, Irwin, it's the least I can do for my only son.'

Boots ignored the comment. 'What I don't get,' he said to Father Gubetti, 'is how you can allow a complete scumbag like John Pianetta to receive the Sacraments.'

Gubetti nodded agreement, much to Detective Littlewood's surprise. 'I know who the man is, Boots. I know what he's done. But I have no right to ban him. The Church isn't here on Earth to save the saved. Our mission begins with the sinner.'

'What about excommunication?'

'The excommunicated are *encouraged* to attend Mass, as they're encouraged to repent and be forgiven. Repentance is the whole point of excommunication.' Gubetti draped his arms over his considerable paunch. 'John Pianetta comes into the presence of Jesus Christ whenever he attends Mass. I believe that Jesus reaches out to him. Every single time, Boots. Jesus reaches out and who's to say that one day John Pianetta won't reach back?'

A decent argument, Boots had to admit, but he wasn't buying. 'Jesus can reach out all he wants, but he'll never touch Johnny's conscience. That's because Johnny's a psychopath and he doesn't have a conscience.'

Gubetti patted his pockets. 'Now where did I leave my cell phone? I need to get on the horn to the archdiocese right now. We've a heretic in our midst who needs immediate excommunication.'

Boots's laugh was genuine enough, but he was still in a hurry. He glanced at his watch and said, 'I have to go.'

Joaquin followed him to the door. 'Listen . . .'

'Not you, too.'

But Joaquin wasn't intimidated. He put his hand on his father's shoulder and said, 'Watch your back.'

Back-watching was Jill Kelly's game. Not to mention plunking bad guys. He and Jill complemented each other. He provided the muscle and she provided . . . Boots smiled as he walked toward his car, eyes constantly moving, acutely aware of the semi-automatic in his coat pocket. In Woodhull Hospital, when they confronted Johnny and his boys, Jill's gun had appeared, ready to use, in an eye-blink. And not a single person in the hallway believed she'd hesitate to pull the trigger. For a few seconds, it was as if she'd stopped time.

Like most cops, Boots had only rarely drawn his weapon. On each occasion, he was seized by a fierce ambivalence. His need to hold fire was as great as his need for protection. Jill Kelly, on the other hand, was only looking for an excuse. At least as far as he could tell.

Boots drove into Manhattan, over the Williamsburg Bridge, then north on Allen Street to New York University Medical Center, a huge complex strung along several blocks of First Avenue, from 31st to 34th Streets. NYU Medical Center was one of the hospitals flooded out when Hurricane Sandy came ashore. It'd taken the better part of two years to restore the Center to full functioning.

Ten minutes later, he stepped onto a unit in the Gastroenterology wing of the main building to find Jill huddled with her uncle, Chief of Detectives Michael Shaw. Shaw was flanked by two aides big enough to serve as bouncers at a Brownsville rap concert.

Shaw didn't see Boots until he turned away from his niece. Still, he managed a thin smile as he extended his hand. 'Ah, Detective Littlewood. There's a Captain in OCCB who doesn't trust you.'

'Only because he doesn't know me as well as you do.'

The line produced a wink. 'Take care of my niece, Boots.'

Boots felt Jill's hand on his arm, the touch as familiar as the shoulder harness he put on every working day. Ahead, Shaw and his entourage turned a corner on their way to the elevators.

'Why did you come here?' Jill asked.

The question, as Boots understood it, was not a rebuke. Jill simply didn't know that visiting one's lover while she stood vigil in a bleak hospital room was more or less obligatory. Like going to Mass on Easter Sunday. Which is not to say that he lacked an ulterior motive.

Boots had to go forward now. There was no U-turn on this road. Still, he'd been imagining the journey with Jill riding shotgun. Without her? In a world of probabilities, his own probability would be cut in half. At the very least.

'First of all, to see how you're doing,' Boots said. 'Somehow I just assumed that you'd be alone.'

Jill shook her head. 'They've been coming all day, the aunts, the uncles, the cousins. The Irish love death, but they answered a false alarm this time. Mom's going home tomorrow. The problem is really about managing her pain. Dr Khan doesn't want to pile on the narcotics unless she stops drinking. He's afraid she'll kill herself.'

Boots somehow managed to keep his rising expectations in check. His tone was matter-of-fact when he spoke. 'And the bottom line? For you?'

'Ready to go.' Jill shrugged. 'Catch me up.'

Boots took the photo of Corry from the inside pocket of his coat and handed it to Jill. 'Her name's Corry. We know she first contacted Open Circle at the Navy Yard stroll and that she sought refuge at Open Circle on Saturday morning. I'm gonna show the photo to her colleagues, see what comes of it.'

'You think those hookers will talk to you?'

'Why not? I'm a charming guy when you get to know me.' Boots ignored Jill's half-hearted smile. 'I've got snitches out there,' he explained. 'Ladies who've been talking to me for a long time. Favor for favor, of course.'

Jill didn't hesitate. She was already turning when she spoke. 'Give me a minute to say goodbye.'

Five minutes later, as they left the hospital to confront the traffic on First Avenue, Jill said, 'They're all over me. The family, I mean. They want me to be more attentive, to spend more time with my mother. I don't know. I don't feel all that guilty. Mom's cirrhosis was diagnosed in its earliest stage. She would've been fine if she stopped drinking. But you couldn't talk to her about rehab. Couldn't even bring the subject up. It was her life to live as she chose.'

'So?'

'So if it's her life to live, why isn't it my life to live? And where was I exactly when she decided to drink herself to death? If, being mother and daughter, we're somehow in this thing together.'

TWENTY-SIX

That evening at eight o'clock, Sanda by his side, Teddy seated himself at a large table in The Waterfront, a bar on Tillary Street near the Manhattan Bridge. The bar was nicely kept, its walls dominated by a series of huge panels depicting the history of the Brooklyn waterfront. Back in the old days, when ships by the hundreds crowded the docks.

They sat by themselves for fifteen minutes, enjoying their drinks, until the brothers Turco walked through the door, saw them and smiled. The older brother was called Turk, the younger Little Turk, though he was the taller of the two by four inches. The Waterfront was a networking bar for aspiring gangsters. One of many.

Teddy waved the Turks over to his table, gave each a dap. 'Whatta ya drinkin'?'

'You buyin'?' Little Turk asked.

'Yeah, you hit the lottery?' his brother added. 'Because this is definitely a first.'

Except for the difference in height, the Turcos looked very much alike. Dark, tightly curled hair, short straight noses and overly broad, almost succulent mouths. They were even balding alike, from back to front.

'This is Sanda.' Teddy ignored the jibes. 'Sanda, this one is Turk and this one is Little Turk.'

The brothers' eyes reflected their mutual judgment. A beautiful woman on your arm was an asset they appreciated. Teddy might have flashed a new Rolex and gotten the same reaction.

'Scotch, Black Label, neat,' Turk said. 'As long as you're payin'.'

Little Turk nodded once and said, 'That'll do.'

'Two Black Labels, neat,' Teddy said.

Sanda hesitated for only a moment before heading off to the bar. Teddy and his friends were about to discuss some business deal she didn't need to know about. Sanda felt no resentment.

And no particular gratitude, either. They'd struck a deal of their own, she and Teddy, a better deal than the one she had. The oldest profession had never appealed to Sanda and she was more than happy to abandon ship. She had money of her own, too, a rainy day fund. Should she be deported, Sanda had no desire to hit the mean streets of Bucharest without a penny in her pocket.

Behind her, Teddy drew the Turks closer. 'You got a market for hash?'

'Not that black shit.'

That was another problem. Most of the hashish that found its way to New York was jet black and as hard as slate. It smelled like old shoes when you lit up and it left a chunk behind that wouldn't burn in a blast furnace. A chunk equal to half its original weight.

'I'm talkin' gold Israeli hash you could mold in your hands. I'm talkin' about perfect hash, perfect look, perfect smell, and strong enough to put you on your ass after a few hits. I'm talkin' about hashish that sells itself.'

Teddy had blundered into the connection when a friend's friend introduced him to an Israeli couple living out in Flushing. Skeptical at first, he'd taken one look at the product and forked over virtually his entire working capital.

'How much?' Little Turk asked.

'Twelve hundred an ounce. Four large if you do a quarter-pound.' Teddy sipped at his beer. 'One thing you might want to think about. This supply I have, it's long term.'

Little Turk leaned back in his chair, his eyes wandering to an exploded reproduction of an old lithograph. Slaves unloading a sailing ship. The slaves were bent so far forward under their burdens that their noses came within inches of the gangplank.

'The good old days,' he said, pointing to the panel.

Teddy ignored the comment. Diversity was part of his game and one of his partners was African. 'Talk to me,' he said.

'If it's what you say it is, we could probably handle a quarter-pound a week. But that's a big fuckin' *if*, Teddy.'

Teddy smiled for the first time. 'Me, I'm a freak for details,' he said as Sanda approached the table. 'I worry about every little thing. But not this, pal. These are the golden eggs and I plucked 'em right out of the goose's ass.'

'You have a sample?'

'In the car. When you're ready to go, I'll walk you out.'

The Turks were committed sports gamblers and they soon fell into an analysis of the Knicks' chances against the Washington Wizards. The Knicks were only six-point favorites and the Wizards were the worst team in the league. Then again, the Knicks point guard was out with a bum knee and Amare Stoudemire was so crippled he could barely get around the court.

Teddy watched the pair take turns making the same basic observations, pro and con, a clown show, really, but somehow satisfying, at least to them. After five minutes, Turk went outside to call in a bet. On the Knicks? On the Wizards? Teddy couldn't tell.

'Hey,' Little Turk said, 'you hear about Johnny Piano and that video?'

Teddy shook his head. Though on full alert, his expression revealed only casual curiosity.

'Well, some dude ran a video on YouTube which he claims is Carlo Pianetta on his knees givin' a blow job. In an alley, no less, with garbage cans piled against the walls. And guess what? This guy he's suckin' off just happens to be so black he's purple.'

Teddy laughed agreeably. Poor Johnny. If not for the tax, he might even feel bad for the guy. 'Have you seen this video?' he asked.

'Yeah, but get this. YouTube canned the video an hour after it went up, but not before it was downloaded. Now it's runnin' on a thousand websites. You wanna take a look, just do a search for "Gay Gangster". You'll find it.'

'And it's definitely Carlo?'

'Nah. I mean, it could be Carlo, but it could be anybody. Meanwhile, what I heard, Johnny Piano's so pissed off he can't sit still for a minute. Face it, Teddy, a guy like that, he lives by respect.'

Little Turk drained his glass. He looked at Sanda for moment, then at Teddy, and finally decided to get his own drink. When he turned back to their table, Sanda was gone and his brother had returned.

'Man,' he said, 'what a beauty. You must be doin' all right, Teddy.'

'Beauty and the beast,' his brother added.

'I think we bored Sanda,' Teddy said. 'She went home to her needlepoint.'

The humor passed so far over the brothers' heads that neither realized that Teddy had cracked a joke.

'There's another story goin' around,' Little Turk said. 'Swear on my mother, even the cops are talkin' it up.'

'About Johnny Piano?'

'Right. You know this detective by the name of Boots Littlewood? He wears three-piece suits, a big guy. He's been workin' in Greenpoint for like twenty years.'

An image popped into Teddy's mind of a store walled off by crime scene tape. The man standing outside the tape had 'cop' written all over him. Even as he interviewed a witness, his eyes had jumped to every passerby, every vehicle on the road. Those eyes had radiated suspicion, but so did every cop's. Teddy's attention had mainly been drawn to the cop's suit. His three-piece, pearl gray, double-breasted suit.

'So, OK, Boots Littlewood. What's that got to do with Johnny?'

Little Turk's story was fairly accurate. After one of his soldiers was ripped off and shot, Johnny Piano, accompanied by a body-guard, tried to visit the man in Woodhull Hospital. This cop, Boots, not only arrested the bodyguard, who was packing heat, but forced Johnny to stand for a frisk.

'Now, get this, Teddy. The cop, he grabs Johnny's nuts, right in front of Johnny's kid, and tells Johnny to back off. I mean, it was personal. Johnny and this cop, they both live in Greenpoint and they go way back. In fact, what I heard, they grew up together.'

TWENTY-SEVEN

Teddy lay in bed at the very end of a most excellent day. The Waterfront Bar had turned out to be a little gold mine. He'd passed out samples to several acquaintances besides the Turco brothers and the response was dramatic. The entire two pounds of hashish in his possession were now spoken for. He'd turned a forty percent profit in a single day.

Of course, he might have doubled his money parceling the hash out in small units, but Teddy ultimately planned to distance himself from the mean streets, especially when it came to drugs. He'd have already done so if he had the right personnel. Teddy needed someone to do his job, to meet with suppliers, ensure distribution, to place and collect loans, to command the crew. Shurie? Too jumpy. Recep? Recep was a man of few words. Too few. Pablo? His main skill was a lack of conscience so profound that even Teddy was impressed. Mutava? Mutava had the skills, but would their vendors and customers work with a black man? Not Little Turk, who'd made his prejudices apparent.

Teddy's thoughts immediately jumped to the video Little Turk claimed to have seen. Carlo Pianetta on his knees, as he'd been when Teddy put a bullet through his head.

A short fantasy drifted through Teddy's awareness. A fantasy in which he confessed to Johnny Piano a moment before firing a bullet into the gangster's forehead.

Like father, like son.

Curled up beside him, Sanda didn't stir when Teddy laughed out loud. Teddy envied Sanda's ability to shut down, to be fast asleep the minute her head hit the pillow. Sleep, for him, was always a long time coming and tonight was no exception. He got out of bed and shrugged into a terrycloth bathrobe. Sanda's landlord didn't send up heat at night, another little fact of life he was forced to accept. At least until he had enough spare cash to rent something nicer, say fronting Prospect Park. Meanwhile, Sanda's apartment fronted the weathered brick façade of what used to be Lon Wing Imports. The business had shut down after a third raid by the feds in search of Chinese knockoffs.

Teddy glanced to his left, toward the Pulaski Bridge. Johnny Piano had been the hot topic of conversation at the Waterfront. The few who hadn't heard about the video and Johnny's encounter with the cop were quickly informed. These were people who had no love for the Pianetta crew and its tax. People who'd like nothing better than to pursue their interests on a level playing field.

Suddenly tired, Teddy returned to bed. He'd sleep now, at

least for a few hours. Or so he thought, until a passing notion in the very last seconds before he drifted off jerked him awake. Johnny Piano's beef with the cop was common knowledge. Littlewood had disrespected Johnny in public and Johnny wasn't a man to be disrespected. If something happened to the detective . . .

If something happened to Detective Littlewood, the NYPD would smash the Pianetta crew. They'd have no choice. After all, the cops, too, were men of respect.

TWENTY-EIGHT

Boots kept his thoughts to himself as he and Jill drove from NYU Medical Center out to Brooklyn, but he was again reminded of his own charmed life. The child of parents who loved each other, he'd never known want. Food on the table every night, every bill paid at the end of the month, a nice warm bed to crawl into at the end of every day. Home from school, Boots could ask his mom, 'What's for dinner?' without fearing there'd be no dinner.

He'd had a friend, Larry Mott, when he was eight or nine. Larry's father couldn't keep a job and there were times when the family survived on canned goods from a local food bank, when they sat in the dark, when Larry came to school wearing pants that had been darned so many times they resembled Frankenstein's face. Boots had witnessed their eviction. He'd watched a cut-rate mover toss the family's possessions into the back of a truck before leaving for a storage depot where those possessions would be held until the storage fee was paid. The Mott family had also scrutinized the process, Larry's mom and dad, his brother and his two sisters, the whole family huddled on the sidewalk. Goodbye, life.

'You go mute?' Jill said. 'What's eating you?'

'Luck,' Boots said. 'Accidents of birth.'

'Say that again?'

'No, let's not. Let's keep our eyes peeled instead.'

'My eyes are always peeled, Boots. I've been watching for a tail ever since we left the hospital.'

Despite himself, Boots looked around. They were on the Williamsburg Bridge and the view to his right, of the Manhattan and Brooklyn Bridges, of the great towers of downtown Manhattan, grabbed his eye. The Freedom Tower, built to replace the World Trade Center, had been completed only a few months before. Even in a world of giants, it soared above the rest, its spire like a defiant upraised finger. The Tower would become a target, if it wasn't already, an enduring goal for the terrorists who twice attacked the World Trade Center before they brought it down. Boots admired the defiance, but he wasn't all that sure he'd want to work in the building, maybe take an elevator to the ninety-fifth floor every morning.

Boots guided the Nissan through a series of right turns that brought them back toward the river, then took a left on Kent Avenue. They were only a few blocks from their destination.

In its heyday, the Brooklyn Navy Yard, all three hundred acres, had employed ten thousand workers. But that was during WWII, seventy years ago, and the intervening decades had not been kind. The Navy was long gone, the complex converted into an industrial park that never quite took. Though dozens of businesses leased space in the Yard, most of its four million square feet sat empty. More problematic, three low-income housing projects, the Ingersoll, Whitman and Farragut Houses, provided an endless supply of drug dealers and prostitutes to work the Yard's outer perimeter. Vice and Narcotics made hundreds of arrests every year, to no good effect. Only gentrification could save the neighborhood, as it had further north on Kent Avenue, but gentrification would be slow in coming. The Whitman Houses had more than four thousand residents, as did the Ingersoll, with the Farragut Houses only a bit smaller.

The city had warmed during the day, with the temperature now in the mid-fifties, and the streets were jumping. Boots felt a familiar tension, an edge sharpened considerably by the events of the past few days. Violence was a dish always on the menu wherever dealers and whores, junkies and johns, converged. Boots took his time, driving slow enough on Navy Street to attract attention, the fifteen-story towers of the Farragut Houses to his left, the brick wall enclosing the Navy Yard on his right.

'You startin' to like this, Boots?' Jill asked.

'God help me, but I believe I am.'

'Forget God. Learn to use that gun in your pocket – where it in no way belongs – and you'll be a lot better off.'

Boots didn't answer. The players needed to be marked, snitches identified. He expected the hard stares, but noted the stares held a little too long, the stares a little too defiant. He would silence them first, if it came to that.

Toward the end of his circuit, Boots happened on five working girls clustered around a short, heavy man in a brown suit, the man doing all the talking, which could only mean one thing: the topic of the conversation was money.

A john? A gangster? The Navy Yard was car-trick heaven. No need to leave your vehicle, no need to take the risk. There were junkies here, too, crack and heroin junkies who'd rip your heart out for a fix. But the man was too old, too short and too fat to be a gangster.

Boots pulled to the curb and looked around before stripping out of his coat. He put his weapon back in the shoulder rig and his coat in the trunk before clipping his shield to the lapel of his jacket. As he straightened, he took a final look around, eyes darting from shadow to shadow.

'Five-oh,' one of the women said as Boots and Jill approached, a waste of breath, what with the other women staring at their shields.

Finally alerted, the man in the suit turned to face the oncoming cops. He had huge cheeks and small eyes and a fawning smile that revealed his sudden apprehension. He knew all about the big cop in the vested suit who'd kicked Steve Ungaro's teeth down his throat. Or so Boots assumed.

'Tell me your name,' Boots said.

'Thomas Ressler. I'm a licensed private investigator.'

'What are you doing here?'

'I'm conducting an investigation?'

'You want to get smart with me? You want to shoot off your mouth, maybe impress the ladies? That it, Mr Ressler?'

Ressler took a step back. He shook his head and put up his hands, palms out. 'No way, Detective.'

'Then answer my question. What are you doing here?'

'No disrespect, right? But I work for an attorney and my investigation falls under the heading of attorney-client privilege. In fact, and I'm not makin' this up, swear to God, I'm under specific instructions not to talk about the case to anyone but my employer.'

'And he is?'

'Nat Kasatamakis.'

Boots smiled, remembering Joyce Kipner, the lawyer who'd shown up when he arrested Al Buffo. If Kipner was an apex predator when it came to mob lawyers, Kasatamakis was a pure bottom feeder. He specialized in no-show prosecution witnesses, in prosecution witnesses who reversed their testimony on the stand, in last-minute alibi witnesses.

'You carrying a gun?' Jill asked.

'Yeah.'

'Where is it?'

'I got a permit for that gun.'

'That's not what I asked you, Tom.'

Ressler sighed. 'In a holster behind my right hip.'

'I'm going to take it now. Raise your hands.' Jill cocked her head to one side, her eyes narrowing, but she smiled as she addressed her amused partner. 'What could I say, Boots? Despite the shooting competitions, I'm not that big on the Second Amendment. I'd be happiest if nobody had guns.'

'Except cops.'

'Exactly.'

Jill removed the PI's weapon, a Browning 9mm, and tucked it into the waistband of her slacks. To her right, a short Latina let out a shrill, 'Ayyyyyy. You go, girl.'

'I'm not your girl,' Jill corrected without taking her eyes off Tom Ressler. 'You carrying any other weapons?'

'No.'

'Turn around and face away from me. I'm going to search you.'

Jill's frisk was thorough, again drawing the approval of an audience that had swelled to seven. Boots listened to the catcalls, the high pealing laughter. You had to be careful with hookers. You got their backs up, they wouldn't so much as spit on you.

You couldn't bluff them, either, and it was nearly certain that most of these women (two of whom were actually men) were currently stoned.

As she finished her search, Jill plucked a billfold from Ressler's breast pocket. She opened it without asking permission and examined his PI license, his concealed-carry permit and his driver's license.

'You're Thomas Ressler?' she asked.

'I already told you that.'

'And you live at 11-15 127th Street in College Point?'

Ressler's mouth opened and he started to speak. Jill could actually see his tongue move behind his teeth. Then his mouth snapped shut and he smiled. *I know where you live.* The bitch had just threatened him.

'Go home, Mr Ressler,' Jill said as she returned his gun and his wallet. 'Your workday is over.'

'You can't just . . .'

Jill leaned forward to whisper into the PI's ear. 'Do you really want me to slap your face in front of all these women?'

TWENTY-NINE

Jill watched Thomas Ressler beat a thoroughly undignified retreat to his car, watched him drive away. Then she turned to Boots and said, 'Your show, partner.'

She didn't need to mention the part about having his back and Boots finally turned his attention to the women. He had a decision to make and precious little time to weigh the consequences. Pianetta had put the pieces together, or enough pieces to get him to the Navy Yard, but he didn't have a name or a photo. That would change if Boots displayed Corry's photo and spoke her name. Ressler would return, most likely tomorrow, asking the same questions, offering the same reward. Jill had bought the good guys a little time, but no more.

Boots examined the hookers, as they examined him. The crowd had swelled to nine, six women and three male cross-dressers.

Two, a man and a woman, were the pale, lifeless white of advanced heroin addicts. The rest were black or Latino. They were all sisters, though, prostitutes trapped at the very bottom of the sex trade, and their day-to-day lives, not to mention their various chemical dependencies, had rendered them nearly feral. Honor played no part in their dealings with cops.

'How'd that case go, Pumpkin?' Boots asked one of the cross-dressers, a man he'd arrested for assault only a few months ago.

'Dismissed. Man decided he didn't wanna testify on account of he's married and what I done to him was righteous. I acted in self-defense.'

'That's what you told me.'

'But you didn't pay me no mind.'

Boots flashed his quick smile, here and gone. 'Well, Pumpkin, being as the man was beaten to a pulp and you weren't so much as scratched, you can hardly blame me.'

Tall and bony with an Adam's apple the size of a mango pit, Pumpkin's mini-skirt revealed stick-thin legs that rose from a pair of huge feet jammed into blue metallic pumps. Now he grabbed his false breasts and shook with laughter.

'Man fucked with the wrong woman. That's all it was.'

Boots nodded. In his mind, the johns were no better than the whores who serviced them. 'How much he offer, Pumpkin? I'm talkin' about the asshole my partner just ran off.'

'Hundred dollars,' one of women said. 'Flashed a Benjamin to prove he wasn't bullshittin'.'

'And what did he want?'

'Wanted to know about some girl got beat up, maybe ain't been around for a few days.'

Boots stared at the woman for a moment. Her face was well-lined beneath the makeup and her eyes reflected a deeply held mistrust. The past hadn't been kind to her and she wasn't expecting anything from the future beyond her next fix. Her pupils had shrunk to mere pinpoints.

'And what'd you say?'

The woman managed a hard, bitter laugh. 'Folks get beat up every day round here. Go missin', too.'

'I won't argue the point, but I'm also looking for a woman, a prostitute I know walked among you, the difference being that

I've got a name and a picture. Now what I'm gonna do, maybe an hour from now, is park my car on Navy Street by the ball fields. Anybody wants to earn a hundred dollars can find me there. But I will say this, and only once. I'm not the trick that Pumpkin beat into the hospital. You lie to me, I'll tear your ass up. Man or woman, I don't give a shit.'

An hour later, as promised, Boots pulled to the curb on Navy Street. By then, he'd approached dozens of women, offering as little information as possible. Twenty dollars being the price of a car trick, the c-note, he assumed, would be motivation enough.

He was right. Two girls detached themselves from the shadows beneath the trees lining the ball fields before he put the Nissan in park. He invited them, one at a time, into the back seat, and questioned each briefly. When it became obvious they were on a fishing expedition, he sent them off without mentioning Corry's name or showing her photo.

'You have a plan B?' Jill asked.

'Not yet,' Boots admitted.

'And you know what's gonna happen when that PI comes back.' Jill adjusted the mirror on her side of the car until she had a clear view of the street and sidewalks behind them. 'Because here's the thing, Boots. The PI's got money to spend, a lot more than we do, and if he throws enough hundred dollar bills around, he'll get a hit sooner or later.'

Boots continued to stare out through the windshield. They were facing the Brooklyn-Queens Expressway, elevated at that point, and the deep shadows beneath the road shifted constantly as the headlights of cars and trucks and busses swept across its supporting pillars. Even now, this late on a weekday night, traffic moved in a steady stream, on the Expressway and on the road beneath.

Five minutes later, two women approached, trudging up the long block, and Boots went back to work. 'Give me a name?' he demanded of each. One couldn't. The other said, 'Mary-Ann.' Both were sent home with no treat to show for the effort.

'Actually,' Boots said, 'I do have a backup plan. If we don't learn anything tonight, we'll come back tomorrow night, show

Corry's photo to every hooker on the street and hope for the best.'

'What about Ressler?'

Boots flashed his quick smile, thinking of Craig O'Malley and the Bulgarian. 'I know two cops at the Six-Four who'd leap at the chance to buy us another night.'

'They'd run him off?'

'That they would.'

'But we're not in the Six-Four.'

Boots shrugged as a woman approached the car. 'Ressler won't know that.'

The hooker groaned when her butt hit the back seat. She took off her stiletto-heeled pumps and rubbed her feet. 'Name's Shoona,' she said.

'Detective Littlewood. And this is Detective Kelly.'

Shoona looked into Jill's eyes for a moment, her gaze frank, though not especially challenging. 'How you doin'?'

'Getting by,' Jill said.

'Glad to hear that.' Shoona leaned back and took a deep breath. 'Most times I get in a car it's for one thing. Nice to be jus' sittin' here.'

'Well, don't get too comfortable, Shoona,' Boots said. 'This isn't a social call.'

'Corry,' Shoona said.

'Say what?'

'Corry. That's who you're lookin for. Reason I know, I seen her drive away with that creep.'

'What creep?'

'Carlo Pianetta. I didn't know his name at the time, just enough about him not to get in his damn car. Corry, she's young and she likes to play the fool.' Now that Shoona had the full attention of both detectives, she settled back, her eyes fluttering, and it was obvious to both detectives that she'd gotten off not long before. Her movements were languid, her words slow in coming.

'You said that Corry *is* young,' Boots said, 'and that she *likes* to play the fool. Does that mean you know, for sure, that she's alive?'

'Uh-huh.'

'Don't bullshit me, Shoona.'

Shoona scratched the side of her face. 'Happens I got Corry's cell number. Happens she called me on that throwaway she's usin'. Happens she needed a little somethin' to get her head straight. I had to carry the shit out to Elmhurst Avenue on the seven train, but I seen right away that she wouldn't be comin' back to Brooklyn anytime soon. Man, her face was all *busted* up. Girl took a serious beat down.'

'Do you think she's living in the neighborhood. That would be Jackson Heights, right?'

'I think she was too ripped up to be makin' any long trips.' Shoona hesitated, perhaps hoping to draw a sympathetic response, but the two cops merely stared at her. 'Corry tole me she was stayin' with her brother. But she was like scared because he was in the habit of sleepin' with a sawed-off shotgun. Corry said he was in the Army and the war made him crazy.'

'Get to the bottom line,' Boots said. 'Do you know where she's staying?'

'No, but I got her number on my cell.'

Boots nodded. Pimps often gave their women cell phones. That way they'd never have an excuse to be out of touch. 'Call her.'

'Gettin' kinda late.'

'Tell her there's some righteous dope goin' around and does she maybe want a few bags for herself. Tell her it won't be around long.'

Shoona's laugh was gentle. 'Yeah, that'll do it.

It didn't. A computerized voice told Shoona that the number she dialed was not a working number. The voice was loud enough for Boots to hear the words from where he sat.

'Looks like the girl wised up,' Shoona observed.

'Did you speak to her about what happened?'

'Uh-uh.'

'You didn't ask her about who killed Carlo, maybe saved her life?'

'Don't know and don't wanna know. Carlo and his people, they kill you soon as look at you. Don't want no business with 'em that takes more than twenty minutes in the back seat of a Cadillac.'

'Fine, but what about a pimp? Does Corry have a pimp?'

'Uh-huh, goes by the name of Stat. But he ain't on the street. He's in jail on account of he shot his brother. Been there for a week.'

Boots took the hundred dollar bill from his wallet and passed it over to Shoona, along with his business card. 'Corry's gonna call somebody when she runs out of dope, most likely you. If you phone me right away, there's another fifty in it.'

Shoona tucked the twenties into her bra. She was getting out of the car when Boots spoke. 'There a man named Ressler, a private investigator. He's asking the same questions I'm asking and he works for the same people you're afraid of. Those people, they get their hands on you, they're gonna squeeze until there's no more toothpaste left in the tube.'

Boots's cell phone began to ring before Shoona cleared the block. He answered to find Detective Cletis Small, he of the precinct gang squad, on the line.

'Got somethin' here you might be interested in,' Small said. 'A pair of Ecuadorean kids, members of *Los Afligidos* from what I'm hearin'. Shot in the head, both of 'em, from the back seat of a car. I'm thinkin' it might tie to the Pianetta thing. I mean, Boots, Los Afligidos is strictly wannabe, a bunch of kids. If one of them did go off, we'd be pickin' up shell casings all night. Whoever capped these boys took their casings with them. This was an execution.'

Boots hung up a minute later. As he put the Nissan in gear and pulled away, his thoughts already turning to his home and his bed (with Jill, of course, in it), he turned to his partner and said, 'It's begun.'

THIRTY

Snugged down in the back seat of his three-year-old Impala, the vehicle large enough to hide all but the top of his head, Teddy Winuk was only visible if you looked past the reflections on the windshield. The two people in the ancient Nissan fifty feet ahead of him, though they glanced around after getting out, clearly didn't notice him. If they had, they would never have indulged in an embrace so passionate it made him instantly yearn for Sanda.

In fact, it was Sanda who'd brought him to Newell Street. Using one of the many websites dedicated to finding anybody, anywhere, anytime, she'd pulled up the address of a property owner in Greenpoint named Andrew Littlewood. A check of birth records produced a single hit for Andrew and Margaret Littlewood, a boy they'd named Irwin. A further search through the database of the *Daily News* had uncovered a story about the arrest of a killer whose name meant nothing to Winuk. But the name of the cop, Irwin Littlewood, and the location of the arrest, the Sixty-Fourth Precinct, pretty much sealed the deal. Teddy already knew that Boots Littlewood resided in Greenpoint, the only question being whether he lived in his father's house. Now that question had been put to rest as well.

Teddy might have driven away at that point. The big cop wouldn't be leaving home anytime soon. But he decided to hang around anyway. Maybe when the lights went out, he'd take a stroll, see if he could find his way to the backyard of Andy Littlewood's two-story home. One thing, the residents on these blocks of Newell Street didn't appear to be concerned with security. Elsewhere in Greenpoint, the lower windows of every building, commercial or residential, were protected by steel bars. Not here.

As the minutes passed, Winuk's thoughts drifted to his cash-flow problems. He was coming to view the problem as a blessing. He'd been jumping on any deal that came along for the past few years, had even worked briefly for a Queens' shylock now doing forty-to-life in the Green Haven Correctional Facility. A little dope here, a jewelry store there, with maybe a hijacking thrown in for seasoning. You had to prove yourself before you collected allies, prove yourself on the street. That had taken time, even though it turned out to be easier than he expected.

Maybe those days were over, but he was still mired in the past, still jumping at every opportunity. And it was no good. He needed to organize, to delegate authority. As it was, nobody was in charge of anything and he spent most of his day improvising solutions to problems he shouldn't have had to deal with in the first place.

No more. No further expansion until he solved—

Teddy's thoughts were interrupted when a car, a Beamer, rolled down Newell Street, its headlights sweeping over the Impala. He glanced to the side as the car passed, just glimpsing a man with a bandage covering most of the right side of his face. A bandage the size of a racing sail that only emphasized his enormous nose.

The name popped into Teddy's mind: Steve Ungaro, Stevie Eagle. That guess was pretty much confirmed when the BMW pulled to the curb at a fire hydrant across from the cop's house and the headlights flicked off.

Teddy smiled to himself. Here it came, opportunity, and he was jumping at it, as he always did, going so far as to indulge himself in a little fantasy that had Ungaro killing the cop, the cops attacking Johnny Piano on all fronts, the empire destroyed, this end of Brooklyn up for grabs. A nice fantasy, but completely wrong, as it turned out. First thing, Stevie Eagle didn't get out of the car, just sat there. Second thing, about five minutes later, a woman slipped out of a narrow alley running between two houses. She passed right in front of him, keeping low until she reached the shelter of a parked car, then dropped to one knee.

Despite the poor lighting – the nearest street lamp was three houses away – Teddy recognized her as the raven-haired woman Boots had escorted into his home. A beauty, for sure, despite the nine millimeter semi-automatic clutched in her right hand.

Teddy watched her inch down the line of cars, coming up behind Ungaro, until she again crouched, this time beside a Toyota parked almost directly across the street from the BMW. He watched the woman's eyes and her weapon clear the hood, watched her line up the shot. A cop, for sure, and a predator to boot.

Another quick fantasy. The woman sprays Stevie Eagle's brains all over the sidewalk, after which he, Teddy Winuk, has ultimate leverage over her and Detective Littlewood.

Teddy went so far as to take out his cell phone, his intention to record the event.

Again, it was not to be. The door to the Littlewood house opened and Detective Littlewood emerged, looking somehow bigger without his three-piece suit. Boots Littlewood wore jeans and a T-shirt and he walked straight at the BMW, coming fast, his hands empty.

A set-up.

If Ungaro made a move, if he produced a weapon, the cop's lady friend would put a bullet through his head, all nice and neat. In New York City, cops got away with shooting unarmed teenagers. Shooting an armed gangster would draw nothing but praise.

Maybe the gangster sensed the trap. Or maybe he just lost his nerve. Either way, he drove off before Boots cleared the sidewalk on his own side of the street.

The woman rose to her full height and said something to her partner that caused him to laugh. Neither seemed overly concerned with the encounter. If Ungaro had come to intimidate, he'd failed miserably. Littlewood picked up his girlfriend, slung her over his shoulder and marched back into the house.

The show over, Teddy relaxed, again thinking he might as well head back to Sanda's, call it a night. He was horny and he was hungry and the temperature had dropped into the forties after a relatively warm day. Still, he lingered to watch an elderly man walk a thickly muscled pit bull up and down the street.

'No, heel. No, heel. Bad dog.'

The animal paid exactly zero attention. It was taking its master for a walk and would not be distracted.

The old man disappeared a few minutes later, leaving Teddy to contemplate the occasional passing car, lights going on and off, a flickering television in a darkened upstairs room. Some notion was tickling the back of his mind, teasing him. Something about the woman, something he'd missed because he'd been too busy staring at her ass when she crouched beside the car in front of his.

Teddy's thoughts immediately jumped to Sanda, his crotch deaf to his commands. He felt like the old man with the dog. But Teddy wasn't an old man and he shifted his focus back to the cop's girlfriend after a few seconds.

Not her butt this time, though it had shown to advantage when she drew down on Stevie Eagle. Littlewood had put his life in her hands. If he'd doubted her willingness to pull the trigger and hit what she aimed at, he would never have left the house.

So?

So, if some bad thing happened to her boyfriend, she'd be inclined, and have the ability, to do something about it. Like kill Johnny Piano? A boy could only hope, hope for the prick to die, hope for the chaos to follow.

THIRTY-ONE

Take out the cop, leave the girlfriend to do her thing, without, of course, dying yourself in the process. A tall order, maybe too tall. Or so Teddy thought as he drove to Sanda's. He was tough enough, not to mention ruthless enough, to pull it off.

But skilled enough?

That last part, about dying in the process, held no appeal. Live to fight another day seemed a lot more realistic.

He was still mulling the possibilities when he entered the apartment to find the bathroom door open and Sanda climbing out of the bathtub. She hadn't heard him come in and he watched her towel herself dry, totally unaware of his presence. But then she glanced at him out of the corner of one green eye, her look mischievous. Sanda's left leg was propped on the edge of the tub as she ran the towel along her inner thigh.

'Hello, Teddy. Did you have a good day?'

'Yeah, and I'm about to have a better night.' Teddy walked into the bedroom, already taking off his shirt, only to find an assortment of velvet-covered restraints laid out on the comforter. He started to ask if they were for her or him, but decided he could swing either way.

Sanda came up behind him. 'Tonight,' she said, 'I teach you about relationship between sex and pain.'

Teddy smiled. 'Guess I better put on my thinking cap.'

'Got a proposition for you,' Teddy said.

'What, Teddy? I have not satisfied you.'

Teddy laughed. 'Not that kind of proposition. A business proposition.'

'Sex is only business I know.'

'Never too late to learn. Anyway, there's serious money in it.'

'Risk, too?'

'Yeah, there's risk.' Teddy described the drug scene he and Shurie had set up in Jackson Heights, the locked-in retailers, the pay-in-a-week policy. 'I'm looking for someone to manage the operation. Take orders, make delivery, collect the money. One thing you wouldn't have to worry about, you won't be on the buying end. You'll pick up product at a location on the other side of Brooklyn and distribute it in Queens. We're gonna deal in standard units, so the product will already be weighed out.' Teddy filled his mouth again. Suddenly, he was starving. 'I'm offering five percent off the top. You take it as you collect it. Maybe two grand a week at the start. Once we get going, it could be anything.'

Sanda didn't respond at first, but her eyes ripped into Teddy's. 'Why do you do this? It cannot be for . . . pussy. You could have many women.'

'Hey, Sanda, don't make a mistake here. I never get sentimental when it comes to business. I'm offering you the position because I have a job that needs doing and I think you can do it. You'll be working with Shurie, by the way. It's his project. I don't wanna hear word one. You have a problem, you take it up with him.'

Far from convinced, Sanda shook her head. 'First time one of your customers gets arrested, he will bring police to me. How I am to trust them?'

'That's the risk part, Sanda, but I did have a little one-on-one talk with our retailers. I gave each of them my lawyer's business card, told them, "Call Mel Abzug from the precinct if you get popped. He'll arrange bail, represent you at the arraignment, get you out if you can be gotten out. On the other hand, if you don't make that call, and I mean from the precinct before you talk to the cops, I'll put a bullet in the back of your fucking head. You want off the hook, better find someone besides me to put on it."'

One more thing to do before Teddy settled down with a beer to watch a little late-night TV. Sanda was already asleep.

'You home?' he asked Shurie.

'Yeah.'

'You alone?'

'Just me, my mom and my five brothers and sisters.'

'You don't think it's time you got your own place?'

Shurie's sigh emptied his lungs. 'C'mon, Teddy, don't bust my balls.'

'All right, you remember you told me about this tracking device, it's like as big as a pack of cigarettes and attaches with a magnet?'

'Yeah, you can buy 'em for a couple of hundred bucks.'

'You still have it?'

'Yeah, sure.'

'What I want you to do, Shurie, is bring the device to me in Brooklyn.' Teddy rattled off Sanda's address. 'And bring me whatever software I need to make it work.'

THIRTY-TWO

Better. That's how Corry Frisk described her condition to herself on Wednesday morning, four days after the assault. Better physically and better mentally, proof being that she now had a word for what happened to her. She'd been obliterated.

Corry's brother, Tommy, had supplied the word. Inadvertently, of course. Tommy never seemed to do anything deliberately except strip and clean his guns, sometimes twice a day. Anyhow, they were in Tommy's little apartment – it had to be about three o'clock in the morning – when Tommy described an assault his platoon fended off in Helmand Province outside of a city called Lashkar Gah. The unit battled a numerically superior enemy for nearly an hour until a pair of helicopter gunships made an appearance, whereupon the enemy disengaged. Eight men, including Tommy's best buddy, died in the fight, while another fifteen were wounded. Twenty-three casualties out of twenty-eight men. They were obliterated.

'I thought I was a done dog. Like a video of my body dragged over the desert would surface on YouTube. Check out the dead soldier. And the funny thing, there's times – I swear, Corry – when I think I did die and this is the afterlife. I mean, when there's so many bullets snappin' past your head, you just figure somebody's callin' your name.'

So, she was obliterated and now she was feeling better, which was natural. Bodies heal. Minds are another thing. There was no restore button on the computer inside her skull and Corry believed that she'd never get well, not in her mind. Any more than Tommy would get well in his. Which is not to say that anyone gave a shit. No, sink or swim, they were on their own.

'Are you gonna do this?' Tommy asked from the front of the gypsy cab he drove whenever he was stable enough to face the world.

'I'm workin' up to it, Tommy.'

There was no going back to the streets. That was the first thing she had to face. Hooker time was over. Just the thought of sliding into a stranger's car filled her with a disorienting fear, as if she'd stumbled and fallen over the edge of a cliff. Like the ground was rushing up to meet her.

By her own reckoning, Corry needed time. Time and space, which her brother also needed. If they were there for the taking, she would already have grabbed them both. Unfortunately, time and space were for sale, pay the price and no freebies allowed.

Tommy's eight-hundred-dollar government disability check, even supplemented by his cab driving, wasn't enough to maintain the status quo. Not given her unfortunate dependency. Tommy hadn't asked her to contribute, but that would eventually come. And what would she do? With two prostitution arrests on her record? Send off her resume?

Dope helped. Shoot up, slide into a hot bathtub lit with candles, let your mind drift. Sometimes the tension seemed to release from every cell in her body. Sometimes she could almost feel her DNA relax, her essence, her most basic self.

Just what she needed, for maybe an hour. Then time and space began to contract, minute by minute, faster and faster, until she was back where she started. In need of a fix.

Corry took a cell phone from her purse, brought it to her ear, then dropped it into her lap. Tommy was driving beneath the elevated subway on Roosevelt Avenue and a seven train was passing overhead.

'You think you could find another street?' she said.

'What?'

Corry waited until the train passed. 'Find a quieter street, Tommy. I don't wanna be screamin' at the guy.'

'Sorry.'

She waited until Tommy made a right onto National Street, then punched a number into the phone.

'Amoroso Construction.' The woman's voice was young and friendly, though her New York accent was pronounced. 'How can I help you?'

'I want to speak with John Pianetta.'

'Please hold.'

The next voice, also a woman's, was decidedly less friendly. 'John Pianetta's office. Who am I speaking to?'

'The woman his kid beat half to death while he was raping her.'

That shut her up. Corry let the silence build for a few seconds, and then said, 'I can identify the man who put a bullet through Carlo's head. I'll be calling again a few minutes from now.'

Corry let her head fall back as she counted off the seconds. She told herself, as she'd already done, many times, that you don't get all that many chances in life, even if you play it straight. When you're a junkie prostitute maybe you only get one.

Besides, and Corry was sure about this, what Teddy did to Carlo was about the two of them, not about Corry Frisk. Teddy saved her, and no denying it, but if it had been someone else, and not Carlo Pianetta, Teddy would have walked away. Probably.

A few minutes later, she had a man on the phone who at least claimed to be Johnny Piano.

'I'm gonna tell you the story,' she said, 'and I don't want you to interrupt me until I finish. Carlo picked me up on Navy Street last Sunday morning at five o'clock. He was real nice, just a horny guy out for a quickie in the back seat. But once I got inside his Lexus, he locked the doors with the child lock so I couldn't get out and then drove to the Pulaski Bridge. I went along because . . . because what choice did I have? But when I asked for the money up front, your kid beat me until I couldn't fight back, until I could barely move. Did he plan to kill me after he finished raping me? I'll never know because ten minutes later this guy turned up out of nowhere. Him and Carlo, they exchanged a few words, then the guy shot Carlo in the head and walked off like nothin' happened. They knew each other, by the way. The man called Carlo by his first name.'

Corry ground to a halt, pretty sure her story had been convincing, especially the mention of Carlo's Lexus. She'd mulled over how to approach Pianetta for a couple of days before she decided to make it as brief and cold as possible. Here it is. Nobody could make this up.

'Do I get to ask the big question now?' Pianetta said.

'Ask away.'

'Do you know the name of the man who killed my son?'

Corry was unable to detect a hint of sympathy in Johnny Piano's tone. 'Yes, I do.'

'Will you tell me?'

'Sure, for thirty thousand dollars. And I'm not gonna retreat from that figure. No, I'm gonna call you tomorrow morning and you're gonna tell me what you decided.'

'How will I know you're not lying?'

'You'll take a good look at my face.'

Tommy pulled over next to a storm drain at the corner and Corry opened the door far enough to flip the cell phone into the drain. Then she closed the door and said, 'How'd I do, Tommy?'

'You did great, sis.'

'All right, then let's go home.'

Two minutes later, as they came up Junction Boulevard, Tommy leaned on the horn. 'Move the fuckin' bus,' he shouted out the window. Then he pounded the steering wheel with his fist when the bus – which could have pulled to the curb – remained exactly where it was. For a moment, Corry was sure he'd reach for the revolver beneath his seat.

Time and space, she said to herself. And soon.

THIRTY-THREE

Frankie Drago walked the final half-block to Boots Littlewood's apartment. He ran every morning now, rain or shine. Well, not every morning, not when a cold winter rain, as gray as the sidewalks, pounded those sidewalks. But the cold didn't stop him. Frankie had changed his life, recovering his health and a bit of his youth in the process. Now, when he remembered those glory days on a high-school baseball diamond, squatting behind the plate, stepping into the batter's box, taking a few practice swings, he didn't feel ashamed. As if he'd surrendered a birthright. No, he remembered that he was the star of the team, that he'd hit two home runs for every one of Boots Littlewood's.

Joaquin's face appeared in the door, drawing a smile. When Boots first announced that he was adopting the kid, Frankie had responded with a quick, 'You're fuckin' nuts.'

Meanwhile, in his own way, Joaquin projected as much confidence as his dad. He was the kid Frankie would have wanted if he'd ever wanted kids. Which, despite his mother's pestering, he hadn't.

'Hey, Joaquin, I heard you were doin' good.'

'My father talkin' about me again?'

Drago's answer stuck in his throat at the sight of Jill Kelly perched on the couch, her long legs folded beneath her. Jill wore one of her boyfriend's T-shirts, the T-shirt big enough to pass for a nightgown. Even without makeup and her hair only vaguely brushed, she was stunning. The black hair, the midnight-blue eyes, the pale Irish complexion, the insolent tilt of her head. Oh, yeah, Boots had finally bitten off more than he could chew.

'Hey,' he muttered, suddenly aware of his sweat-soaked track suit. Purple, of course.

'This is Frankie Drago,' Joaquin said. 'Frankie, meet Jill Kelly. *Detective* Jill Kelly, as she likes to be called.'

Jill nodded before returning to her morning coffee. She knew all about Frankie Drago, knew he'd been to jail for killing his sister and knew that he and Boots had been friends since high school. Knew, also, that Frankie had become a kind of informal snitch.

Boots made his appearance a moment later, wearing his suit pants and a white shirt open at the neck. 'Frankie,' he said, his tone cheerful, 'you come right from the shower?'

Boots was in a good mood. Jill's mother had agreed to enter a rehab program, the first weeks to be spent in-residence. He and

Jill would drive her from NYU Medical Center to her place of confinement in the Bronx as soon as they finished breakfast. That would free up Jill to guard his body full time.

'I'm killin' two birds with one stone,' Frankie said. 'Doin' my run and doin' a favor for a friend.'

'And who would that be?'

Frankie turned to Jill. 'Does he do this to everybody? Or am I a special case?'

The questions. drew a smile from Jill, but no response. The woman had the eyes of a professional poker player, always busy, alert for a tell.

'Let's take a walk,' he told Boots. 'It's nice out.'

'So?' Boots asked as they strolled down Newell Street.

'So, I been hearing things. On and off, from certain people.'

'Like?'

The bookmaker shook his head. 'What's the matter with you, Boots? Why did you fuck with these guys?'

'They were interfering in my investigation. Still are, for that matter.'

'You're so full of shit. Look, all the time I've known you, from back when we were kids, you were always careful. Angles, that's what you were about. Now you're buttin' heads with a guy who'll kill you in a minute. Like some mountain sheep with his balls in an uproar. I don't get it, Boots. I don't.'

Boots had already heard this many times, from his son and his father. But he liked the bit about the sheep crashing their heads together. The point – in the sheep's case – was to impress a lady. To the victor belongs the spoils. Or at least one part of the spoils' anatomy. But his game was more complicated. First, he had Jill. Not the beautiful woman Frankie imagined bedding. Detective Littlewood's Jill Kelly was a walking insurance policy.

'Frankie, if you came here to lecture me on my mid-life crisis, consider your mission accomplished.'

'No, it's more than that. You remember askin' me to keep my ears open, right?'

'Right.'

'Well, two things I'm hearin' that you need to know. First, the man who shot Silvy Mussa wore a rosary with colored beads and a skull instead of a crucifix at the end. You know, like that bullshit gang in the projects, *Los . . .*'

'*Los Afligidos*. The Afflicted.'

'The afflicted? What's that supposed to mean?'

'It's a cry for help from a small group of Ecuadoran kids surrounded by large, powerful gangs.'

Frankie took a step back. 'Pardon me if I puke.'

They walked in silence for a minute, until Boots's patience wore thin. 'So, what else?' he asked.

'Johnny's not gonna retaliate against you. His kid talked him out of it.'

'Why's that?'

'Because they decided that you're playing Johnny for a sucker. Like you want Johnny to take a shot at you and they're not gonna fall into the trap. Also, Johnny's people are spreading the word that Johnny took care of the scumbags responsible for Carlo's death, that he evened the score and now it's back to business as usual.'

Boots considered the implications for a moment before speaking. 'How do you know this?'

That produced a quick flush. 'I got it from Johnny, himself.' Drago shrugged. 'What could I say, Boots? He knows that we know each other. It's not like I could refuse.'

'Do you think he's playin' it straight?'

'What I think, Boots, is that he'll bide his time. Maybe he'll eventually forget. Maybe he won't. But for right now, you don't have to worry.'

THIRTY-FOUR

Boots collected Jill and they headed out under rapidly darkening skies. More rain, just what he needed. But the gloom definitely complemented the first task of the day. He and Jill were to pick up Jill's mom at the hospital and transport her to a rehab facility in the South Bronx. Boots found himself wishing the rush-hour traffic would intensify, though it was already horrific. Last night, when he asked Jill if she wanted him to come along, her quick assent surprised him. He'd expected an out-of-hand refusal. Had counted on it, in fact.

The two hours Boots spent minding the car while Jill arranged the discharge didn't help. He listened to the radio for a while, a call-in sports show, but the news was bad. The Steinbrenner family was sticking to their austerity pledge. Rather than acquiring new talent in the free-agent market, they were hemorrhaging talent. Cano, Granderson, Andy Pettitte and the greatest closing pitcher in major league history, Mariano Rivera. Gone, baby, gone. Along with his hopes for next season. Boots shut off the radio with an hour to go, figuring he'd be better entertained by the crash of a jackhammer pounding the asphalt a block away.

With all that time to think, Boots should have been prepared for the woman in the wheelchair, but he wasn't. Boots had been in the hospital and he knew you were supposed to ride to the front door in a wheelchair. After that, you were on your own, assuming you could walk without falling down, which Theresa Kelly obviously couldn't.

Theresa Kelly was fifty-five years old, according to her daughter, but she looked much older to Boots. Even more, she looked tired, someone who'd simply worn down, crushed by her burdens, self-made or not. The whites of her eyes were filmed with yellow, her skin as well.

Boots watched Jill guide her mother into the back seat, then slide in beside her and close the door. When she settled against the seat, her mother spoke up.

'Jill?' her mother said. 'Please introduce us.'

'This is my mother, Boots, Theresa Kelly. And this, Mom, is my partner, Boots Littlewood.'

For the first couple of miles, as they headed north on First Avenue, Boots concentrated on the heavy traffic. The Kellys remained silent behind him, their expressions equally grim. This was the end game, an inevitable stop on the express Theresa Kelly had been riding for many years, maybe the last stop. Theresa Kelly was far too sick to enter an ordinary rehab facility. She needed skilled nursing care and the only site in New York that provided it to recovering alcoholics and addicts, Citizens Rest, was itself housed inside one of the largest nursing homes in the city.

Boots piloted the Taurus straight up First Avenue, through

Midtown, the Upper East Side and Harlem, to the Willis Avenue Bridge. He was halfway across the Harlem River when Theresa Kelly spoke up.

'My husband was a policeman, a detective,' she said. 'Did Jill tell you?'

'Yes, she did.'

Boots glanced in the rear-view mirror. Theresa Kelly's hand was shaking, a steady tremble that Jill smothered by taking her mother's hand in her own.

'Do you know what's so very interesting?' Theresa asked.

'I don't,' Boots said.

'How someone can be so far away and so present at the same time.'

'Like a circle. Sometimes I think of my mother that way. There are times when she seems to fade, and maybe I don't think about her for a couple of weeks. But then she's right there with me, as if she never died.'

Jill laughed. 'This isn't the end,' she said, her tone firm. 'It's the beginning. Only a fool would see it any other way.'

'Even if it *is* another way?' Theresa asked her daughter.

'Especially if it's another way. I mean, if the reality turns out to be shit, you can at least enjoy the fantasy.'

'Language, Jill. Language.'

Citizens Rest offered no surprises. A massive white-brick cube broken by windows and doors, it took up an entire block of Longwood Avenue just off Southern Boulevard. The home, like every other nursing home in the city, made do with Medicaid reimbursement rates that did not allow for proper staffing, much less frivolous decoration. Boots knew the inside would be nearly as barren as the home's exterior and he was more than happy to be told to watch the car while Jill handled the paperwork.

The drizzle had turned to a steady rain by the time Jill returned an hour later. She motioned Boots to slide over and got in behind the wheel, her attitude brusque. Do it or else.

'They threw me out,' she said, 'and I won't be able to visit for at least two weeks. I need something to do and driving is the only game in town.'

Boots maintained a somber expression. He even nodded wisely, as though the prospect of two uninterrupted weeks with Jill Kelly wasn't the best news he'd heard in months. Guarding his precious body by day, in his bed at night. Thank you, Lord.

Or maybe not the Lord, who, if Boots remembered right, frowned on fornication.

'Remind me again,' Jill said. 'What are we doing today?'

'We're doing the one job every cop on the force looks forward to.'

'And what's that?'

'Random canvassing in a cold downpour. And you better turn the wipers up to high if you don't plan on killing the both of us.'

THIRTY-FIVE

Surveillance? Turning the tables on the cops? The idea had a nice ring to it when Teddy Winuk set out that morning. Do unto others what they would do unto you, only do it first. Like putting a tracking device on the big cop's piece-of-shit Ford Taurus. Teddy glanced to his left, at the image on Shurie's laptop, a little yellow car moving along a map that covered six or seven square blocks of the city. Nice.

Unfortunately, Teddy's euphoria was short-lived. Never renowned for his patience, he quickly discovered that covert surveillance was as boring an activity as human existence had to offer. After making a quick stop at NYU Medical Center, Littlewood had shut down the Taurus by a fire hydrant on 39th Street. There, an hour later, it remained.

Parked on the next block, Teddy felt like a coiled jack-in-the-box. Somebody open the lid. Please. He text-messaged his associates, only to find them already pursuing their interests like the dependable earners they were. Shurie had found a buyer for the hijacked refrigerators and was in the process of making delivery. Recep was doing collections in Canarsie and Howard Beach. Pablo's job was a little trickier. As the crew's Spanish speaker, he'd set up a meeting with a man who claimed to represent a Mexican cartel, *La Familia Michoacana*. LFM would supply them with marijuana, cocaine, heroin and methamphetamine, the only issue being whether they could handle the volume.

As for Mutava . . . well, Mutava was a big problem. The African communities in New York were tightly knit, with lots of rivalries between clans and nationalities. The Africans weren't angels, not by any means, but they distrusted outsiders when it came to borrowing money and they rarely used drugs.

Bottom line, Mutava wasn't an earner and never would be.

Teddy had spent a year in a foster care group-home, back when he was eleven. He and Mutava, whose parents were being detained by Immigration, had formed an alliance against the older boys. At one point, Teddy watched Mutava plant a homemade shiv in a kid's back. Teddy would have been glad to help, but he was busy slamming his aluminum baseball bat into a second boy's kneecaps.

If left to himself, Teddy would simply carry Mutava, earner or not. But Teddy had junior partners and they were gung-ho capitalists who insisted that everyone pull his own weight. No exceptions.

Teddy glanced at the laptop's screen, then at the rain spattering on the hood of his car. The cop's Taurus hadn't moved and the dark skies hadn't lightened. On impulse, he called Sanda.

'Whatta ya doin'?'

'I was planning trip for groceries, but now with rain . . .'

'Why don't you meet me in Manhattan? We'll ride around together, talk a little more business.'

Was he asking Sanda? Or was he ordering her? Teddy could sense the wheels turning in Sanda's brain. Finally, she said, 'Where are you?'

Twenty minutes later, while Sanda was still en route, Littlewood's Taurus moved off. Teddy called Sanda to find she was in a gypsy cab, stuck at the entrance to the Williamsburg Bridge.

'Nothing moves, Teddy. I am thinking the bridge is closed off.'

'Then tell the driver to turn around. I can't wait anymore.'

Careful to remain two blocks behind, Teddy trailed the cop, his girlfriend and some old lady to a nursing home in the Mott Haven section of the South Bronx. They were taking the old lady out of the car when Teddy passed.

Teddy didn't have to be told that hanging around this particular neighborhood wasn't a good idea. He could smell the hostility. Meanwhile, the little car on the monitor had moved to Fox Street where it remained, motionless. Teddy, unable to contain himself, decided to make sure the detective was still inside the car.

Littlewood had a newspaper propped on the steering wheel when Teddy came past, a tabloid. He seemed oblivious to any threat, probably because of the rain. The few pedestrians on the sidewalk hustled right along, even the ones with umbrellas. If some few were predators, they weren't looking for prey.

Resigned now, Teddy made a right at the next intersection. He found a parking place and shut down the engine, only to have the windshield fog over. For the next few seconds, he watched a city bus swim across the streaked glass. Then he started the car and flicked the wipers on. Even so, the image through his windshield was blurry, ditto for the side windows, and you couldn't make out anyone's face. It was a perfect day for a hit. Come up on the detective with the side window rolled down, pull to a stop and lean across the seat. Bang, bang, bang. Simple as that. And Teddy already had the gun, a .40 caliber Colt tucked away in a hidden compartment beneath the center console.

Teddy made a valiant attempt to dismiss the idea out of hand. He'd been telling himself to stop acting on impulse for a long time. This was just another example of his inability to discipline himself. If he didn't want to spend most of his life in a cage, he had to limit his risk, his exposure. He needed to start thinking long-term. Ten years from now, would it make a difference whether the cop lived or died?

The argument failed to convince him. First, Littlewood spent most of his time in the company of his girlfriend, by far the more dangerous of the two. Now he was alone. Second, given the old lady and the nursing home, the cop was probably off duty, which would make him less cautious, especially this far from home. Third, it was a half-block from Fox Street to Longwood Avenue, two blocks to Bruckner Boulevard, and maybe six blocks to the eastbound Bruckner Expressway. He would be over the Throgs Neck Bridge and into Queens long before the cops responded.

Teddy made a second run along Fox Street, looking for security cameras. He didn't find any attached to the low-rise apartment buildings on either side of the road. No surprise. The South Bronx was poverty heaven and rents were minimal, as were the services provided by landlords. Teddy made the right onto Longwood Avenue, a commercial street lined with shops. Most of the shops had cameras mounted above their doors, but that didn't bother Teddy. The two-way road was six lanes wide. If he swung out into the center lane, no camera would record his license plate, even assuming one or two picked up his car.

Teddy was reaching for the keys in the ignition when the little car on the map started to move, its initial surge signaled by a particularly irritating beep, beep, beep. Teddy paused long enough to draw a deep breath. Was he disappointed? Relieved? His cell began to ring before he framed an answer.

'Hey, boss,' Pablo said, 'I believe we have a positive situation here that needs your blessing.'

'Where?'

The intersection Pablo named, Stillwell Avenue and Avenue P, was out in the ass end of Brooklyn, about a million miles from the South Bronx. But postponing the trip was a risky proposition, at best. *La Familia* had put an acceptable offer, in terms of price and volume, on the table. Now Teddy's presence was necessary to close the deal. But Teddy Winuk wasn't ready to abandon his project. He'd been close, very close, close enough to taste victory on the tip of his tongue. With a little luck, he'd close the deal before the end of the day.

'Set something up for later,' he said. 'Maybe over the weekend or early next week.'

'Jeez, boss . . .'

'I'm in the Bronx, Pablo, and there are ten flooded highways between me and you. So give the fellas my apologies, but I'm not gonna make it this afternoon. I got other things to do.'

THIRTY-SIX

It was after one o'clock when Boots and Jill finally reached the intersection of Roosevelt and Elmhurst Avenues in the Jackson Heights section of Queens County. This was where Shoona had delivered an unspecified amount of heroin to her battered friend, Corry. Boots took in the pizza shop, Solliano Sicilian, where the pair, according to Shoona, made contact. He and Jill were standing beneath the elevated subway tracks on Roosevelt Avenue, sharing a single umbrella. The rain, now merely steady, had begun to slacken.

Like every other New York cop, Boots and Jill had paid their dues on the street. There was no jumping from the Academy to a cushy job behind a desk, no matter how powerful your connections. You were assigned to Patrol when you graduated, which meant that you worked in every weather. A blizzard on the way? A hurricane? You didn't get to hunker down in front of your flat-screen, maybe with a quart of beer and a giant bag of corn chips at your elbow. Off-duty cops were called into work during weather-related emergencies, while overtime was mandatory for those still on duty.

By comparison, today's rain was a minor inconvenience.

Boots and Jill decided to kill two birds with one stone. Inside the shop, they ordered slices and sodas, which they quickly downed. Then Boots flashed his shield and a reassuring smile. It was certainly possible, and perhaps even likely, that one or another of the all-Latino staff was illegal. Boots didn't want to frighten anyone.

'Something I'd like you to take a look at, if you don't mind,' he said, pulling out Corry's photo. 'You ever see this woman?'

Two of the three Latinos working behind the counter nodded to each other. '*Si*,' the older one said. 'She was comin' in here . . .'

'Monday, it had to be, on account of I don't work on Tuesday or Wednesday.' The second man spoke without an accent. 'Man, her face . . .' He raised his hand to his cheek. 'It was out to fuckin' here.'

'You wouldn't, by any chance, know where she's staying?'

They didn't, and neither did the delivery men standing under the awning outside. These men also worked in every kind of weather, but they hadn't made a delivery to the woman in the photo.

Boots and Jill turned away. They'd already discussed their approach to the canvas they intended to conduct. First they'd work Roosevelt Avenue, six blocks in either direction, both sides of the streets, then Elmhurst Avenue and the smaller side streets. Roosevelt Avenue, where they stood, was the borderline dividing Elmhurst and Jackson Heights. Both communities were residential and dominated by low-rise apartment buildings. If Boots and Jill struck out in the stores, they'd come back tomorrow and speak to the workers who maintained those buildings. Boots was fairly certain of one thing. Given her condition, Corry couldn't have come very far when she met Shoona two days after the attack. She had to be less than a half-mile from where he stood, though in what direction he had no idea.

'Yo.'

Boots turned to a boy who couldn't have been more than sixteen. 'Yo?'

The boy ignored Boots's tone. 'Alvino has something to tell you,' he said, 'but he doesn't speak English. He wants me to translate. My name's Marty.' Marty indicated a man forty years his senior who immediately broke into rapid-fire Spanish.

Alvino kept his head down as he spoke, but he told his story well. On Monday, toward evening, he was returning from a delivery when he saw the woman with the broken face. She was in the company of a black woman and she naturally caught his attention when she came out of the shop. At the same time, he noticed a young man on the other side of Roosevelt Avenue. The man was just standing there, in the rain, watching the front door. When the injured woman crossed Roosevelt Avenue, he followed her.

'Can you describe him?' Boots asked.

The man was dressed in camouflage, like a soldier, which is why Alvino first noticed him. But his hair was very long, way too long for the military. Plus, he kept shifting his weight, like he was too excited to stand still.

'Now, this is important, you say that after the woman left the restaurant, she crossed Roosevelt Avenue and her brother followed on the other side of the street.'

'*Si.*'

'Which street did they do down? Ninetieth Street or Elmhurst Avenue?'

Alvino shook his head. He'd lost interest at that point. Nevertheless, Boots and Jill were elated. Alvino had nailed Corry's brother, who slept with a sawed-off shotgun, according to Shoona.

Most likely, Corry had been laying low for the past few days, but her brother lived in the community and he stood out.

'You know,' Jill said, 'I think we're gonna put this one down.'

'I agree. We'll probably locate Carlos's victim. But that doesn't mean she can identify the man who shot Carlo. Or that, if she can, she will.'

'At least we can warn her off. Given enough time, Johnny will find her, just like we . . . almost have.'

Boots found canvases to mostly be exercises in futility, but this time he got enough hits to keep him eager. Corry's brother, though, not Corry. Jill was doing the talking for both of them, her effect on the men they interviewed obvious.

The rain slowly diminished as the afternoon passed, with the temperature rising into the fifties. By the time four o'clock rolled around, Jill and Boots had both stored their coats in the trunk of the Taurus. They'd uncovered six individuals as well, each of whom recognized Jill's description of the long-haired soldier with the jumpy attitude. The proprietor of Jackson Liquors claimed that his first thought, when the nervous soldier walked through the door, was that he was about to be robbed. Another told the detectives, 'I don't know, man, but he looked like he'd definitely get in my face if I said the wrong thing.'

Nevertheless, despite the hits, they were no closer to locating Corry or her brother when they walked into a Dunkin' Donuts near 86th Street. Desperately in need of caffeine and sugar by that time, they ordered a half-dozen assorted donuts and extra-large coffees.

Boots carried their tray to a counter by the window overlooking Roosevelt Avenue. He bit into a cinnamon doughnut and said, 'Don't look up, but I want you to check out the car approaching from behind me.' He waited a few seconds, until the car passed out of sight. 'This is the fourth time I've seen that car,' he said, 'and the first two times were back in the Bronx.'

'You sure?'

'I don't have to tell you what model that is, right?'

'It's a Crown Vic.'

'Right, a Ford Crown Victoria. You recognize it because Ford sold hundreds of thousands of them to police departments and taxi fleets over the years.' Boots waited for Jill to nod. 'Now, that particular vehicle is a first generation Crown Victoria, a line Ford stopped manufacturing in 1997. Meanwhile, when it passed me on Fox Street, goin' slow, I saw that the body was perfect and the paint job looked brand new. Plus, Ford put the biggest engines they had into the Crown Vics they sold to the State Police.'

'And one of those engines was under the hood of the car that just passed us?' Jill smiled. Boots looked like a clod, the sort of cop you assign to knocking down doors. But it was all a disguise, which was another thing she liked about him. 'How do you know, Boots? I mean what size engine he had in the car.'

'I saw him coming the second time and I listened as he went by. But I wasn't suspicious because I just assumed he was looking for a parking space, like I assumed he was a car nut and the Crown Vic had been lovingly restored. Now that he's here, though, in Queens . . .'

Boots let the obvious go unsaid. They were being followed, and from a distance, which meant the Taurus was bugged.

'Johnny Pianetta sent you a message this morning,' Jill said. 'Through Frankie Drago. He said he was backing off. He didn't want a confrontation.'

'Right.'

'You think he was lyin'? You think he sent this guy to follow you?'

'Nope and nope.'

'So, who do you think he is?'

Boots stuffed the last of his doughnut into his mouth, then wiped his fingers on a napkin. 'That, Jill, we won't know until we ask him.'

THIRTY-SEVEN

Teddy Winuk was familiar with the concept of denial, had even written a paper on the subject for his Psych 101 course. He'd used debtors to illustrate his various points, though he failed to disclose that his knowledge of debtor psychology stemmed from his experience on the street. Deadbeats like Ben Loriano simply didn't – or, better yet, couldn't – admit that the day of reckoning would eventually and inevitably arrive.

The essay, which earned him an A-, had been pronounced insightful by Morris Chernowitz, his instructor. But not insightful enough, apparently, to protect Teddy from the same defect.

Funny, Teddy thought as he sat behind the wheel of his Crown Victoria, how it's possible to be in denial about denial. He'd been following the two cops around all day – to Manhattan, to the Bronx, and finally to Queens – without ever asking himself what they were doing. Well, that wasn't exactly true. The first two stops had been about dumping the old lady in a nursing home. But then Littlewood had made a beeline to the intersection of Elmhurst and Roosevelt Avenues, where both cops got out. That was the first difference. The second was the placard that Littlewood stuck behind the Ford's windshield: ON OFFICIAL POLICE BUSINESS.

Teddy's thoughts were interrupted by the tap of a horn. To his left, a smiling, middle-aged woman mouthed the words, 'Are you leaving?' She wanted his parking space, but she wasn't going to get it. He shook his head and returned to his thoughts, staring out through the windshield. The rain had stopped, but the gloom, if anything, had deepened.

The two cops had begun at a pizza parlor near the subway stop at Elmhurst Avenue. He'd watched them from across the street, watched them display what must have been a photograph to the employees inside, watched two of those employees nod their heads, watched the cops begin a meticulous canvas of the stores on Roosevelt Avenue.

All without asking himself whose picture they were showing.

Teddy was standing in front of a urinal at Casa Colombiana when it finally hit him. This was all about Carlo Pianetta, about his murder, about finding the woman Carlo was raping when Teddy put a bullet through his head. Otherwise, there was no reason for what the cop did to Johnny Piano or Stevie Eagle.

This was something Teddy should have figured out a lot sooner. Still, the news wasn't all bad. If the two cops had gotten a hit, they would have abandoned the canvas. But they were still searching. Or they were the last time he'd driven past them. No more. Teddy glanced into the side mirror and saw the big cop turn onto 85th Street. In no obvious hurry, he was strolling along the sidewalk toward the Crown Vic.

Teddy reached for the keys in the ignition, the urge to flee instinctive. A waste of time, as it turned out. The woman cop with the laser-beam stare was coming toward him from the other end of the block. And she wasn't strolling along the sidewalk, like her partner. She was out in the street with her badge clipped to the lapel of her navy-blue jacket, blocking his escape.

Panic had never been part of Teddy's lifestyle and he instantly calmed once he understood there was no running away. Even if the odds were stacked against you, there were still better and worse strategies to pursue. Like shutting down Shurie's laptop, pulling the keys, jumping out of the Crown Vic, locking the door and crossing the street.

'Police, hold it right there.'

The woman's voice was as sharp as her stare. Plus, Teddy didn't need eyes in the back of his head to be sure the big cop was coming up behind him. He turned to face the woman.

'Officer, what can I do for you?' he said.

One thing for sure, he couldn't let himself be provoked, couldn't give them an excuse to search his Crown Vic. The gun, if they found it, would earn him three years in prison. And there was another, very pressing problem he needed to handle: a witness to the crime of murder. Could she identify him? He hadn't thought so at the time, but he wasn't all that eager to bet the next twenty-five years of his life on a fleeting judgment.

'I want you to step over to that building and put your hands on the wall.'

Teddy complied, but it wasn't the woman who frisked him. No, it was Detective Littlewood who tossed him, the same Detective Littlewood who'd wrapped his fingers around Johnny Piano's nuts.

Take it, Teddy told himself. No matter what they do to you. Just take it.

But there was nothing to take, except his wallet, which the big cop held in his hand as he backed away.

'I'm Detective Littlewood,' he announced. 'And this is Detective Kelly. Who are you?'

'You want my name?'

Littlewood smiled a thin smile that instantly vanished. 'That would be a good start.'

'Theodore Winuk.'

'Winuk? Where have I heard that name before?'

'I don't know.'

'You're not from Greenpoint?'

Teddy knew where this was going. If he kept answering questions, the cop would have talking about his sex life in a few minutes. 'I'm sorry, Officer—'

'Detective,' Boots corrected.

'Detective. And I don't mean any disrespect, but I'd like to know why you searched me. Have I broken some law?'

'You never heard of stop and frisk? We can search anyone, anytime, for any reason. And by the way, that bullshit about disrespect? An honest citizen would have been much more indignant. You gave yourself away.'

The cop pulled out Teddy's credit cards, his Social Security card, his driver's license and his registration before tossing the wallet back. Without explanation, he took a small notebook and a pen from the inner pocket of his jacket and began to copy the information on the documents, including the account numbers of the credit cards.

'This your address?' he asked. 'New Utrecht Avenue in Bensonhurst?'

It wasn't, but Teddy nodded. He had no fixed address at the moment. His bills went to a mail drop on Greenpoint Avenue.

'Tell me why you've been following us,' the second cop, Detective Kelly said, her tone relatively neutral. 'Please, I'm curious.'

Littlewood added his own two cents before Teddy could reply. 'Yeah, and also, while you're at it, explain how you made yourself believe that you'd get away with it. Because it's obvious that you're a deluded asshole who doesn't know the first thing about conducting a surveillance.'

One of Teddy's first mentors had drummed a maxim into his head, repeating the message dozens of times. Don't talk to the cops. You'll never convince them not to arrest you if they have probable cause. And if they don't, they'll eventually let you go.

'Like I already said, Detective, I don't mean any disrespect, but I'm not answering any more questions. I've already identified myself.'

'Is this the point where I smack you?' the big cop asked. 'Is this the point where I punch you right in the face?'

Teddy drew a breath. He didn't particularly feel like being punched in the face, but if that was the price he had to pay, then so be it. 'You do what you have to do, but I'm through answering questions. If you want to speak to my lawyer, his card's in my wallet.'

'I know. I've already seen it. Mel Abzug, works out of a second-story office in Williamsburg. That's a long way from Bensonhurst, but I'm gonna let that go. Now, give me your keys so I can search your car. And I don't wanna hear word one about your rights. You've been following me around all day, interfering in my investigation. I really can't have that.'

THIRTY-EIGHT

I t was pushing eight o'clock by the time Boots and Jill finished booking Teddy Winuk for the crimes of interfering in a police investigation and unlawful surveillance. This was an exercise in futility and Boots knew it. Yes, they had Winuk's laptop and the tracking device planted in the Taurus. Yes, they'd established the connection between the two. But the search of Winuk's Crown Vic was patently unconstitutional, as Assistant District Attorney Thelma Blount had been quick to point out.

'It'll never get past a Mapp hearing,' she'd explained. 'The judge will throw out the laptop, without which you have exactly *nada*.'

Boots had nodded agreeably. He hadn't been thinking long-term, his only objective to confine Winuk until Carlo's victim was located. Unfortunately, he wasn't likely to accomplish even that modest goal.

On another day, Boots might have arranged to hold his suspect at the precinct for twenty-four hours before shipping him off to

Central Booking. That couldn't happen now because Winuk's lawyer, Mel Abzug, was already present. Mel would have his client bailed out before midnight, or so he loudly proclaimed.

Boots and Jill decided to console themselves with dinner at The Brooklyn Star, one of gentrifying Williamsburg's many hip restaurants. They invited Joaquin along, but he was expecting a call from his estranged girlfriend, Polly Boll, and begged off.

At the restaurant, after a round of drinks, Jill ordered roast chicken, and Boots a grilled pork chop that despite having marinated for hours, turned out to be tough.

'I could've beaten Winuk's ass from morning to night without him opening up,' Boots said. 'A genuine tough guy, Jill. A striver.'

'A striver and a killer.'

'Are you that sure?'

Jill ignored the amused tone. 'I'm sure this is the man I saw on the Alltel video. Not that it really matters. We're not gonna pin it on him.'

'Not tonight, anyway. And not tomorrow, either. But I've already located two snitches who know him. Down the line, we might get lucky.'

'Are you going to make him a project?'

'That I am, Jill. I don't want him on my streets and I intend to remove him, if not for killing Carlo, then for something else.' Boots sawed at his pork chop, the blade of the knife compressing, rather than cutting, the meat. 'What's critical now is what you tell Karkanian.'

'Why me?'

'Because you're Karkanian's spy. Did you forget?'

That part was true enough. Karkanian would expect Jill to reveal Teddy Winuk's existence. Jill smiled to herself.

'What's the joke?' Boots asked.

'I'm trying to imagine myself telling Karkanian that Winuk can't be working for Johnny Pianetta because he murdered Pianetta's oldest son. How do I know? Call it feminine intuition. The man walks like a killer.'

Jill gestured to their waiter. The bread pudding at the Brooklyn Star was also a killer. She ordered for both of them – to her knowledge, Boots had never refused dessert.

'So, what's next?' she asked.

'The first item on our list is Corry. That's because, if you're right about Winuk, finding Corry will be first on *his* list.'

'You don't think we scared him off?'

'I don't think Teddy Winuk does fear. But even if he did, the stakes are too big. Twenty-five to life? He'll try to beat us to the only witness. He has to.'

'And then what?'

Jill's question remained with Boots as he and Jill made the short run from the restaurant to Newell Street. Carlo's victim had been left alive, and not through any mistake. More than just sparing her, the shooter might very well have pulled the trigger in order to save her. So, now that his own liberty was at risk, what would the white knight do if he found the damsel in distress?

Rather than circle the block for the next hour, Boots parked the Taurus on Calyer Street, a few blocks away from his home. Here the neighborhood was solidly industrial and it was easy to find parking at night if you didn't mind a little walk. Boots didn't mind, his thoughts having turned to the hours ahead. As unpleasant as the circumstances were, Jill was truly free for the first time in years and Boots expected to take full advantage.

The temperature, if anything, had risen, and they walked with their coats thrown over their arms, alert to a danger intensified by the gathering fog. Lost behind windows filmed with condensation, the occupants of the passing cars and vans were little more than blurry shadows. They might have been sitting with their hands in the laps or holding sawed-off shotguns. You had to be ready, as Boots knew from bitter experience, and both cops turned their attention to an approaching vehicle as they neared the front door of Andrew Littlewood's house. A second later, the door to that house flew open to reveal Stefano Ungaro and the gun he carried in his right hand.

The epithet Ungaro shouted must have been directed at Boots Littlewood because it described an act Jill could not possible do to her mother. Yet Ungaro fired at Jill Kelly first, pulling the trigger twice in rapid succession.

The world began to narrow for Boots as the door opened. It shrank until it was too small to include Jill Kelly, who toppled over backwards. It shrank until it grew too small even for Joaquin, who'd been home when Boots called from the precinct. It shrank until a single thought seized his awareness, excluding every other consideration.

Kill or be killed.

Boots reached that bottom line in milliseconds, amazed to find himself unafraid. He was thinking clearly, and he'd continue to think clearly as long as he focused on the task before him. His right hand was moving toward the Glock in his shoulder rig before Ungaro pulled the trigger for the first time. The flow seemed utterly natural, a gesture he'd made so many times that no calculation was necessary.

For the next few seconds, time for Boots moved with the stately grace of a water ballet, and at the speed of light, every second broken into a thousand segments, every second infused with desperate urgency. Yet Boots, far from bewildered, continued to evaluate his options. He knew that he wouldn't free his gun before Ungaro turned on him, knew it as Ungaro fired his second shot into Jill Kelly. Therefore . . .

Boots flipped his trench coat at Ungaro, holding it by the collar so it would flare out as it fell across the man's right hand and arm. The move caught the gangster by surprise and he hesitated initially as he tried to shake the coat off. When that didn't work, he pulled the trigger twice. The automatic fired the first time, the bullet ripping past the big cop's shoulder, but then the hammer snagged on the coat's fabric.

There would be no third attempt on Detective Littlewood's life. Boots leveled his Glock and fired twice at the center of Ungaro's chest. Although both shots ran high, both ripped into the gangster's flesh. The first took out a significant chunk of his lower jaw. The second destroyed his right collar bone, leaving him in pain so immediate and overpowering that his pistol dropped from his fingers and he screamed in agony.

Far from sympathetic, Boots kicked Ungaro's weapon off the stoop and smashed his Glock into the side of the man's face. Then he followed Ungaro to the ground and laid the hollow end of the Glock's barrel on his left eye.

'Don't shoot him, Boots. I'm alive.'

'Are you wounded?'

'My vest . . .' Jill groaned as she pulled herself to her feet.

'The vest stopped the rounds, but it feels like I broke a couple of ribs.'

'Go inside,' Boots said, his tone unsympathetic, 'and check on Joaquin.'

'Don't kill Ungaro, Boots.'

The gun didn't waver. 'Just do it.'

As the seconds ticked by, Ungaro made an effort to communicate. But the blood flowing from what was left of his jaw and mouth impeded every word. Later on, Boots was never sure whether Ungaro said 'Kill me' or 'Don't kill me'. Finally, the door opened behind him.

'I found a note from Joaquin. He went back to his girlfriend. Your father's not here, either.'

'He's spending the night with his bride-to-be.'

Boots finally backed off, rising to his feet. He could hear a police siren on McGuinness Boulevard a few blocks away. He found its rise and fall oddly comforting as he finally turned to his partner. Jill had shrugged out of her blazer and opened her blouse to expose a pair of bullets lodged in the body armor she wore beneath. Her midnight-blue eyes reflected the pain she was in, but there was bewilderment, too. It wasn't supposed to come out this way.

'You'll live,' Boots observed after a moment. 'Which, by the way, makes us even.'

THIRTY-NINE

Teddy Winuk left Kings County Criminal Court at three o'clock in the morning. Despite the obvious setbacks, he felt good. First thing, he hadn't caved in to the big cop, hadn't said a word. Second, the arraignment judge, a woman named Li Xiu Ying, had listened to his lawyer's impassioned plea and dismissed the charges, with the Assistant D.A. barely putting up a fight. Third, Sanda Dragomir was sitting behind the wheel of the Crown Vic when he stepped onto Schermerhorn Street.

'We're goin' back to where you picked up the car,' he said as he slid into the seat beside her. 'We have work to do.'

Sanda made a right on Boerum Place, heading for Atlantic Avenue and the Brooklyn-Queens Expressway.

'You have a driver's license?' he asked.

'I have license from Ohio. I buy this online, yes?'

'How'd you do that?'

'I buy on website called Silk Road before FBI shut this down. With bitcoins money.'

Teddy looked at Sanda and grinned. Another unexpected talent, another reason to want her on the Winuk team. 'I'm impressed,' he said.

'Thank you. Now, I will drive to nearest subway and go home.'

'C'mon, we're gonna hit a couple of after-hours joints. It'll be fun.'

'Fun? In Jackson Heights?'

In fact, Roosevelt Avenue in Jackson Heights was lined with businesses catering to Colombians and rumor had it that million-dollar drug deals were routinely cut in its various clubs and restaurants. Jackson Heights was also Shurie Banerjee's home turf and Teddy knew it well enough to be sure that a beautiful woman on his arm would be the ice-breaker he needed.

Teddy had made one move before the two cops pinched him. He'd flagged down the delivery boy who spoke to the cops outside Solliano Pizza. A twenty would almost certainly have done the trick, but Teddy, in a generous mood, had flashed a fifty.

The kid hadn't hesitated. He described the woman with the broken face and the long-haired man wearing the camo gear, then took the money. Teddy didn't hesitate, either. He drew the same conclusion Boots and Jill had drawn only an hour before. The search would be for the man, not the woman.

For all his hyperactive metabolism, Teddy suddenly found himself tired. He leaned back against the seat and closed his eyes, though he didn't sleep. In his heart of hearts, he knew he should have walked on by when he first heard the woman's moans. Either that or kill her as well, which he hadn't wanted to do, and still didn't.

'Where is it I am going to?' Sanda asked.

'Roosevelt Avenue, under the el. And take it slow. I've got a long day ahead of me and I could use a little downtime.'

By six in the morning, when the after-hours clubs shut down, Teddy and Sanda had spoken to three individuals who'd run into the long-haired man in the camo gear. They confirmed that he was ex-military and provided a first name: Tommy.

'Some of these guys,' a fellow vet explained, 'they come back different. Tommy's one of those guys. The kid's got a hair trigger, which I was real careful not to pull.'

All three men believed that Tommy lived in the neighborhood. They didn't know exactly where, but close by.

Teddy had thought twice before bringing Sanda along. This sort of business didn't need informed witnesses. But the individuals who'd spoken to them, all men, had spent the first moments of the encounter staring at her breasts. Teddy had watched her play them with her smile, her thick, husky voice, her crazed English. Talk about priming the pump. After a minute or two, their mouths were going a mile a minute.

'I'm gonna put you in a cab,' Teddy said. 'Send you home.'

Sanda looked at him for a minute, her eyes reflecting an odd disappointment. 'Can we have breakfast first?'

Teddy grinned. In fact, he was starving. 'Sure.'

They found a small coffee shop on Roosevelt Avenue two blocks away. Teddy expected a few questions, maybe a demand for reassurance. But Sanda didn't ask what they were doing, or why she'd been asked to come along, or why she was being sent home. Instead, she focused on practical matters. She'd met with Shurie, at Teddy's request, and she believed they could work together. In any event, she was prepared to run drugs from the stash-house in Brooklyn to their customers in Queens. There was a small problem, though. She needed a car, which she couldn't buy on her own.

'I have Ohio license, yes, which I used once to show police after being stopped on Long Island Expressway. This was good. They give me warning and let me go. But if I use Ohio license to register a car—'

Teddy raised a hand. If she wanted to register her car in New York, she'd need a New York driver's license. That wouldn't be a big deal if the Ohio license was legit, but it wasn't. Teddy drained his mug and signaled the waiter for a refill.

'Did you talk to Shurie? About the car?'

'No.'

'Then that's what you need to do.' He smiled, deliberately softening his remarks. 'I don't want to get involved in the day-to-day mechanics of the operation. That's why I recruited you in the first place. Shurie? You'll need his muscle to keep your customers in line, but the truth is that he couldn't organize a hotdog wagon. Solve problems, Sanda. Solve problems and you'll always be valuable.'

FORTY

I t was Jill's superior, Captain Karkanian, and not Boots who took Ungaro's attack personally. Acting on his own authority, Karkanian had Johnny Piano yanked from his home, dragged into the Six-Four and locked in an interview room. There he was detained for the next four hours, despite the protestations of Joyce Kipner, superstar lawyer to the mob. The punitive nature of this detention was established before Kipner's arrival when Karkanian made a little speech about the consequences of attacking police officers.

'We're gonna hit every street operation you run. We're gonna flood Amoroso's construction sites with highly motivated building inspectors. We're gonna offer a sweet deal to any defendant who can put your ass in a cage, including Ungaro, who's going to recover. That means you're fucking dead, Johnny. That means it's time to buy yourself a coffin.'

Two hours later, Johnny decided to give an off-the-record statement. This was against the advice of his lawyer, but he did it anyway. The contents were predictable. Johnny had nothing to do with the attack, didn't know it was going to happen and would have prevented it if he did.

'A man like Ungaro, you kick his teeth in, he's gonna come back at you. Detective Littlewood might have figured that out before he did the kicking.'

Boots wasn't present for any of this. He spent the first three hours after the attack at Woodhull Medical Center while a pair of emergency-room doctors, both young and male, calculated the extent of Jill's injuries. After a close examination, too close for Boots, they decided that a couple of ribs were either broken or badly bruised. There was no need to determine which because the non-treatment for both was identical. Give it a month and you'll be good as new.

Jill's responses to the doctor's questions, and to the debriefing conducted by an NYPD Shooting Board following her release, were limited to a series of monosyllabic grunts. Every breath hurt and the lieutenant who conducted the examination was properly sympathetic. The incident, he assured her, was a no-brainer.

'You and Detective Littlewood, you're heroes,' he announced. 'My guess, your partner will be up for a Combat Cross.'

Chief of Detectives Michael Shaw, Jill's uncle, had later confirmed that judgment to Boots. 'You did well, lad, you and Jill both. And that business with your coat? Wonderful, Detective, absolutely wonderful.'

Jill and Boots weren't released until after three o'clock in the morning. Both were exhausted, the adrenaline having deserted their bloodstreams hours before. Jill was especially reluctant to speak. Her ribs were on fire and the short walk from the hospital's entrance to a cab left her drained. But she couldn't stay silent forever and she knew it. There were things that needed to be said, though not with the cab driver listening. Or in front of Joaquin and Andy, both of whom had returned to Newell Street.

'You saved my life,' she finally said. She and Boots were standing on the curb outside his door.

'I was only thinking about myself, about surviving. And by the way, just in case you've decided that you failed here, if Ungaro hadn't shot you first, our roles would have reversed, the only difference being that you would've killed him.'

'No question,' Jill said. 'That's the way it would have come out.'

'Glad we agree.' Boots laid his fingers on Jill's cheek, a gesture she might have resisted at another time. 'Now ask yourself this.

Why did Ungaro shoot you first when I'm the one he came to kill? Unless he heard about what happened at Woodhull after Silvy Mussa got shot. And if that's the case, then you did protect me, with your reputation, if not with your gun.'

Jill smiled at that. 'Does that mean you're gonna give me your medal?'

'Probably not,' Boots admitted.

Boots never really got to sleep that night. His thoughts continued to churn when he closed his eyes, like bingo balls tumbling in a cage. Except there was no one to stop the cage and choose a ball. By six, he'd had enough. He got out of bed, took a quick shower and headed for the kitchen where he made a pot of coffee and toasted a slice of bread. A few minutes later, he carried both into the living room where he found his father asleep in a chair. Andy looked old to his son, old and tired.

I've got nobody but myself to blame, Boots reflected. I knew exactly what I was doing.

But that wasn't strictly true. When Boots ran into Ungaro at Open Circle, he'd simply popped from everyday consciousness into his personal red zone. Choosing played no part in the process. Still, if Joaquin had been home last night . . .

'If I'd been home, the scumbag never would've gotten in the house,' Joaquin announced as he emerged from his bedroom. 'Not that way.' Joaquin's voice woke Andy Littlewood, who groaned as he stretched. An old man's groan that spoke of stiff-ened muscles and porous bones.

This was stereo guilt, which Boots didn't need, but then he remembered that his son, like most private investigators, had a concealed-weapons permit.

'You're packing these days, Joaquin?'

'Always a good idea, Boots, when your father's partnered with a woman named Crazy Jill Kelly. If Ungaro had broken that window when I was home, he wouldn't have been around when you and Jill arrived.'

Boots laughed as he walked over to the front window and slid the curtains back a few inches. The reporters had gone home. Thank you, Lord.

Jill made her appearance twenty minutes later. She was

hurting, but wasn't about to use codeine or any other narcotic to relieve the pain.

Boots and Jill had gotten lucky twice. The first time when Ungaro fired into Jill's vest, instead of her face. The second time when they were interviewed after leaving Woodhull. Clearly out to protect the job, the lieutenant who conducted the interviews had confined his questions to the moment of contact.

Ungaro emerged from inside the house? Check.

Ungaro had a gun in his hand? Check.

Ungaro fired first? Check.

Ungaro's bullets hit a member of the force? Check.

Shooting justified? Check.

Job off the hook? Double check.

At no point had either been asked what they were doing before Boots parked the Taurus on Calyer Street. As a result, the very existence of a witness to Carlo Pianetta's murder remained unknown to OCCB and Captain Karkanian.

'I'm going with you this morning,' Jill announced, her tone defiant.

Last night, while still in the emergency room, Jill had called Citizen's Rest, where her mother was undergoing rehab. She'd fought her way through to the unit's director, a Ms Hammond, but that was as far as she'd gotten. Theresa Kelly was slated, as were all new residents, to spend the first two weeks of her treatment isolated from outside influence while she detoxed. No media, no visitors.

'The story's already big time and my name is scheduled for release tomorrow morning,' Jill had explained. 'I don't want my mother to find out by reading the newspapers.'

'First, Detective, your mother isn't allowed newspapers. Second, your life is not in danger. Third, your mother can leave the facility anytime she wants. She's not a prisoner. Fourth—'

Jill hadn't waited for the fourth reason, or any other reasons. She'd hung up, her frustration obvious. Theresa Kelly's husband, Jill's father, had been killed in the line of duty. Now her daughter had been attacked. At the very least, she ought to learn about the attack, along with Jill's condition, from Jill.

'Did you hear me, Boots? I said I'm coming along.'

Detective Littlewood's grin vanished as quickly as it appeared.

'Wouldn't have it any other way, partner. Without you I'd be lost. But I need to make a call before we go. It'll only be a minute.'

Boots carried the house phone into the bedroom and dialed Frankie Drago's number. Though he was unaware of Karkanian's threats, he knew that retaliation was likely. If Frankie became a target of that retaliation, he could be sent back to prison. That would leave Boots unable to bet the Yankees when opening day finally rolled around.

'Hey, Boots, are you OK?'

'You heard about what happened?'

'I heard Ungaro shot a cop and I naturally wondered if it was you.'

'It was my partner and she was wearing a vest. But I didn't call to chat. I called to advise you to shut down until further notice.'

'Jesus, Boots, my mom had to get new dentures and they're gonna cost two grand. Where am I gonna get the money if I shut down?'

'I don't know, Frankie, but from what I hear, in prison they pay you thirty-five cents an hour.'

FORTY-ONE

Corry Frisk's eyes were glued, not to the task at hand, but to the mirror as she guided a trimmer across her brother scalp. Tommy's eyes were riveted to the same mirror. He was sitting on a chair in the bathroom, watching his shoulder-length hair drop from his head to the floor. Behind the pair, in the bedroom, Tommy's new clothes were laid out on the bed. Levi jeans, a blue sweatshirt bearing the NY Giant's logo and a pair of low-end Nike athletic shoes, still in the box. A zip-up fleece jacket hung from a hook by the front door.

'You hurtin'?' Corry asked. She, herself, had popped two OxyContin tablets and was feeling no pain whatever.

'I'm good.'

Corry continued on without disputing the claim. This wasn't

about salvation. This was about passing muster in a dangerous world and she trimmed her brother's hair evenly. If they weren't in a hurry this morning, she would have sent him to a barber.

Tommy swept up the hair while Corry made them a blueberry-pancake breakfast. Call it a pre-victory celebration. When they finished, at eight thirty, she and Tommy went for a ride. The temperature was already in the mid-fifties and the clear blue of the sky was broken only by a few scattered clouds. Fluffy clouds, to be sure.

'What happened to winter?' Tommy asked.

'Winter's over for you and me. We're going where those chilly winds don't blow.'

Corry was referring to Florida and Tommy's friends, most of whom were vets and sure to understand what Tommy and his battered sister were going through. All they had to do was get there. All they had to do was survive.

Corry would have liked to take a walk, if only to measure Tommy's effect on the general public, but the closest patch of green was a cemetery near Astoria Boulevard. Her own appearance wasn't likely to pass unnoticed, either. The swelling was almost gone, but the cuts and the bruises remained. It would take another week before she could pass for normal.

'You waitin' for anything in particular?' Tommy asked.

Corry shrugged as she took a throwaway cell phone out of her purse. She flipped it open, punched in Amoroso Construction's number and brought it to her ear.

'Amoroso Construction, good morning, how can I help you?'

'Let me speak to John Pianetta.'

'One moment, please.'

The woman with the hard voice picked up next. 'Mr Pianetta's not in yet. I expect him in an hour.'

'That's funny, because I told him I'd be calling at nine.'

'What, you don't read the papers? You're the only reason he's comin' in at all.'

Ten minutes later, they were parked in front of a candy store on Junction Boulevard, reading identical copies of the *Daily News*. A small photo of John Pianetta appeared on the lower-left corner of the front page, a photo taken in better days. Pianetta was shaking a priest's hand in front of a church.

Gangster Questioned in Attack. (story p.3)

The story described a police shootout in Greenpoint, a close call for two cops who'd been attacked by a gangster long associated with the Pianetta crime crew.

Corry tossed the paper in the back seat. Pianetta had a good reason for being late, but that didn't mean he wasn't playing her in some way.

'Funny,' she told her brother, 'how you can convince yourself that you're runnin' the show when you're really fucking desperate.'

Like Tommy had gotten his hands on a dozen OxyContin tablets, but she'd already taken most of them and there was no money to buy more.

With no real option, they drove into Astoria where they found a parking spot on Vernon Boulevard that offered a view of the East River on the far side of a small park.

'What you think,' Tommy said after a few minutes of silence, 'is let it be them and not us.'

Corry encouraged her brother with a nod. Tommy had a habit of starting his conversations in the middle, then working forward and backward.

'Them who?' she asked.

'The Humvees were the worst, but even the MWRAPs . . . I mean, when you were in an MWRAP and got blown up, you mostly survived in one piece. Like it didn't kill you, so you'd think you were all right.'

Tommy stopped to watch a man let his dog, a golden retriever, off the leash. On a mission, the dog shot into the park, ears back, tongue lolling. It traced wide circles in the grass, coming within a few yards of its master, then darting off at the last minute.

'Most patrols were conducted on foot, but . . .'

'But you still had to get there.'

'Exactly. Usually that meant a convoy, anywhere from three to ten vehicles traveling in a line over some narrow road. We knew we'd run into IEDs because there were IEDs on all the roads in the south.'

Corry looked down as a police cruiser came up behind Tommy's car. The two cops inside gave them hard looks, but didn't stop. Tommy waited until they turned a corner before pulling away. In all likelihood, if they weren't on a call, they'd circle back.

'So, you were saying, Tommy?'

'So, I'm sayin' that you think, OK, I'm still in one piece, so I'm all right. But then one day you're goin' down that road and you think, please, Lord, make it them and not us. Make it the guys in front of us or behind us. Blow them up and not us. Please, Lord. Please, please, please.'

Thirty minutes later, Corry was on the phone with John Pianetta. Or someone pretending to be John Pianetta. 'What's it gonna be, yes or no?' she asked.

'Just like that?'

'Just like that.'

'Thirty grand is a lot of money.'

Corry took a breath. 'Not for you.'

'How would you know?'

'Call it a lucky guess.'

'You got a big mouth, lady.'

'Look, I appreciate that you're under a lot of stress, what with shooting the cop and all. But I got problems of my own. You don't give me a straight answer in the next five seconds, I'm gonna hang up.'

'OK, fine, tell me where and when.'

'Two hours from now in Fort Greene Park. There's an open area, a meadow, at the southeast corner by DeKalb Avenue. I'll be standing in the middle.' Corry hesitated for a moment, then added, 'I'm expecting to see your face.'

'You think I'm gonna come alone?'

'You wanna bring a couple of bodyguards, feel free. As long as you're there. And by the way, if you try to drag me out of the park, I'm gonna start screaming.'

FORTY-TWO

Boots decided to start where he began, at Solliano Pizza, the only definite location where Corry and her brother had been sighted. The shop was located at the intersection of Elmhurst Avenue, Roosevelt Avenue and 90th Street. Boots intended to search for Corry's residence, which meant that Roosevelt Avenue, solidly commercial, could be excluded from the canvas. Nevertheless, there were still a dozen streets and hundreds of low-rise apartment buildings to explore. Jill had been stone-faced on the ride out to Jackson Heights, but she wasn't likely to hold up if they were on the street for hours.

Boots had suffered a fractured rib during his rookie year when he was smashed from behind with a pool cue. If he remembered right, he'd passed the better part of the following week on his couch while the Yankees lost five games in a row.

'I'm thinking that Corry chose the pizza parlor,' Boots said before they got out of the car, 'because it was close to her brother's apartment.'

Jill opened the car door. 'Didn't you draw the same conclusion yesterday?'

'Yeah, but I was hung up on identifying her and I didn't make the right search. I started with local businesses, hoping some restaurant made a delivery to the brother's apartment. I should've gone residential right away.'

Boots matched his stride to Jill's somewhat halting gait as they walked the block to Solliano Pizza. Both knew they were on thin ice. Jill had been placed on medical leave, an automatic given her injury, and Karkanian had personally impounded Boots's weapon, another automatic. Boots now carried a backup piece that wasn't registered with the job. If he got caught with it, he'd face an NYPD disciplinary board. If he got caught without it, on the other hand, say by the wrong people . . .

Boots and Jill arrived as one of Solliano's workers raised the iron grate protecting the store's front window. The man paused for a moment, his expression quizzical, only to have Boots wave him off.

'Two things, Jill. The delivery men told us the guy in the camo gear who caught their attention was standing on the other side of Roosevelt Avenue. They also told us that Corry walked across Roosevelt Avenue after she finished her business with Shoona. But that's where Elmhurst Avenue and 90th Street come together, and nobody was sure which street she took. Now we have to make a choice.'

'I pick Ninetieth Street.'

'Why?'

'Elmhurst comes in at an angle.'

Boots paused as a 7 Train pulled into the station. The 7 Train was another reason there were few residences along Roosevelt Avenue. The din was tooth rattling.

'I don't think I understand your logic,' he said when the train halted, 'but I'll bite. From here it's a matter of luck anyway.'

The housing along 90th Street was typical for this part of Queens, a mix of single-family homes on tiny lots, two-story attached garden apartments and low-rise, brick apartment buildings. Nothing fancy here, no luxury of any kind. New York's shrinking middle class lived in neighborhoods like this in each of the city's outer boroughs. At one time they would have been predominately Italian and Jewish. Now they hailed from every populated continent.

Their badges clipped to the lapels of their jackets, Boots and Jill split up to work both sides of the street, knocking on doors, describing the man they were looking for, moving on. When they were confronted by an apartment building, they rang the bell for the superintendent, leaning on it until someone replied. The supers in New York were famous for ignoring tenant complaints, especially out here where Christmas tips were few and far between.

They came together again at the first corner. Boots examined Jill closely. If she was in pain – which she had to be – she was keeping it to herself. She looked more determined than grim.

'One hit, Boots. A woman in mid-block. She recalls seeing a long-haired man wearing camo a couple of times, but has no idea where he lives.'

'Does she remember where she saw him?'

'Walking down the block. *Probably*. And don't ask from which direction, because she doesn't recall.'

Two hours later, they stood on the corner of 90th Street and Thirty-Fourth Avenue, three blocks from where they started. They'd interviewed several people along the way who remembered seeing Corry's brother, but nobody who could place him. Most important, they'd spoken to the super, or one of his workers, in each of the multi-family apartment houses. These men serviced the individual apartments and they knew their tenants. One and all, they denied ever having seen the long-haired soldier.

'You still up for this?' Boots asked.

'I'm good, Boots. Really.' Jill shook her head. 'I once broke my ankle. Sky diving on a day that was much too windy. This is nothing by comparison.'

'Then let's get moving.'

Boots had long subscribed to the old adage, it's better to be lucky than good. That's because you could always claim that a piece of good luck resulted entirely from your hard work and many brilliant insights. On this day, his and Jill's first break came when Boots decided to walk back to Roosevelt Avenue, the better to recharge his caffeine level. Afterward, they'd canvas Elmhurst Avenue.

They got their second break on 90th Street between Thirty-Fifth and Thirty-Seventh Avenues when a mail carrier walked through the door of a red-brick apartment house. A middle-aged black woman, she didn't miss Jill's raised hand or the badges clipped to the cops' lapels when she turned into their path.

'What can I do for you?' The woman's large eyes didn't widen or narrow. Nor did her neutral expression change.

'Is this your regular route?' Jill asked.

'That it is. Four square blocks of paradise. I've been out here for the past five years.'

'Good, because we're trying to locate a man who lives in the neighborhood. You'd remember this guy for sure. He's young, in his twenties, and he walks around in a camouflage jacket and pants. His hair hangs to his shoulders.'

'Oh, sure. I know who you're talking about. Thomas Frisk. In fact, I've spoken to him a couple of times while I was filling the mailboxes in his lobby. I got a nephew, my sister's boy, who did two tours in Iraq.'

'His lobby,' Jill asked, 'which is exactly where?'

'Right across the street. He's in . . . Three B or Three C. I forget which, but he gets a disability check the second Thursday of every month.'

Jill took in the situation and smiled to herself. Boots had personally canvassed the five-story apartment house on the other side of 90th Street. He'd questioned the building's superintendent, who'd denied any knowledge of a long-haired ex-soldier living in one of the apartments. Jill didn't ask herself why the man had lied. Human beings lie for good reasons, bad reasons or no reason at all. That said, not everyone who lies to the cops has the misfortune to be standing outside, hosing down the sidewalk, when the cops discover that lie. Boots was already crossing the street, his shoulders hunched.

FORTY-THREE

Detective Littlewood was halfway across the street when Jill's half-shouted demand wormed its way into his consciousness. 'Stay cool, Boots, I'm not supposed to be on the job. Plus, I don't think I'm really up for a brawl.'

Boots didn't intend to harm the man he approached, though he did mean to frighten him into cooperating voluntarily. An Irish immigrant, his brogue intact, the man had identified himself as Shawn Doyle. Now he turned off the hose and sucked down a quick breath.

'Don't tell me why you lied, because I don't give a shit.' Boots came close enough to lean over the smaller man. 'Just tell me where he lives. In Three B or Three C?'

'I figured the lad had enough problems—'

'What did I just . . . Hey, lemme see some ID. In fact, lemme see your green card. You don't have one, I'll march you straight down to immigration.'

'Boots, hang on.'

'What?'

'I think he's sorry.' Jill caught Doyle's jittery eyes. 'You are sorry, right? For lying to the cops, which is not a crime, but a definite act of defiance. You know, like an upraised finger. That's why my partner's upset.'

Doyle stepped back until his shoulders touched the wall behind him. 'All right then, I was foolish, lyin' to you like I did. But I was only tryin' to do the right thing behind a man who fought for his country.'

'And now you're going to do the right thing by telling us if he lives in Three B or Three C.' Jill smiled. 'Call it penance.'

'Tommy lives in Three C, but I'm sayin' it won't help ya.'

'And why is that?'

'Because he moved out a couple of hours ago, him and his sister.'

'For good?'

'Aye.'

'How do you know?'

'Because I saw him with my own eyes loadin' suitcases and a duffel bag into a van. "Are you goin' on vacation?" That's what I asked the lad. "No," he says, "I won't be comin' back. Anything left in my flat, it's yours now."'

Boots looked at Jill and smiled. Corry had followed his advice without ever hearing it. The advice to get her ass out of town.

'You have keys to the apartment?' he asked.

'That I do.'

'Get 'em.'

None of the furniture in Tommy Frisk's one-bedroom apartment had been removed, not the flat-screen or the small stereo or even the knick-knacks, but the closets and dresser drawers were empty.

Boots sat Jill in a chair while he methodically searched the apartment. He was looking for any indication of where Corry and her brother were headed. As a law enforcement matter, locating the pair would be relatively easy. A simple subpoena, for one thing, would produce a list of their outgoing calls. If you worked the list hard enough, you'd find them. And Tommy's disability payments would provide another trail when he got around to changing his address with Social Security, as would visits to any of the Veterans Administration's hospitals or clinics.

These were avenues of investigation unavailable to John Pianetta or Teddy Winuk. They'd get no further than this apartment, after which they'd return to the business of creating mayhem on Boots Littlewood's turf. And Boots would gladly return to his own duties at the Six-Four. He was starting to miss his routine, the basement workouts as well as the rhythm of the squad room.

Last night's confrontation hadn't been without an effect, but it wasn't the one Boots expected. Just a year before, Boots had killed a man. That had made a difference, knowing that he could pull the trigger. He'd crossed a line, as Jill was quick to point out. But not this time. No, he was already on Jill's side of the line when Ungaro came through the door and he didn't feel particularly different this morning. Maybe that had something to do with Ungaro's survival. Maybe not.

Boots turned over the couch cushions and thrust his hand into the couch's interior. He came up with a handful of lint, a discarded envelope from the Social Security Administration and four Winchester 7.62 millimeter, hollow-point rifle cartridges. Boots tossed away the lint, but thrust the envelope and the cartridges into his pocket. He didn't know exactly what he planned to do when he finally reported in, but he was determined to leave the apartment clean.

Jill took out a cigarette and lit up, instantly producing a craving in Boots so intense that it bordered on demonic possession. 'Tell me what you're thinking,' she asked as she blew a thin stream of smoke toward the ceiling.

'I'm trying to make sure they can't be followed by Winuk or Pianetta.'

'Then what?'

'Then . . . then I don't know what. Look, if I write this up – I mean everything we've done over the last few days – OCCB's gonna find Corry. No question, no doubt.'

Jill pulled on her cigarette. 'So, what should we do?'

'I don't know.'

Boots finished his search without finding any indication of where Corry and her brother had gone – all to the good – and he felt his attention shift as he took a seat next to his partner. For the past four days, he'd been focused on protecting Carlo's victim. Now the victim, herself, had put the issue to rest. So, what next? What to tell Karkanian, if anything? And what to do about a young man named Theodore Winuk? Boots had already made several calls, both to his snitches and to uniformed cops in the Six-Four known to work the streets hard. Although Winuk's name was recognized by several, Boots had been too preoccupied to ask for details. That would come later.

'So, what do you say we head back to Greenpoint?' he asked.

'To do what?'

'To eat lunch and talk about our next move. If we have a next move.'

Jill allowed Boots to help her to her feet. With their objective accomplished, the codeine prescribed for her last night was starting to look better and better. Her ribs were on fire. She winced as she eased her purse over her shoulder, winced again when her cell phone began to ring.

'Boots, would you grab my phone. It's buried at the bottom of my bag.'

Boots readily complied, glancing at the screen as he handed the phone over. 'It's from Karkanian.'

Resigned, Jill put the phone to her ear. 'Damn,' she whispered to Boots, 'I can't get away from this guy, even when I've been shot.'

FORTY-FOUR

Corry Frisk experienced a moment of panic as she crossed DeKalb Avenue and entered a pathway leading between a pair of towering sycamores. She'd lived too much of her life on the street to have any illusions about men like Johnny Piano. The attack on her had also taken its toll, and the time between getting into Carlo's Lexus and this very moment seemed a mere eye blink, as though she'd be drawn back to that long night if she made the simplest mistake. Even the blue skies and the unseasonable warmth – the temperatures were already in the low sixties – appeared to mock her.

Better off dead. The words bounced from one corner of her awareness to the other. Better off dead than a strung-out junkie whore afraid to work the streets. Better off, better off . . .

Maybe thirty grand wasn't all that much money, but it was enough to get them out of town, she and Tommy. Enough to put a roof over their heads, enough to get her in a methadone program, enough to get Tommy into some kind of rehab. The money was the difference between hope and hopeless.

The neighborhood of Fort Greene, Brooklyn, was more or less typical of gentrifying communities in New York. Not far from the Navy Yard where Corry had worked, Fort Greene's original housing included hundreds of generous townhouses built after the Civil War in the Italianate style. Long Island University, the Brooklyn Academy of Music and the Paul Robeson Theatre were all in Fort

Greene, as was Brooklyn Tech, one of the city's best high schools. No surprise, then, that gentrification came early to the neighborhood. But if the yuppies who poured in were able to force out the mostly black tenants by driving up rents, the enormous housing project that dominated the area between the northern end of the park and the Brooklyn-Queens Expressway, the Walt Whitman Houses, guaranteed economic integration. In Fort Greene, the poor and the wealthy, if not the rich, continued to rub shoulders.

Fort Greene Park on that day reflected this dynamic faithfully. The warmth had drawn hundreds of people onto its thirty acres and the paths were crowded with mothers pushing strollers and baby carriages, kids cutting school, elderly men and women in search of a sunny bench, pet owners walking dogs of every size and shape, from Yorkshire terriers to scarred pit bulls.

Corry was naturally encouraged by the presence of so many witnesses. If Johnny decided to take her down, he'd have to do it in front of them. And he'd have to wait until she told him about Teddy, which also meant that Johnny had to be there himself. Otherwise, she'd walk away.

If they let her.

Although Corry wore a pair of oversized sunglasses beneath a floppy hat with a six-inch brim, she nevertheless drew a few sharp glances as she walked past a kids' playground and onto a sunlit field. A hundred yards across at its widest point, the little meadow described an irregular oval bordered with leafless trees. Corry made her way to the center of this oval, her heart rate increasing with each step. Yeah, you could tell yourself better off dead, but the better part depended on how you came to die.

Take a breath, she told herself. Take a long, deep breath. You're liable to start shaking any minute. Talk about a tell. The men you're gonna deal with live on fear. Fear is like food for them.

Corry closed her eyes for a moment as she pulled herself together. When she opened them, three men, led by John Pianetta, were approaching from the western side of the clearing. A short, middle-aged man, his face all jowls, walked on Pianetta's left. The man on his right was much younger. He had the eyes of a hawk and Corry assumed he was the muscle.

Corry let Pianetta come to within four feet before she raised her hand. 'Close enough,' she said, surprised to find that her fear was rapidly being displaced by a swelling anger.

'Whatever you say, lady.' Pianetta stopped his entourage with a wave of his hands. 'So, here we are.'

'You bring the money?'

'What, you're not gonna introduce yourself?'

Corry took off her glasses and raised her chin. 'You know me now?'

Though Pianetta didn't answer, the question produced the desired effect. When the gangster stretched out his left hand, the older man passed him a brown paper bag.

'What about you?' he said. 'What proof do I have that you're not gonna lie through your teeth?'

Corry pointed to her face. 'Same answer.'

'You'll have to excuse me, lady, but you could've caught that beating anywhere. Maybe you were fucking around on your old man and he found out. Maybe you cheated your pimp and *he* found out.'

'It doesn't bother you? What your son did to me? Not even a little bit?'

'You want sympathy, call Oprah. Me, I'm here on business, so I'm askin' you again, show me some proof that I can trust what you're sayin'.'

Corry knew, going in, that this moment would come. Still, she hesitated, as though considering her response. Then she said, 'Carlo wore a brown leather coat, full length, which he took off and left on the back seat of the Lexus. That was after he parked the car under the bridge.'

'That's good, because my son was partial to leather coats. But unfortunately, the cops impounded his car and—'

'Yes or no?' Corry stretched out her hand, palm up. 'Pay or go home.'

Pianetta's mouth tightened. Women like Corry didn't make demands on men like John Pianetta. Even if they had something to sell, they came on bended knee. Meanwhile, as Corry was quick to recognize, Johnny Piano was in a bind. He had to find out who killed his son. It was expected of him by men like the pair who flanked him.

'I want the story,' Pianetta said as he handed over the bag. 'I wanna be convinced. Start with when the guy showed up, the guy who killed my son. I don't give a shit about the rest it.'

Corry opened the bag and looked inside, taking her time. She found six packs of banded, well-worn hundreds. Though she ran her thumb over the bills, she didn't count them.

'I fought your son,' she finally said. 'I fought him with every ounce of strength in my body. Big mistake, because it only turned him on, right? Me struggling, him punching me in the face? "C'mon, bitch, c'mon bitch, c'mon bitch." That's what he kept sayin' as he pounded me, over and over again.'

Corry stopped suddenly. She glanced around, at the clear sky and the twisting branches of a leafless elm. I'm alive, she thought to herself. I'm alive.

'I basically gave up,' she said. 'He'd do what he'd do, and then he'd kill me. Then and there, you understand, in the cold, on the concrete. I was helpless. But then this guy came up behind Carlo. From out of nowhere on a Saturday morning when the streets were empty. I watched his face as he walked up and his expression didn't change. He looked curious, like he was trying to decide about something, but he only said Carlo's name. That's when Carlo realized somebody was there.'

'Did Carlo recognize him?'

'He did when he finally turned around. Carlo told the guy that I was just a whore and he should mind his own business. But the guy paid no attention. And he didn't say a word, either, just kept looking at Carlo. I think he might still be looking, except Carlo said . . . he laughed when he said it, laughed way back in his throat . . .'

'Said what?'

'Said he'd be through in a minute if the guy wanted to take a turn. That's when the guy shot Carlo, one time, in the head.'

'He didn't say nothin'? Just drew and shot my son?'

'He didn't say a word to Carlo, or to me, either. And he didn't stick around afterward. He just walked away like nothing happened.'

Corry paused for breath. Time for the payoff. Time for the ghost behind the curtain to emerge. 'This guy, he was in his twenties and tall, better than six feet. His hair was light brown and he wore it pretty short. I knew him right away because I ran into him a few times at a bar in Brooklyn called the Waterfront. He had green eyes—'

'You could see this in the dark? His fuckin' eyes?'

'—and his friends called him Teddy.'

The old guy on Johnny's left was first to react. His face tightened as far as his jowls would permit and he grunted. Johnny's chin came up a second later. He looked at the old guy, then shook his head in disgust.

'He had the gun with him, this Teddy?'

'Yeah, he pulled it from inside his belt.'

'And he just shot Carlo without sayin' a word?'

'He said "Hey, Carlo" when he walked up, but that was it.'

Corry took a step back, then another. Now that they had what they wanted, all three men were looking at her the way Teddy looked at Carlo. If she was going to make a clean getaway, now was the time.

'Where ya goin'?' Johnny asked.

'To spend my money.' Corry took another step.

'Nah, nah, nah. That's all wrong. No, the way I see it, you got two choices.' Johnny Piano's smile had too much pleasure in it to be genuinely menacing. 'You could toss that bag to me right now, or you could make me find you and take it back. Simple, right? The easy way or the hard way.'

But Corry had a third choice, one she'd prepared well in advance, and she chose that moment to put it into play. Spinning on her heel, she broke into a fast walk, putting just a little more distance between herself and Pianetta before speaking into the cell phone concealed in the breast pocket of her coat.

'Kill 'em, Tommy,' she said. 'Kill 'em all.'

FORTY-FIVE

Karkanian's voice sounded in Jill's ear before she could say hello. 'Tell me where you are,' he said.

'Jackson Heights.'

'In Queens?'

'Last time I checked.'

'Now tell me that Littlewood's with you.'

'Whether it's true or not?'

'I don't have time for your bullshit. Just answer the question.'

'He's here.'

'Are the two of you alone?'

'Yes.'

'Go to speaker.'

The command was pretty much unnecessary. Boots already had his ear to the phone and there was no mistaking the stress in Karkanian's voice. The man was as nervous as a teenage boy entering an adult prison.

'OK, boss,' Jill said. 'We're on speaker.'

'Detective Littlewood, are you listening?'

'I am,' Boots said.

'How long have you been in Jackson Heights?'

'About four hours.'

'Both of you?'

Boots glanced at Jill and shook his head. 'Captain, do you wanna tell me what's goin' on? Or do I need to contact my union lawyer?'

'Four hours, right? In Jackson Heights?'

'Yeah,' Jill said, 'and we must've spoken to fifty people.'

'OK, that's good. Littlewood, do you remember that gangster you confronted under the Pulaski Bridge on Monday morning, the same gangster you confronted again at Woodhull Medical Center?'

'Now I know I need a lawyer.'

'Well that gangster, John Pianetta, was shot dead in Fort Greene Park an hour ago, along with two of his known associates.'

Jill was first to speak. 'Make my day. Tell me he died in pain.'

'No such. All three men were shot from a distance and died within a minute.' Karkanian's relaxed tone conveyed his relief. Jill and Boots, both under his command, were off the hook. 'Now, I'm very busy, so let me just say this once. The shooting went down at the southeastern corner of the park and the scene's crawling with media assholes. You are not to go there. You are to report forthwith to an MCC parked at the northwestern edge of the park. That would be Myrtle Avenue and St Edwards Street. Forthwith, detectives. Which means, in case you didn't understand me, right the fuck *now*.'

The forthwith part was just for show, as all concerned knew. Absent a helicopter, the trip from Central Queens to a Mobile Command Center in downtown Brooklyn would take at least forty minutes. That would have been true even if Boots and Jill, as they started down 90th Street, hadn't run into Theodore Winuk coming up the block.

Far from startled, or even apprehensive, Winuk's eyes narrowed when he saw the two cops. He shifted toward the curb, but didn't slow down until Boots drove a fist into his stomach. Then he doubled over and dropped to one knee.

'I'm not mad,' Boots told Jill as they continued on down the street. 'In fact, I assumed he'd come back.'

'So, why did you hit him?'

'Because he expected me to react and I didn't want to make him suspicious. I already know, of course, that he won't find anything in the Frisk apartment. If the issue was in doubt, I would've taken stronger measures.'

FORTY-SIX

Boots and Jill didn't discuss Teddy Winuk on the ride to Fort Greene Park. Short term, the only compelling issue was whether or not to reveal what they knew about Corry and Tommy Frisk. Karkanian had said that Pianetta was taken out from a distance, which necessitated the use of a rifle. Boots had found rifle cartridges in the vacated Frisk apartment. Was that a big deal? Was it evidence?

Millions of rifle cartridges were manufactured and sold every year. And even if the ballistics unit was able to identify Winchester as the manufacturer of the bullets that killed Pianetta and his associates, it would prove nothing. Winchester-manufactured 7.62 millimeter cartridges were sold all over the world.

'What's Corry's motive?' Jill asked. 'Why would she take the

risk? Because Johnny's kid attacked her? It's not enough, especially with Carlo dead. There's gotta be another reason for walking
into the lion's den.'

'True enough, but it'd be a pretty good joke if she and her
brother pulled it off.' Boots slipped into a momentary silence as
he drove up onto the Kosciusko Bridge. Newtown Creek, a block
from where Carlo's body was found, lay directly below them.
Out in the distance, the Pulaski Bridge spanned the creek. 'Think
about it. We've been doin' everything in our power to protect
Corry, right? But all the time she's been the predator. Personally,
I'm startin' to feel like a jerk.'

NYPD Mobile Command Centers come in a number of sizes,
from ordinary vans to busses to eighteen-wheelers. The one Boots
and Jill reported to was the size of a Winnebago and clearly
marked. Inside, long shelves with chairs set before them supported
six computer monitors and the Center's communications system.
The shelves ran three-quarters of the way from back to front.
The remaining space, separated by a partition, was given over
to the sort of leather chairs that might be found on a private jet.

The back of the MCC was unoccupied, the computer monitors
blank. In front, a lone man sat with a newspaper on his lap. Not
Captain Serge Karkanian, as Boots expected, but Chief of
Detectives Michael Shaw, Jill Kelly's uncle.

'Ah,' Shaw said without rising, 'Come in and find a seat.'

Boots felt his thermostat ratchet up a degree or two. He was
going to have to jump through a few hoops and he really wasn't
in the mood.

Shaw ran the pale fingers of his left hand through a shock of
white hair that had fallen across his forehead. Like the detectives
he commanded, Shaw wore a suit instead of a uniform, this one
navy blue. According to Jill, Shaw's many suits were meticulously
hand-tailored, but this one fit his narrow frame loosely.

As Boots dropped into a chair, he found himself wondering
if the man, closing in on seventy, was ill. Shaw's voice seemed
a bit shaky, too, but the man always spoke in a near whisper,
forcing you to lean toward him. This was a tactic Boots commonly
used to draw suspects into his orbit.

'Tell me what you've been up to this past week,' Shaw said

to Boots. 'Since your encounter with the deceased John Pianetta on Monday morning.'

'We've been searching for the woman Carlo was raping when he was murdered.'

'And did you succeed? No, scratch that. Did Captain Karkanian direct you to find this woman?'

'He never gave us an assignment of any kind.'

'Did you keep Captain Karkanian informed of your activities?'

'Cut the crap, Uncle Mike,' Jill said.

Shaw's laugh, like his smile, was little more than a faint whisper. 'OCCB didn't uncover the existence of Carlo's victim until this morning. Karkanian's as dense as he is ambitious, but he does have one cardinal virtue.'

'What's that?'

'For police officers like yourselves, the job's collective mission, to protect and serve, applies to the general public. To other police officers, like Michael Shaw and Serge Karkanian, the entity we protect and serve is the job itself. So I've been askin' myself a question this morning. Was the job served and protected by the way you, Boots, goaded Stefano Ungaro and John Pianetta?'

Jill started to speak, but her uncle merely raised his hand. 'My office has received calls from a dozen reporters. They don't question the Ungaro shooting. They concede it was justified, But they want to know why it happened in the first place.'

'Well,' Boots said, 'now they've got some real meat to chew on. Johnny Piano, infamous mafia don, gunned down in a public park? They'll forget about me soon enough. Remember, Ungaro's not dead.'

Shaw stared at Boots for a moment, then shook his head. 'I paired you with Jill because I thought you might steady her. Now you've become like her.' He picked up a remote and pointed it at a twenty-inch monitor. 'I'm going to ask both of you a question at the end of this presentation. I'm expecting an honest response, Jill. If you lie to me, I swear I'll bury you.'

Boots expected the image on the monitor to be generated by one of the job's mobile video units. Instead, he found a Google Earth photo of Fort Greene Park and the surrounding blocks.

'The death examiner took one look at the severity of the

wounds,' Shaw said, 'and told investigators they could only have been made by a rifle. But nobody heard a sound. And if the shooter was in the park, he must've been invisible. The park was crowded at the time and the witnesses we've interviewed didn't notice anything out of order.'

Shaw focused a laser pointer at the glowing monitor and used it to outline a grassy field in the lower right-hand corner of the screen. 'We're getting a relatively consistent story from the witnesses closest to the shooting. Pianetta and his men were standing in the middle of the field talking to a woman. At some point, a package changed hands, going from one of the men to the woman. Then the woman walked away, even as the men were shot. She never turned around.'

'Are there any security cameras in the park?' Boots asked.

'No, and no cameras here, either.' Shaw moved the laser to a building across the street. 'You're looking down at the roof of a five-story townhouse. The townhouse is up for sale and currently unoccupied. Approximately an hour ago, one of the uniformed officers assigned to canvas the block discovered that the basement door had been forced, most likely with a pry bar. CSU is on the roof as we speak. They report finding shoe impressions near a low wall facing the park.'

Boots looked at Jill. 'How far you think that is?' he asked. 'From the rooftop to the center of the field?'

'A hundred yards, tops.'

'Think you could do it? I mean take out all three?'

'With a silenced rifle? Boots, they'd never know what hit them, especially if my partner in the field positioned them so they were facing me. They'd be dead before they knew they were under attack.'

Shaw again raised a hand. 'I said there'd be a question at the end of the presentation. I'm going to ask it now. Do either of you have any knowledge of this woman or the individual who fired the rifle?'

There it was. The hoop Boots had been expecting all along. He looked at Jill. Her tight expression revealed only the pain she must be in. As for her uncle's threat . . . well, she'd faced him down before. The issues for Boots were more complex. First thing, he wasn't related to Michael Shaw and had no reason to expect Shaw to protect him. Nor would it be above Michael Shaw to punish Jill by punishing Boots. *This is your fault, Jill. Boots wouldn't be working inside the Midtown Tunnel if you'd only told me the truth.*

Boots chuckled. In fact, there was no decision to make. Three murders had to count for something, even if the slain were unworthy, even if they were violent gangsters who committed murders of their own. Boots's desire to protect Corry Frisk had come as a matter of instinct. He'd known what Johnny would do if he got his hands on her. But he'd wildly underestimated the woman. Corry had something to sell, something that would draw Pianetta into the open, and that could only be the identity of the man who killed Carlo. Did she actually know who did it? Or had she run a con? And did it matter?

'We ran down the victim,' Boots said. 'Carlo's victim. We tracked her to her brother's apartment in Jackson Heights. Unfortunately, by the time we arrived, they'd packed their clothes and told the super they weren't coming back. I had the super let us in – technically, the apartment was vacant – and searched it right before Karkanian's call. I found these behind the couch cushions.' Boots handed the Winchester cartridges in his pocket to Shaw. 'The victim's name is Corry Frisk. Her brother is Tommy Frisk. He's ex-military and known by local merchants to be a little off.'

Boots looked at Jill again. Was she disappointed? Too bad. 'And one more thing, Chief. If there's a departmental violation here, it's not on us. No, it's on Captain Karkanian. I think the violation is called failure to supervise.'

'I'll take that into consideration. So, you've nothing more? Carlo's victim, her soldier-brother, a few cartridges, that's it?'

'That's it.'

'What about you, Jill? Do you have anything to add?'

'Nope.'

'Then we're all on the same page. Excellent.' Shaw steepled his fingers, the better to contemplate the ropy veins that covered his hands. When he spoke again, though he continued to whisper, his anger was apparent. 'Over the next twenty-four hours, you, Boots, as lead detective, will write up day-by-day reports of all you've done over the past week. You will put those DD5s in

Captain Karkanian's hand by close of day tomorrow, after which you will join your partner on medical leave. No more bullshit, Littlewood. It's sink or swim time for you. I can't allow myself to be fucked over by precinct detectives.'

FORTY-SEVEN

Nose to the grindstone, shoulder to the wheel. Teddy Winuk was as happy as (to use his own words) a pig in shit. He didn't even resent the casual blow that had dropped him to his knees. It's exactly what he would have done if his and the cop's positions had been reversed. In fact, he would probably have delivered a serious beating to anyone who disrespected him so blatantly. But the cop had merely continued on down the street, and for good reason. When Teddy finally discovered the address of the woman he sought, he was treated to a pleasant surprise. She was gone, along with her brother, off to parts unknown.

Teddy had been returning from Jackson Heights to Sanda's apartment in Greenpoint when WFAN interrupted its sports programming to deliver the best news of the day. The great Johnny Piano, untouchable mafia don, had been shot dead in a Brooklyn park, along with his closest advisor, Mike 'The Rock' Marciano.

Usually moderate in his use of alcohol and narcotics, Teddy and Sanda had partied the night away, alternating shots of Chivas with snorts of first-cut cocaine. The neighborhood was wide open now, exactly as he'd hoped. Johnny Piano's surviving kid was too young to hold his father's crew together. It was every mutt for himself and no tax to pay. What you made, you kept.

Teddy wasted no time once he got past his hangover. He quickly organized four local drug dealers. These were men who worked in neighborhood bars, often with the approval of the bartenders. Teddy offered to supply them with product at prices markedly below those charged by the Pianetta crew, and to offer protection as well. As tired of paying the tax as Teddy, they'd not only agreed to go along, but introduced Teddy to other dealers, a few of whom were in need of a small loan. To tide them over.

At one point, maybe a week in, Teddy realized that he was doing exactly the opposite of what he'd resolved to do only a short time before. Consolidation was out the window, as was a command structure that distanced him from day-to-day operations. But what could he do? Opportunity wasn't just knocking on his door, it was hammering.

Three weeks in, as Thanksgiving approached, Teddy realized that he needed to make another jump. He and his boys had always handled problems as they developed, using the personnel at hand. Now he had to acquire muscle he could bring into play at a moment's notice. The remnants of Johnny's crew were fighting among themselves, but they'd eventually return to the business of making profits. Other strivers, like the Turco brothers, were also making moves. In the end, you were only entitled to what you could defend.

Teddy solved two problems at the same time. One of his junior partners, Ato Mutava, would never be an earner and Teddy was close to cutting all ties with the man, despite their long history. Now Teddy ordered Mutava to form a standby security force, five men, each of whom would draw a salary. There were many in the African communities that dotted New York who'd fought in one or another of Africa's civil wars. Most wholeheartedly embraced the future and they pursued their opportunities, especially education, with a relentless energy that left other immigrants breathless. But there were a few deviants among them, men willing to sell their skills if the price was right. Teddy only needed a few.

Teddy parked his car in front of the apartment he shared with Sanda Dragomir at five o'clock on a Tuesday afternoon, three weeks after what the newspapers were calling the Fort Greene Massacre. He went upstairs to find Sanda perched on her stationary bike, pedaling hard. She wore pale blue shorts and a matching tank top made of a silky fabric that clung to her sweat-soaked body.

Teddy's first thought, when he came through the door, was that she'd somehow known he was on the way. But that couldn't be true. No, desirability was a way of life for Sanda. Meanwhile, her work performance more than equaled her performance in bed. Teddy's Jackson Heights operation was running like clockwork.

'You interested in moving?' Teddy said as he kissed the back of her neck. Even now, he could barely keep his hands off her.

'We are going to Park Avenue, to live with rich people?'

'More like one of the brick townhouses fronting McGolrick Park.'

'Where is this park?'

'On Russell Street about a mile from here. I can get a deal on the top two floors. It's nice, Sanda. You look out the window, you're staring at trees and grass, not a wall. Plus, it's three times as big as what you have now.'

Teddy walked into their tiny kitchen and opened the refrigerator to find a turkey resting on the top shelf. Thanksgiving was two days away. Personally, he didn't give a shit about Thanksgiving or any other holiday. But the celebration was important to Sanda, who embraced all things American.

'You Americans don't know what you have,' she'd told him. 'In Romania, you learn when baby not to let anyone know of what you are thinking. You hide yourself away and learn to be only for self. Everyone has hand out. Not only police, but teachers at schools and doctors in hospitals. If you don't have rich relations to protect you, then you are nothing.'

Teddy had seen too many people living on the streets of New York to be all that impressed, though he didn't doubt her sincerity. And he'd eat her Thanksgiving dinner, too. Sanda was a good cook and she didn't complain when he plopped himself in front of the TV while she went about it.

Sanda came up behind him as he grabbed a beer. She laid a sweaty palm on his neck and said, 'Tonight I brine turkey, yes? Like top chef.'

'And what about now?' Teddy was thinking of dinner, but Sanda surprised him.

'And now I take shower with silly man named Teddy Winuk to scrub my back.' She wrapped a towel around his neck and twisted it tight. 'You are my prisoner. I will do with you as I wish.'

Teddy raised his arms. 'Anything you say, Sanda. Just don't hurt me any more than necessary.'

Teddy Winuk took his customary seat in the back booth of Kopetnik's Diner on Manhattan Avenue a little after nine o'clock the next morning. With no fixed address, and no fixed schedule, Kopetnik's generally served as an impromptu office for meetings with his junior partners. Occasionally, however, men came along to pitch deals of one kind or another. The one he expected to hear today would be delivered by a man named Wilhelm Kennedy.

Tobacco on the move was at the center of every hijacker's favorite fantasy. Cigarettes could be sold off in a heartbeat, and there were profits galore, what with a pack of smokes running twelve dollars in the city. Opportunity wasn't lacking, either. Trucks carrying thousands of cartons, each carton containing ten packs, crisscrossed the five boroughs every day. They'd be easy meat if they didn't also contain a tracking device that alerted a company dispatcher if the vehicle deviated from its preprogrammed route by as little as fifty feet.

Wilhelm Kennedy claimed to work for Wizard Enterprises, a cigarette warehouse in the Bronx that maintained a fleet of twenty box trucks. A truck mechanic by trade, he passed his days in Wizard's garage, doing whatever job the fleet supervisor assigned him, including the installation and maintenance of tracking devices.

'I can disable the tracking device on a Wizard truck in under a minute,' he'd told Pablo. 'The trick is knowing where it is.'

There were flies in this ointment. For one thing, if the system was disabled that fast, the cops would immediately suspect an inside job. Would Kennedy stand up to the heat? That remained to be determined.

Teddy ordered his standard breakfast from Inga, Kopetnik's long-time head waitress. Corned beef hash and two eggs over, hold the potatoes.

'You gonna be with family tomorrow?' Inga asked as she wrote down his order. 'For Thanksgiving?'

Teddy thought it over, then said, 'Yeah, I am.'

Ten seconds later he was forced to revise his expectations

when he glanced out the window to find, not Pablo and Wilhelm Kennedy, but Detectives Littlewood and Kelly, heading for the front door.

FORTY-EIGHT

With no choice in the matter – Teddy had his back to the wall furthest from the front door – he stayed put as the two cops approached, merely reminding himself to keep his mouth shut. He'd let his lawyer do the talking. After all, that's why they called them mouthpieces.

'You're not carrying, are you, Teddy?' the big cop, Detective Littlewood, said. 'You don't have a gun on you?'

From the look on his face, the man had to be hoping. The other one, Kelly, was off to the side, waiting for an excuse.

'No, I don't.'

'I believe you, Teddy, but I gotta search you anyway.'

'Does that mean I'm under arrest?'

'No, you're not. We just want you to come down to the station. There's something – actually, a few things – we need to show you. Now, please, stand up and place your arms away from your body.'

Teddy raised a hand. 'I'm not resisting, but do we need to do this here? I have breakfast in the diner almost every day. People know me and they're gonna think I'm being arrested.'

Teddy watched Littlewood glance at his partner, who shook her head. The movie was about to begin and she would be the bad cop. Teddy thought of Sanda and some of the games they played. Kelly was beautiful, as beautiful in her own way as Sanda. But Sanda was all about seduction, while the cop's frigid eyes transmitted little beyond contempt.

'Tell you what,' Boots finally said, his tone affable. 'We're parked around the corner on Freeman Street. If you agree, I'll do the search there so you won't be embarrassed. How's that work for ya?'

Two minutes later, Teddy stood with his hands on the roof of an unmarked Toyota while Kelly, not Littlewood, ran her hands over his body. Teddy assumed the rough handling was meant to demonstrate a bit of that contempt he sensed, but he found the scene erotic. If this was a porno film, their clothes would be coming off in the car. All three of them.

They drove the five minutes to the Sixty-Fourth Precinct in silence. Though Teddy wasn't handcuffed at that point, the two cops stayed close as they walked him past a sergeant seated behind a desk, through the lobby and up three flights of stairs. They encountered other cops at every point and Teddy had to fight a dream-like sense of being drawn into a nightmare place he didn't want to be, and from which there was no escape.

All part of the drill, he told himself as they walked through a door marked DETECTIVES and into a large room. Several smaller rooms off to one side were obviously meant for inter- rogation. No more than ten-by-ten, they stood with their doors open to reveal hard plastic chairs set around small tables.

The cops' next move would reveal their intentions. Would they shove him into one of the interrogation rooms or ask him to have a seat at one of the desks in the squad room? How bad was it going to get?

'Hey, Boots, the boss wants to see you.' The small black man who spoke was seated at the only occupied desk. 'He's been askin' for you all morning.'

'Me alone, or both of us?'

'Both of you.'

'Damn.'

Teddy wasn't fooled. They were going to put him on the stove and set the heat low, see what the stew tasted like when they returned.

Littlewood grasped Teddy's arm and guided him into the middle interview room. Teddy had been in similar rooms before and he dropped into the chair behind the little table, the hump seat, without being told.

'Do I get to make a phone call?' he asked. They'd already confiscated his cell phone.

Kelly came around the table to handcuff his right wrist to a steel ring attached to the chair. The chair, itself, was bolted to the floor.

'Grow up, jerk,' she said. 'This is not the Supreme Court and nobody's looking. You're here for as long as we want you.'

Littlewood flashed a quick smile. 'You have to forgive my partner. She's a judgmental sort by nature and she's decided that she doesn't like you. In fact, we have a little bet going. You want to know what it is?'

Say no, Teddy told himself, even as his mouth formed the word yes. The need to discover what the cops had on him was overwhelming. After all, they didn't have to be investigating the hit on Carlo. It might be anything.

'Is that a yes?' Littlewood asked.

'Yeah.'

'OK, I think you killed Carlo because he was raping that woman you were looking for in Jackson Heights. I think you played the hero and rescued her. My partner thinks you killed Carlo because he was your rival. She thinks when you came upon Carlo, you saw an opportunity to advance your own interests and you took it. Rescuing Carlo's victim never crossed your mind.'

Detective Littlewood dropped a hand to his prisoner's shoulder. 'One piece of advice? If you take the case to trial, keep citizens who think like my partner off the jury. You let her on the jury, you're dead.'

Some things you can't fight, like the emotions stirred up by a sudden fall from smug satisfaction with your life to a growing fear about spending the next twenty-five years in a maximum security prison. But fear wasn't the right word for what he was feeling at the moment. No, just now Teddy felt exactly as he'd felt so many times when his stepfather beat the crap out of him for no good reason other than wanting to hurt someone. The mess he was in right now just felt unfair.

Meanwhile, some other part of him acknowledged the accuracy of Kelly's judgment. If it'd been someone else, a stranger, he wouldn't have pulled the trigger. He'd have hurt the man, maybe pistol-whipped him, but not killed him. Probably. But that didn't change the simple fact that killing was the right punishment for Carlo's crime. Teddy Winuk had done the world a favor.

As time went on, Teddy was confronted by another, more basic, consideration. He'd gulped down a mug of coffee before leaving Sanda's apartment for Kopetnik's, and another cup at the diner. His need to drain the snake was growing and he was now uncomfortable enough to cross his legs and shift his position.

Teddy glanced at the mirror next to the door. Was someone looking in, maybe gloating? In his opinion, the cops weren't all that far removed from a mafia crew. Arresting you wasn't enough. They had to humiliate you, too. Say by making you ask to use the bathroom, like you were still in Fourth Grade. By making you admit that they were the masters and you were the dog.

Littlewood and his partner were trying to break him down, but it wasn't going to work. Teddy felt his resolve stiffen. Let them prove that he killed Carlo. Don't give them any help. Sanda would provide him with an alibi if he needed one, but it probably wouldn't go that far.

As the minutes continued to pile up, Teddy's thoughts returned to the sense of loss he'd felt when Littlewood first marched him into the precinct. His plans were falling into place, one after another, and the money was pouring in. Only a few hours ago, he'd felt nearly invincible. Now he had to admit that he'd made a big mistake going out to Jackson Heights, a big mistake when he first decided to follow the cop. If he'd only minded his own business, the cops wouldn't know that he even existed.

The door popped open to reveal Littlewood's bowling-ball head. 'Sorry about the wait, Teddy, but . . .'

The door closed before Teddy could protest, leaving him angry again. That was good, that was the attitude he needed to cultivate. Hate them enough to give them nothing. They might slap him around, and they'd definitely bully him, but they wouldn't beat a confession out of him. Those days were over.

FORTY-NINE

Detective Littlewood opened the door and pushed through. He was holding two mugs of coffee in his left hand and some of the hot liquid spilled over the rim and onto his fingers as he came into the room.

'Ouch,' he said as he laid the mugs on the table, then pushed one in Teddy's direction. 'I filled 'em too high.' He took the chair closest to Teddy, leaving his partner sitting on Teddy's left. 'First thing, I'm gonna read you your rights.'

'I know my rights and I don't want to talk to you without a lawyer present.'

Ignoring the outburst, Littlewood read a standard Miranda warning from a standard form, one the job printed in lots of five thousand. He laid the form on the table and said, 'Unlock Teddy's cuffs, partner, so he can sign the form. And leave 'em off. He doesn't need to be restrained. Right, Teddy? You're not gonna try to run away?'

Teddy didn't respond to the question, although he sensed, as he signed the form, that Littlewood had offered a deal and he'd accepted. 'I don't want to talk to you,' he said. 'I have a right to silence and I'm takin' it.'

'Did anyone ask you to open your mouth?' Kelly broke in. She had her arms folded over her chest, leaning away from him like he smelled bad.

'My partner's right, Teddy. I haven't asked you a single question and I don't expect to. I'm here to show you. For example, this is the weapon used to kill Carlo. A scuba team fished it out of Newtown Creek about a week ago.'

Kelly pulled the gun, an H&K P30 chambered for 9mm cartridges, from a paper bag. She laid it on the table in front of her prisoner, then backed away. The serial numbers had been filed off and an evidence tag hung from the trigger guard.

Teddy stared at the gun for a moment as he waited for his thoughts to settle. On the one hand, the only way the cops could know the make and model of the pistol he used to kill Carlo was if they fished it out of the creek. That part, at least, was true. But the cops still had a long way to go before they tied the gun to him and proved it was used on Carlo. Teddy had snatched up the shell casing before he left the scene, so the most they could prove was that Carlo had been killed by a 9mm handgun. One of millions sold by various manufacturers every year.

'Not impressed?' Boots asked.

Teddy shook his head, more in disgust than anything else.

'OK, I know you're not a fool, so I'm not gonna tell you the gun has your fingerprints on it. Fingerprints on guns are bullshit anyway. In fact, I personally know cops in ballistics who in their entire career never lifted a print from a gun. But DNA? Well, that's another matter. When you handle a gun, the oil on your hands, along with skin cells, attaches to the grip and the trigger. You've probably convinced yourself that sitting on the bottom of Newtown Creek for ten days degraded the DNA to the point where it can't be tested. But you'd be wrong, Teddy, very wrong.'

Kelly finished her partner's thought. 'Bottom line, we've got a warrant and we're gonna take a DNA swab before you leave.'

'Tell it to my lawyer.'

'I'm tellin' it to you, Teddy. Fuck your lawyer. Just like I'm tellin' you that our snitches claim that you had an ongoing dispute with the Pianetta crew. That's motive, Teddy, which juries appreciate.'

Teddy tried to convince himself that everything he'd been told was a lie, that cops lie at the drop of a hat, but it wouldn't wash. The gun did, in fact, belong to him, and he was, in fact, having trouble with the Pianettas. Meanwhile, his bladder was about to explode.

'Why don't I get the machine?' Littlewood answered his own question by leaving the room. Now Teddy was alone with Kelly, a deceptively slender woman in a green pants suit. Looking at the two of them, you'd have to conclude that he could kick the crap out of her. Not that he was stupid enough to try.

'I have a question,' she said, 'or maybe a couple of questions.'

'Didn't your partner tell me you weren't going to ask any questions?'

'He was speaking for himself, Teddy. Now, first question. Did you take stupid pills on the day you decided to conceal a tracking device on my partner's car? And what did you tell yourself at the time? That we wouldn't notice you following us? My partner and me, at first we thought you were trying to find the woman who saw you murder Carlo. But that didn't make sense because you couldn't have known we were looking for her when you installed the device. No, you had something else in mind. Wanna tell me what it was?'

Teddy stared into the cop's eyes. They were a blue so dark it was nearly invisible. And even though her eyes revealed nothing, they hinted of possibilities he didn't want to consider.

Kelly broke the silence. 'You were naive when you convinced yourself that you could shadow us without being spotted. You were an amateur going up against professionals. And you're being naive here, too. But let me get back to the topic at hand. I think you heard about my partner confronting Johnny Piano in Woodhull Hospital. I think you figured if something happened to my partner, the NYPD would come down on the Pianetta crew like a ton of bricks. I think you were out to kill my partner. That's not nice, Teddy. And I'm not gonna forget, either.'

Relief flooded through Teddy when he saw Littlewood's face appear in the doorway. Talk about intense. Had the bitch threatened him? He didn't want to think about it and now he wouldn't have to.

'Showtime, folks.'

Littlewood pushed a rolling cart topped with a keyboard and a monitor ahead of him as he came through the door. 'Wi-Fi,' he said, pointing to the monitor. 'No cables. I tell ya, Teddy, what with all the technology, it's a wonder that you criminals get away with anything. There are cameras everywhere now, including the road between the Pulaski Bridge and the Alltel Petroleum Depot. Those cameras, by the way, were fully functional on that Saturday morning when you murdered Carlo.'

Littlewood shifted the mouse. He was about to click on the play button when he stopped abruptly. 'Oh, yeah, something else you need to know before we get started. On that Saturday, November fourth, a good citizen reported a shot fired. The citizen was living on Box Street, about two blocks from the bridge, and his call was received by a 911 operator at 7:42. The footage you're gonna see now begins at 7:44 and runs to 7:49. Take a look, tell me if this is you.'

A voice in Teddy's brain commanded him not to look, a voice he was compelled to ignore. His gaze was drawn to the monitor as iron filings are drawn to a magnet. For the next four minutes, he watched a figure, obviously a man, walk the block from Paidge Avenue to Newtown Creek, watched the figure disappear into the shadows, only to appear a moment later and retrace his steps to Paidge Avenue.

'That could be anyone,' Teddy said when Littlewood hit the pause button. Again, relief rushed through his body and his mind. He'd been fully aware of the cameras when he decided to ditch the gun, which is why he'd stayed on the far side of the street.

'That's what we decided, too. Worthless for purposes of identification, put it to the side. But then I started thinking, this guy, he's slick. He knows where the cameras are and he's avoiding them because he just murdered Carlo Pianetta. But what about before he murdered Carlo? When he was only out for a stroll? Was he just as alert? Was avoiding cameras part of his lifestyle? Teddy, you can believe me when I tell you that these were questions I had to answer. So, what does a cop do when he gets curious? He hits the street. And what happens when he gets lucky? That, my boy, I'm about to show you.'

The mouse disappeared in the big cop's hand and he raised a finger before pausing. 'There's a Housing Authority warehouse on Ash Street, two blocks from the Pulaski Bridge,' he said, 'with cameras running the length of the roofline. This footage was taken by those cameras on Saturday, November fourth , between seven thirty-three and seven thirty-nine AM. You can check out the time-and-date stamp for yourself.'

Teddy watched himself come into view, then disappear, then appear again beneath the next camera. Like he was passing through dimensions. And maybe the quality wasn't all that great, but no juror would look at the images and conclude that it couldn't be Teddy Winuk on the screen. The best he could hope for was a maybe.

'Now,' Littlewood said, 'you're probably asking yourself how we're gonna link the man approaching the Bridge with the man who walked down to Newtown Creek. The answer, of course, is clothing. The light pants, the open pea jacket, the knit cap. What's your lawyer gonna tell the jury? It's a coincidence?'

Teddy knew that everything he'd seen or heard since he entered the room had been prepared in advance. Every fucking syllable. They were ripping away his resistance. Like he was ten years old and losing a fight. Like he wanted to cry uncle, make a full confession, anything to get out the room.

'I need a toilet,' he said.

'Hey, all you gotta do is ask, Teddy. You want something to eat, to drink? I can do that, too. C'mon.'

Teddy followed the big cop through the squad room and down a short hallway to a closed door.

'Through here,' Littlewood said.

He pulled the door open to reveal a windowless room just big enough for a toilet and a sink. An exhaust fan on the outer wall hummed away.

'Knock yourself out, Teddy. And you don't have to leave the door open. I'll wait out here.'

Teddy's physical release was immense, but again he felt like a schoolchild who'd been waiting all morning for permission to use the boy's room. He was now certain that he'd be arrested, certain that the cops had enough to put him in the cage, certain that bail was a long shot and it'd be at least a year before he stood trial. That didn't mean the case against him was strong. The face of the man approaching the Pulaski Bridge was blurry, the features indistinct. So, yes, it could be him, but it didn't have to be. What he needed was a solid alibi.

A few minutes later, when Teddy re-entered the squad room, the door to the Squad Commander's office was open. Inside, seated on a straight-backed chair, staring right at him, was the final nail in his coffin.

'Teddy,' Sanda Dragomir said, 'how many times I have told you? For love I do not exist. I am sorry for this, but it is simple truth.' She hesitated a moment, as if she expected a reply, then finally smiled. 'I am to become real American, Teddy. I am to be legal in the land of the free. Yes?'

FIFTY

Boots glanced through the window at his prisoner. Teddy was seated behind the table, his wrist again handcuffed to his chair. Captain Serge Karkanian stood next to Boots, his eyes also fixed on their suspect. Karkanian had been really pissed when Boots and Jill, without a trace of remorse, told him they'd been investigating Carlo's murder. For a few minutes afterward, Boots thought Karkanian would suspend them on the spot.

'You think he's softened up?' Karkanian asked.

'I think he's already mush,' Jill said. She was standing behind the two men, impatient now. 'I think, inside, Teddy's the consistency of vanilla pudding.'

Winuk was sitting with his elbows on the table, his chin in his hands, all but certain that he was going to spend the next twenty-five years in prison. Though he fought to maintain control, his emotional state was sliding toward a place called despair.

In fact, the case against him wasn't all that strong. Sanda Dragomir, their prime witness, was an illegal immigrant who maintained herself by selling her body. No juror would like the deal she'd cut with the state, a green card in return for her testimony. A good defense lawyer would tear her to pieces.

The only true witness to what happened, Corry Frisk, had been located by OCCB within a week, as Boots predicted. Initially, she and her brother were put under surveillance and photographed. Corry's photo was then placed in a standard photo array, along with eleven other photographs, and shown to the two men and six women who'd witnessed the Fort Greene Massacre. The witnesses had studied the faces closely, as they were asked to do, but Corry's likeness went unrecognized.

When OCCB, with the cooperation of the Pensacola Police Department, finally approached Corry, she simply handed them her lawyer's business card. Likewise for her brother, Tommy. They were living in a trailer park, surrounded by well-armed veterans of the wars in Iraq and Afghanistan. Tommy's pals.

Without Corry Frisk, and with Sanda far from a disinterested witness, the case would rest on the video, a shaky foundation according to the prosecutors consulted by OCCB. Not that the DA wouldn't prosecute. He'd charge Teddy with murder, all right, but offer manslaughter by way of a plea bargain. Given that Teddy didn't have a record, he'd probably do three years.

Fortunately, Teddy Winuk was not only unaware of these developments, but he probably didn't suspect that he was being played as much by what he didn't know as what they'd already shown him. Too bad. Winuk was as ready as he was ever going to be, at least in Boots Littlewood's opinion.

Boots entered the interrogation room carrying a large Pepsi and two small bags of potato chips. He laid them in front of his prisoner, then took his former seat. Jill Kelly was not in the room.

'Tell me something, Teddy,' he said. 'Tell me where you wanna go with this.'

'What do you mean?' The words emerged slowly, as if the man was testing his ability to speak.

'Lemme spell it out. On Saturday, November 4th, you left Sanda's apartment around seven thirty in the morning. Before you left, you jammed a semi-automatic handgun behind the waistband of your trousers. Sanda saw you do this and she'll testify to it. From seven thirty-three until seven forty-nine we have you on Ash Street, two blocks from the Pulaski Bridge, out for a stroll. Three minutes later, after hearing a gunshot, an honest citizen living a block from the bridge called nine one one. Four minutes after that, we have you, on multiple cameras, walking to the shore of Newtown Creek. Finally, we have a semi-automatic handgun recovered forty feet from where you stood.'

Boots shut down abruptly. The kid needed a little time now, time to consider his possibilities. Teddy wasn't stupid. Boots hadn't said a word about the woman they were both looking for in Jackson Heights. A ray of hope?

'Am I under arrest?' Teddy finally asked.

'No, but you will be soon.'

'On what charge?'

'What do think? Spitting on the sidewalk? Littering? You'll be charged with the premeditated murder of Carlo Pianetta. I'm asking you where you want to go with that.'

Teddy finally smiled, a tight smile, but one that spoke of his intention to communicate. 'How 'bout home and to bed?'

'That's good. But I was thinkin' you might want to get your side on the record. How you stumbled upon a rape in progress, how you took steps to rescue the victim the only way you knew how. Afterwards, who knows? You acted on instinct when you pulled the trigger and you acted on instinct when you ran away.

The main thing is that you didn't harm Carlo's victim, even though she could probably identify you. You let her live.'

Teddy opened the Pepsi and one of the bags. He shoved a handful of chips into his mouth and washed them down. 'Are you recording this?' he asked.

'No, Teddy. The evidence is stacked against you and we don't need to play games. Everything you say is off the record until you decide otherwise.'

'Then tell me what happened to this woman you claim that I rescued.'

'She's not cooperating, at least for the present.'

'What about the future?'

'If she's subpoenaed to testify before a grand jury, she'll have to appear. What she'll do if she's put under oath is anybody's guess. But you're the one who needs her, not us. All we have to do is convince a jury that you shot Carlo. Why? Because you and Carlo were fellow criminals and you were at odds with him. This we can also prove.'

The two men sat in silence for the next several minutes while Teddy finished the chips and his soda. 'What's gonna happen to Sanda?'

'She'll be given a green card and relocated. To California or Florida, if she has her way. Sanda hates the cold.' Boots laughed. 'Meanwhile, her heart could've been sculpted from ice.'

'It's not her fault, not really.' Teddy stared down at the table for a minute. 'I mean, she warned me, but I didn't listen. And if I did take a gun when I left her place, which I'm not sayin' I did, I wouldn't have let her see me do it if I expected to run into Carlo ten minutes later.'

'How's that tune go?' Boots said. 'Bad luck and trouble, follow me all my days?'

'The punch you don't see coming is the one that knocks you out.'

'Like you never expected us to recover the gun?'

'More like I know you were lyin' when you told me you found DNA on it.'

'Is that because you wiped it down before you tossed it in the creek?'

Boots felt the tension lift as both men laughed. Exactly as he'd hoped. Teddy was grasping at straws, though he didn't know it.

'So, whatta ya think I'll get?' Teddy asked. 'If I'm convicted?'

'If you go to trial? Or if you take the plea bargain?'

'If I take the plea.'

'Manslaughter with a five-year sentence. You'll probably do three.' Boots leaned over the table and let his voice drop to a whisper, as though he was about to reveal a secret. Which, in fact, he was.

'But the state is the least of your problems, Teddy.' Boots let that sink in before continuing. 'The hit on Carlo was big-time news, which you'd have to expect, him bein' a known gangster caught with his pants down. So, there's no hidin' the fact that we closed out the case by arresting you. You hear me? Once I start the booking process, the New York Police Department's Division of Public Information will notify every reporter and news agency listed in its computerized files. And the media will come, Teddy. They'll come by the hundreds and they'll be standing outside when you get to star in your own perp walk. Now, I could put a coat over your head, so the photographers don't get a shot of your face, but somehow I don't think what's left of the Pianetta crew is gonna be fooled. They got lots of trouble these days, between the hits on Carlo, Johnny and the Rock, the cops busting their operations and strivers like you muscling in. Guaranteed, they're lookin' for someone to blame.'

Boots straightened up. Teddy's features had squeezed together as Boots explained what should have been obvious. Once Teddy's name was out there, his life would be on the line every minute of every day. And it didn't matter whether he spent those days on the streets or on Rikers Island awaiting trial.

Jill Kelly entered the room and took a seat to Winuk's right, as before. When she spoke, it was obvious that she'd been listening. 'You're a smart boy, Teddy. You've got an Associate's degree – in business, no less – and you kept your grades up all the way through. But now here you are, trapped in a corner with no way out. How do you explain that?'

Teddy rallied at that point, motivated, probably, by Jill's contempt. 'What do you want from me?'

'We're recruiting you, Teddy.'

'What?'

Jill crossed her legs, then lit a cigarette. She offered the pack to her prisoner. 'Want one?'

Teddy shook his head.

'The way I see it, you've got two choices. First, you can ask for protective custody and hope nobody gets to you. But that means twenty-three-and-a-half hours a day by yourself in a cage for at least the next four or five years. And even assuming that you're not picked off on your way to your half-hour of exercise, you still have to ask yourself what's gonna happen when you're released. You'll be on parole, so you can't just disappear, and Tony Pianetta's not likely to forgive and forget.'

'What's the second choice?'

'I think you know.'

'You want me to rat on someone?'

'No, Teddy, we want you to become a *permanent* rat.' Jill laughed. 'But if you like, you can try thinkin' of yourself as a double agent. You don't have a lot of time, by the way.'

The door opened to admit Captain Serge Karkanian, accompanied by a detective sergeant named D'Shawn Robinson. Short and barrel-chested, Robinson had the pitiless eyes of a drill sergeant.

'Theodore Winuk, meet your future.' Boots repressed a smile. The wheels in Teddy's head were already turning, with every possibility he imagined preferable to a bullet through the back of his skull. 'Two things to consider before me and my partner say goodbye. First, there's no statute of limitations on a homicide. We can take you off the street ten years from now. Second, there's no statute of limitations on the kind of Sicilian revenge likely to be enacted if I leak your name to Anthony Pianetta. Which, if you try to fuck us over, I will surely do.'

FIFTY-ONE

'I don't know,' Boots told Jill as he put the Taurus in gear and headed off. 'I mean, it's only a week till Christmas and I'd give anything to have my mother home.'

They were on their way to the Bronx, their immediate goal to pick up Theresa Kelly, who was being released from the rehab unit at Citizen's Rest. Maybe she was sober now, but there was no healing a cirrhotic liver and the woman was still very sick.

Jill and Boots were rapidly approaching the end of their mandatory medical leaves. The idle time had been rough on Boots, his only two consolations the weight room and the wounded Jill Kelly. He couldn't wait to get back to work. And there was plenty of work to do, according to Cletis Small, who occasionally stopped by for lunch.

The story Detective Small consistently related was more or less the story Boots had been anticipating since he learned of Johnny Piano's murder. A dozen crews, including Teddy Winuk's, were vying to occupy the sudden void and the competition was increasingly turning violent. He had his work cut out for him.

Boots was still weighing various lines of attack when Jill spoke up. 'I had a liver biopsy last week,' she said, instantly driving all consideration of the future from her lover's awareness. 'To see if my liver was a match for my mother's. It is, as it turns out.'

'What does that mean?' As far as Boots knew, transplanted livers always began their journey inside a cadaver.

'It means I can donate a piece of my liver, Boots. To keep my mother alive.'

'I didn't know that was possible.'

Boots kept his disappointment to himself. Jill had undergone a biopsy without letting him know, another barrier he'd failed to overcome. Meanwhile, she was confiding in him now and he settled behind the wheel. Jill would proceed at her own pace, if at all.

New York was in the middle of an early cold spell and the temperature was in the upper twenties as they made their way from Brooklyn to the Bronx. Skies were clear and the sun bright, perhaps by way of compensation. The view of midtown Manhattan from the crest of the Kosciusko Bridge was stunning, every edge sharp. The spire of the Empire State Building seemed to pierce the sky, a spike into flesh.

'They're going to spit him out eventually,' Jill said. 'You know that, right?'

Boots ignored the change of subject. 'Who?' he asked.

'Teddy Winuk. I've seen for myself how OCCB uses registered informants. They'll rent him out to other agencies, favor for favor, one of yours for one of mine. Narcotics, Vice, the DEA and the FBI, everybody takes a turn. Then one day he'll get arrested and find out that he has no friends.'

'I have plans for him, too,' Boots said. 'I may not be able to go after Winuk directly, but I can target his operations and his associates. I mean to drive him out of the Six-Four. What OCCB does with him after that is none of my business.'

'What makes you think you're going back to the Six-Four?'

The question was pertinent, though Boots preferred not to think about it. Tomorrow morning, he and Jill would present themselves to Brooklyn Borough Command for assignment. Cops were usually returned to their home units after a brief medical leave. But not always.

They drove in silence for a time, until Boots tapped his finger against the steering wheel. Despite his best effort, the quiet was too much for him. 'What's the latest on Corry Frisk? Any news?'

Like Boots, Jill had remained in touch with several colleagues. One, Violet Hamilton, sent Jill text messages whenever something new developed.

'Corry's standing pat, which is exactly what I'd do in her situation. And by the way, Karkanian's somehow decided that Corry and Tommy Frisk had nothing to do with the Fort Greene homicides. He's looking at a Sicilian crew from New Jersey.'

'Tell me they're not headed by a man named Tony Soprano.'

Jill laughed. 'For jerks like Karkanian, the mob is still about people with vowels at the end of their names. OCCB doesn't have a single one of the Mexican cartels under investigation and we know they operate in New York.'

An hour later, Boots found a parking space next to a fire hydrant and pulled in. He put the car in park, slid the seat back and reached for a paper bag. The discharge process at Citizen's Rest would take an hour, at least, and he'd brought coffee and a *Daily News* along. As a matter of habit, he checked the Ford's rear-view and two side mirrors to make sure they were properly aligned. This was not something he would have done a month before.

'When they take out part of your liver,' Jill said, 'it's not a small part. They take nearly half.' She paused long enough to button her coat. 'But you want to hear something funny? It doesn't matter, because your own liver grows back.' She reached for the door, but then dropped her hand to her lap. 'You want to hear something else that's funny?'

Boots took a red thermos bottle out of the bag and unscrewed the top. 'Sure,' he said. 'I could use a chuckle.'

'The surgeon, Dr Sugarman? He won't do the surgery unless Mom stays sober for at least six months. Sugarman's polite, so you have to read between the lines. After that it gets simple. Why take all the risks if she's going to drink herself to death anyway?'

'The risks to who?'

'What?'

'The risks, Jill. To you or your mother?'

'To me, of course.' This time Jill pulled the door handle, releasing the lock. 'Sugarman forced me to look at pictures of the surgery. He said that he wanted my informed consent to be fully informed. Boots, they start the cut under your breastbone, then sweep around below your ribs on both sides. The first thing when I saw the pictures, I was reminded of the Y-cut that pathologists use. And I also knew, before Sugarman said a word, that I'd have a scar as thick as a clothesline.' Jill hesitated for a moment, then looked at Boots from the corner of her eye. 'Would you still love me, Boots,' she asked, 'if I made you count the stitch marks with your fingertips? Blindfolded?'

Boots laughed a bit too long, but just a bit. The woman's façade was bulletproof. What was happening underneath was anyone's guess. He watched Jill push the door open and put one foot on the curb.

'Here's what worries me the most, Boots. I'll be laid up for the next ten weeks. No lifting anything over ten pounds, and no gun range, either. I think I'll go mad.'

'Does that mean it's going to happen?'

'I haven't decided yet, and I'm not going to, not until I'm convinced that mom's gonna stay sober. According to Sugarman, she has a two-in-three chance of being alive in five years if she receives a piece of my liver. That probability falls to zero if she doesn't have a transplant.'

*   *   *

Thirty minutes after Jill disappeared, Boots lifted his eyes from the newspaper to check his mirrors. His timing was perfect and he watched a familiar Lincoln double-park behind his Taurus, watched Michael Shaw's bodyguard open the Lincoln's rear door, watched the Chief of Detectives emerge. Bathed in sunlight, Shaw looked more sallow than ever, and if his ivory-handled cane was mostly for show, he leaned on it nonetheless.

Though Boots made a conscious effort to control himself, he was annoyed enough to wait until Shaw tapped the cane against the side window before he popped the locks.

Shaw lowered himself into the front seat and arranged the cane between his feet. He said nothing as his bodyguard eased the door shut and walked back to the Lincoln, finally positioning himself on the curb side facing his boss. Boots took a moment to admire the man's dedication. He wore only a suit and it was very cold.

'I hope you don't mind our having this conversation in your car, Boots.' Shaw stared out through the windshield. 'I'm becoming senile, you see, and I can't remember whether I bugged my own Lincoln.'

'Does that mean you want this conversation to be private?'

'I do, Boots.' Shaw gave it five seconds before speaking again. 'You defied me, you and Jill both, and it doesn't matter if the story had a happy ending. I have to do something.'

Boots glanced at each of the mirrors, then back through the windshield. 'Crawling's not part of my game plan,' he said. 'In case that's what you're after.'

'It's not.' Shaw leaned forward onto his cane.

'Then . . .?'

'Can't you do better than this? You made $92,000 last year.' Shaw swept the car's interior with his eyes. 'Or did you lose too much betting the Yankees with a felon named Frankie Drago?'

Boots rolled with the punches. Did they have proof? Did Frankie Drago, the only man who could provide that proof, give a statement to Internal Affairs? Boots refused to believe it. This was about intimidation, as if the job didn't have enough leverage.

'I did my time on the street like every other cop,' Shaw said. 'I earned my gold shield after four years on patrol and I started my detective life in the north Bronx. For the next twenty years, I either worked the streets or supervised detectives who worked the streets. I learned to separate talented detectives from worker bees along the way, purely as a matter of self-defense. Do you understand? I learned to recognize talent and to use talent to my advantage, always reserving my best detectives for highly publicized cases that must be closed. They never failed me.'

Boots checked the mirrors again, sighting the bodyguard. The man was shifting his weight from foot to foot and his breath steamed the air. As if his boss gave a shit.

'Is this the carrot?' Boots asked. 'The carrot before the stick?'

'You know, I wasn't kidding a few weeks ago when I said you're becoming just like her. I mean, Jill, of course. And by the way, Jill's going to the Academy where she'll be a shooting instructor. As I understand it, she'll be assigned to improve the scores of the least talented cadets.'

Boots considered the prospect for a moment, then shrugged. The Academy's shooting program wasn't a bad spot for Jill. At least she'd get to practice after working hours.

'And, you, Boots, are being promoted to Detective First Grade. You put down Carlo's murderer, dealt with Stefano Ungaro and protected my niece, as I asked. You deserve to be a hero.'

'I knew the turf,' Boots said, recalling Open Circle and the Navy Yard stroll. 'I knew where to look first. Not that I accomplished anything. Winuk's still working my streets.'

'Your streets?' Shaw sounded his wheezy laugh. 'You presume too much. The streets were there before you were born and they'll be there when you rot. If anything, it's the other way around. The streets possess you, not you the streets. But you'll be happy to know that you're going to get what you want. Tomorrow, assuming we reach an understanding, you'll be reassigned to the Six-Four.'

Boots recalled Ronald Reagan's debate line: there you go again. The hoop was rising. All he had to do was jump through it. But Shaw was right about one thing. Throughout his career, he'd made an effort to minimize risk. Now he missed it.

'Nothing to say, Boots?'

'*Nada*, Chief.'

Shaw's voice hardened, though he continued to speak in a near-whisper. 'I've already told you about the use I made of the most talented detectives on my way up. Now I'm telling you that I've continued to make use of them. The four men and two women who comprise my Special Investigations Unit are superb investigators, one and all. They're also at my disposal. My eyes and ears, so to speak.'

'I can't say I'm surprised.' Boots was focused on a simple fact. He wasn't being invited to join this unit. He was being sent back to the Six-Four. 'In your place, I'd do the same thing.'

'I wasn't asking for approval, but I thank you nonetheless.' Shaw took off his hat, a narrow-brimmed fedora. He ran his fingers through his hair, then returned the hat to his head. 'From time to time, mainly because my office is a sieve when it comes to leaks, I need a true outsider to conduct an investigation. That outsider must be talented, obscure, and not currently assigned to my office. A man, for instance, who insists on working in a backwater Brooklyn precinct, running down burglars and stickup men. A man who's taken great care to hide his light under the proverbial bushel. That would be you, Detective Littlewood.'

'And Kelly?' Boots asked. 'Detective Jill Kelly, too?'

'I'm explaining, not negotiating. And I don't require your assent. When the time comes, you'll accept your assignment. And not because you're afraid of Michael Shaw, though you should be. You'll do it for the adventure. You see, Detective Littlewood, given what you've been through, you're certain to find your little precinct as boring as it really is.'

Shaw yanked the door handle, then waited for his bodyguard to come over and pull the door fully open. Up ahead, Jill appeared in the entranceway of Citizen's Rest, along with her mother. Theresa Kelly was in a wheelchair, but she got up and took a few steps when her brother-in-law approached. Though Boots was looking at Shaw's back, he knew the man was smiling. His arms were outstretched, his cane dangling from one hand as he briefly embraced his sister-in-law. Jill stood off to Shaw's left, clearly amused. She turned to Boots and winked.

Boots started the Taurus, then turned up the heat. A week, a month, a year from now, Michael Shaw would come calling. And Boots would accept anything short of a suicide mission. He was no hero. In fact, when he really thought about it, he was pretty much a coward. That's why he'd insist on having Jill Kelly by his side.

Up ahead, Jill said something to Uncle Mike, then lit a cigarette. Boots could only imagine how much it aggravated a man like Shaw to face off with a woman who never took a backward step. Jill's dismissive smile only broadened at her uncle's response.

Boots got out and circled the car. Theresa Kelly was walking toward him, her hand on her daughter's arm. A lot stronger than the last time he'd seen her, she let go of Jill's arm and allowed Boots to help her into the back seat.

'Detective Littlewood, it's good to see you again.'

'And you, too, Mrs Kelly.'

Boots hustled back to his own side of the car and settled in behind the wheel. He waited for Jill to fasten her seatbelt, then pulled out into traffic.

'Guess what, Boots? I'm headed to the Academy as a firearms instructor.'

'Your uncle told me. I assumed he meant it as a punishment.' Boots caught Theresa Kelly's eye in the rear-view mirror. 'You warm enough back there?'

'I'm fine, Detective . . .'

'Do me a favor. Call me Boots. I reserve Detective Littlewood for criminals and superior officers.'

'All right, then.'

Now that she was off the booze, the docs had upped Theresa's pain meds and her eyes were hazed. Boots laughed to himself. Doctors loved euphemisms, but Theresa's pain med of choice, according to Jill, was plain old morphine. The woman was stoned and she'd almost certainly have to deal with an ongoing addiction if she got a piece of Jill's liver. Or would her doctors keep on supplying the morphine, maybe figuring, since they'd gotten her addicted in the first place, that they owed her one?

'Did Uncle Mike really tell you I was being punished? Because I swear to you, I would have paid him to arrange the transfer.'

Boots crossed beneath the Bruckner Expressway, elevated at this point, and turned left onto Bruckner Boulevard. He was heading for the Whitestone Bridge, connecting the Bronx to Queens. Earlier that morning, Jill had invited him to dine with the Kellys, mother and daughter. After which, she was quick to assure him, he'd be spending the night.

Call it a small victory, a tiny chip in Jill's case-hardened façade.

'No, he didn't actually say he was punishing you. But he did say that we defied him and he had to do something about it. Maybe he just hopes to keep you out of trouble.'

'Right.' Jill leaned forward to lower the heat. 'You know, Boots, the new Academy has a below-ground firing range.'

The old Police Academy on 19th Street in Manhattan, after fifty years of service, had finally closed down a month before. At the same time, the NYPD's firing range on City Island had shut its gates to all but sniper training. The new Academy in College Point, only a couple of miles from the Kelly homestead, had its own firing range. And unlike the outdoor range on City Island, it wouldn't be the subject of voter petitions signed by locals protesting the noise.

'So, it's all good, right?' Jill said. 'You'll meet me after hours and we'll practice together.'

'Toward what end? You want me to compete?'

'Actually, I was thinking, given your temper, that it would be a good idea if I made you lethal. Would you like to be lethal, Boots?'

Boots thought it over for a moment as he worked his way around a pothole repair crew. Finally, he glanced at Jill and said, 'Outside of counting your stitches blindfolded, there's nothing I'd like more.'

3 1491 01178 0735

Niles
Public Library District

JUL 3 1 2015

Niles, Illinois 60714